To Barbara Gale,
With whom I share much,
Much affection,
Richard

CONFESSION

Richard Freis

SARTORIS
LITERARY
GROUP

"A traditional publisher with a non-traditional approach to publishing."

For my Family,
Near and Far

1

I am Lazarus, Father, risen from the grave. Or rather from the sea, where I tried to drown myself. I tried to drown myself, and the sea would not accept me. It pushed me away from itself, back into a life that I didn't want to live.

How hard did you find it, sizing me up? An old man, washed up at the rectory door after your morning mass, whose speech bore the marks of distinction and who looked like a fisherman barely sobered up from a drunk.

Of course, I'm not one of your regular parishioners. I came to you because I can't yet humble myself to confess the truth to a priest I know. And also because the bishop once mentioned your name in my hearing.

We were playing golf together, a foursome, two laymen and two priests. The bishop was not being indiscreet. He is, after all, a CEO, whatever else he may be, and he finds help quietly discussing his problems with others who face similar situations. In this case, he was not speaking to me, however, but to the other priest. They were mentioning how insistently conservative you are. I took this to mean that you would be severe in naming a penance for sin.

You see, I'm trying to control even my own penance. I could indeed make the case for the most severe penance. But also I think I hoped, with the instincts of thirty-five years as an attorney—the man who has all the words, as Becca called me—to show you that what I did was inevitable,. Perhaps, since God's mercy is greater than mine, it was even forgivable.

But despite Becca's reproach, this morning I could find no words. Faced by my muteness and confusion, you suggested that I write down for myself what happened before I return to make my confession.

So I have come back to this house on the coast, the setting of so much of my experience, the scene of my life's two great fragmentations. Perhaps facing this keyboard I will be able to elude the urgent, spontaneous voices of accusation and defense and more clearly touch the reality of what has happened, remember so I can see.

See four days.

A life.

2

Thursday morning, only Thursday morning, four days ago, I was still rooted in my ordinary life. Solidly rooted, as I thought, or rather, as I took for granted. Would I have acted differently, if I had foreseen there was nothing solid about it, but only a routine that had lasted so long I assumed it would last forever? A routine I relied on as if it were God's plan.

Every morning I stood by my office window as I finalized in intention my schedule for the day. I assumed time was mine to arrange in this way. Thursday, too, I stood in my office on the twenty-third floor of the Center Building, where Burden, Cassel, Fairchild and White have our law offices. I am George Burden.

I was aware, around and behind me, of the furnishings, which our young decorator had chosen, as he self-consciously told the firm's overseeing committee of partner's wives, "to give an impression of power so assured that it need not assert itself." This young man was the son of a colleague. He had moved after his high school years to San Francisco, but recently returned home. "Home," he said, in a maxim he often served up with an air of fresh discovery, "still exists in Mississippi."

My diplomas and a lifetime of recognitions rested in their familiar places along the wall.

My B.A.—in English literature, my adolescent passion—bore the seal of Ole Miss, where I am now a trustee. At the time, that would have seemed an improbable outcome. My father was an attorney, a career he was able to hold onto with some success in spite of the drinking that made such hell of his life and mine. I didn't know then whether I wanted to become an attorney in yet another effort to please him, or to do something else, something that would allow me to be as unlike him as possible.

I decided to become a writer. One of my professors knew William Faulkner. On the basis of some overheard remarks, I picked up *Sanctuary*, expecting to find scandal. Instead I was nailed to the page by the book's power over words. Even now I can quote the passage where town boys, watching Temple Drake enter the gymnasium for the dance, saw her "vanish in a swirling glitter upon a glittering swirl of music." For a year I introduced similar phrases into everything I wrote, and felt a flush of superiority when my teachers red-penciled them out.

During my first three years at Ole Miss I pursued my pleasure in matching words to the world. Through it I found myself part of a group of young writers. I loved the intense and (for me) cautiously beery friendships. When I was made to read the Latin poet, Catullus, I felt a knowing bond with his boozy, admiring, touchy friendships with other poets. But not with the tormented love affair that shaped the heart of his poetry.

In a Latin book I discovered at home, I found written inside the front cover under my grandfather's name—William Burden, Latin 2, Dr. Hamilton—a poem of Catullus. The paper was faded to the sepia of an old photograph and mottled with brown stains. But the hand in the faded black ink remained young and strong:

> *Odi et amo. Quare id faciam fortasse requiris?*
> *Nescio, sed fieri sentio, et excrucior.*

Was this a fragment of a passion of his own? Or simply a verse he liked? Below, the fresh ink shockingly black, I, his grandson, inscribed my own translation:

I loathe at the same time I love. You ask me: How can this be so?
I can't explain it, but oh! It nails me to a cross!

But this was not a record of experience. Through those years I remained chaste.

I don't know whether I could have made a writer, but what saved me from ending up as a professor of English somewhere was my father's death. At the end of my junior year I received a call from my grandmother saying that my father had collapsed. Before I reached home, I was an orphan. His death released in me a strong desire for security and a strength of ambition I didn't know I had. I took pre-law courses during my senior year at Ole Miss, went on to Harvard Law School, and then returned to Jackson to begin my career.

On the adjacent wall hung prints of wild turkeys, not only because I enjoy hunting, but to let prospective clients know that I enjoy it. I may be a member of the Harvard Alumni Club, the prints reassure them, but I remain a son of Jackson.

And on the shelf behind my desk, fifteen year old pictures of myself, the children, and Julia: myself, tall, big-limbed, my suit wrinkled by the heat, alert eyes, beaked nose and strong chin tracing a likeness to my father; Julia, almost as tall as I, her large-boned figure in maturity relaxing into competent grace, blue eyes gazing from her square face levelly at the camera.

My mind veered away from the pictures.

One-thirty meeting with Cash at the Governor's Mansion ...
Leave for lunch at eleven-thirty ...

The illusions of distance made the city small. Across the street behind the big brick wall I could see the back of the Mansion, cars official and personal, someone taking out garbage. The jumble of buildings stretching before me were a history of the city, old and new: the Old Capitol where Jefferson Davis had argued for secession; church steeples; multicolored plastic-paneled structures applauded as modern thirty years ago, now dated and obvious in their intrinsic ugliness; and the newer office buildings of the recently recovering downtown. Half a mile away the great neon letters atop the Customer's Bank, facing the highway beyond, floated in reverse against the skyline. Beyond them stretched the Fairgrounds and the Coliseum and the highway itself which marked the edge of the city and led to the spreading suburbs to the east.

I suppose I can claim to be one of perhaps two dozen men who has done the most in the last fifteen years to envision and build the city as it has grown in that time. Looking at it, I felt its solidity reflected back in myself.

Why did I linger there? What need for reassurance did I feel? I tried to return to my schedule.

Lunch eleven-thirty ...

My secretary buzzed and told me Martin Fairchild wished to see me when I was free. I asked her to call him in and went to the doorway to meet him. Martin was approaching down the long corridor that connects the inner suite of offices and, on our floor, the library. A visitor stepping from the elevators on either side of the reception area into the firm—the parquet floors and oriental carpets, the dark wood, gleams of brass and copies of *Fortune* and *The Wall Street Journal*, the switchboard operator in her glass-paneled booth behind the receptionist's desk and the impatient runner with a package in his hand waiting for the elevator down—sees only one side of the firm. The hallways and offices, although well appointed, have the air of work spaces, barer, more stripped for efficiency. This familiar setting pulled me from my distraction into the professional alertness habitual there.

Martin reached me and took my extended hand. He followed me into my office and remained standing while I took my seat behind my desk.

Martin Fairchild is about five years younger than I am, just over fifty, with a thin face and slightly receding hairline and blue eyes that blaze with his seriousness and intelligence. In this morning's pin-striped gray suit and dark maroon tie he exhibited the quintessential Martin look, precise and self-contained, as if he had been somehow cut out and pasted upon the background.

"What is your day like?" he asked. "I'd like you to help me think out how to handle Jack Harper."

"Late this afternoon?" I said. "My morning's packed, and I'm tied up already for lunch. Then I meet Cash at one-thirty. It may go until three."

"What does the Governor want?"

"It's always politics. A group on the coast wants to start an arts festival to attract more tourism. It's a risk. Those things always have a large overhead and difficulty attracting the audience to guarantee a profit. Now they're looking for a start-up grant from the Council for Economic Development. Since Julia and I have lived down there so much, Cash thought it might be helpful if I'm present."

"Three's a bit late for me," Martin said, running a thin hand across his forehead in thought. "What about early tomorrow?"

"I'm sorry. Julia made me promise we'd take a long weekend at the coast house. *Promise.* She was quite definite about not wanting these particular plans adjusted. Sunday is my birthday. Fifty-fifth, if you can believe it. I can't. We're leaving tomorrow morning." I paused. "I have five minutes now if you want to fill me in. Then we could play it by ear."

12

Martin sat down in one of the blue wing chairs in front of my desk.

"This is the problem," he began at once. "I think Jack's son is ready to sell land the school board wants in Madison. But Jack doesn't want to let it go. Both he and his son have to agree in order to sell it."

His luminous eyes looked puzzled.

"I don't really understand it," he continued. "The project is a good one, land for the city to build a bigger high school. It's ideally located. Jack's always had a shrewd eye for the dollar, but he's also been generous to his town. The son's frustrated, but he's very loyal to the old man. I need your knack for sizing his resistance up and turning it around."

"I'll tell you what," I said. "Let me think it over and call you this evening. How many times have you talked with Jack?"

"To tell you the truth, only once, at his office, and it didn't get very far. He seemed anxious to close the conversation quickly."

"Okay," I said. "I'll give you a call."

Martin rose from the chair, his expression now more relaxed, and left.

The truth is I could already see that Martin hadn't approached Jack in the right way. It's a trait of Martin's. He pays attention to the problem, but doesn't pick up the personal factors in the situation. People will usually tell you what's on their minds, if you let them talk long enough. They may not tell you up front, they may not be aware of it themselves. But if you listen, you can read it.

My hunch was that Jack Harper was holding onto the land because he and his wife had a house on that property when they were first married. They started their family there. Dot Harper'd died recently, after a struggle with cancer that left them all hurt. Letting go of the land now probably felt to Jack too much like letting Dot go all over again. Martin needed to talk to him someplace where it wasn't business. He could make Jack see it as an expression of the family meaning of the place, a use that would honor what Dot valued. She did a lot for the public schools.

Almost eight-thirty...

My mind wouldn't focus. I'd awakened anxious at five and the anxiety kept ratcheting up. I'd had a moment of respite at the health club, amid the cheerful morning tiredness and camaraderie. I decided when I joined the club several years ago that I was too old to work out creditably on the weight floor. It gave me a humiliating sense of competing with the younger men where I wasn't stronger than they. Surprisingly, I know, for someone from the coast, I only learned to swim well as an adult. I love moving along the surface of the pool, watching the shifting perspectives of the bottom as the water works its illusions, rhythmically counting out the laps, feeling the spontaneous sense of balance and control as the water rides past me.

This morning, walking back to the lockers after my swim, something—perhaps it was the air conditioning—suddenly made me chill. I began to tremble, then to shake so violently I was afraid someone would ask me if I were ill.

Trying to control myself, I walked over and slipped into the Jacuzzi. Wave after wave of warmth invaded my shaking body; comforted and calmed me. I knelt beside one of the jets, my arms folded on the warm tile that edged the tub, my head resting on my arms, and shut my eyes. I floated in darkness, the soft fist of water pummeling my chest. An unaccustomed thought flashed into my mind, so intensely I was forced to notice it. How good it would be to let go, infinitely surrender.

Then I heard the laughing voices of two other members of the club engaged in some verbal horseplay. I raised my head and moved away, as if I were about to be discovered doing something shameful.

I had to get down to work. There was a meeting at nine about the distribution of office space between senior and more recent members of the firm. Like many apparently small issues this one had become potentially explosive.

Life is a series of problems to be solved. I'd always relished that and felt comfortable about handling this one. But I'd hoped to make some phone calls before giving it my attention.

Now it was too late. I knew why I was distracted, but I didn't understand the force of the distraction. I only half recognized the further feeling that accompanied it. My palms were sweating. Spontaneously, I wiped them against my blue suit coat like a child wiping jam from his fingers. What was this panic?

3

The noon light fell through the half-closed blinds in a striation that shaped itself to everything it flowed upon. My eyes idly followed as it flattened itself along the top of the struggling air conditioner, angled squarely over the gray table and chairs, heavily cut and as polished as plastic, which stood between the window and the bed, and rippled across the blue and purple spread, intricate and ugly in its pattern as the back of a cheap playing card, tangled at our feet. Finally the light died, fading in its course through the shadowy, damp-smelling interior of the hotel room to a dim streak staining the opposite wall.

Our anonymous, our intimate home.

All morning this hour had been my world, rehearsed in imagined episodes that eclipsed my office surroundings. This scene unrolled and unrolled itself until someone jolted me from it. Then it recaptured me, unrolling itself yet again. I was afraid that my distraction must be evident to anyone who dealt with me through the morning, but my body and imagination were on automatic pilot, and no effort of my will was able to control their working.

This struggle had been growing for weeks.

Each day I encountered this civil war in myself as if it were new, refusing to face how fully my life was slipping from my control. From the concealed places of my mind, desire and terror made expanding forays into the public world of my days. I was exhausted from resisting them. Increasingly I wanted to surrender, simply to accept the truth: the rest of my life had assumed for me the unreality of a fantasy, only these hidden hours felt real.

My center was no longer in myself, but in Becca.

Becca. Her name spoke itself in my mind. I raised my head, careful not to disturb her: I wanted to hold her with my eyes.

Her body lay still in the latticed light. In the soft striation her black hair shone almost lilac. She lay turned toward me. Her mouth as she breathed in sleep left a faint damp ring against the pillow.

15

This girl, younger than my youngest daughter, was my lover. Her beauty and her presence in my days defeated my capacity to make an adequate response: even my gratitude was so large that it almost paralyzed me.

My glance, intimate as a hand, explored her. A thread of semen crossed by a stripe of light shone silver-white across the dark triangle between her thighs. It was a sign of my possession.

I reached over and touched her. My arm against her young skin was large, loose-jointed, fleeced with wiry gray hair.

My hand reaching over her hip mapped the rough skin of her buttocks, rounded the contours of her hip where the pelvic bone protruding raised a hard tor under the smooth skin and created beneath a dimpled valley, descended the slope where the soft skin of her belly joined the curve of the thigh, found then in its progress the dark, enclosed triangle, a soft brush to the hand, and touched the rose-pale petal-wet center through which I could seek, but never fully possess, her elusive innerness. I took that beauty with my fingertips. Into those infinitely alert receptors flowed a world, the total horizon of my attention. Body and soul, she filled me: now I was nothing but her presence.

"Becca," I whispered, "I couldn't live if you left me."

She stirred, but she didn't open her eyes or speak.

At the beginning of our affair, Becca had less to shed than I, fewer scruples, less fear, fewer habits of restraint. But always when we made love she lay as if spelled in sleep, following the lead of my prompting. This passivity, this grant of mastery, this apparent total surrender to my desire enchanted me. More, it explored me, it showed me depths of passion I hadn't imagined were in me. In this initial ecstasy every gesture of desire was a blaze of being, bearing life forth from nothingness. And yet this very passivity had turned my assurance of mastery into its terrifying opposite.

For behind her mask of surrender lay a secret depth of privacy, a depth I couldn't see. No matter how perfect Becca's compliance, she receded always before me. Her body became for me a reservoir of ambiguity, an indeterminate figure into which I could read infinite meanings.

What was she really thinking in that interior world which eluded my inspection? Did she genuinely love me? Did she want to leave me? Had she already left me within?

Now gazing at her my desire, yes, and my inerasable tenderness, were invaded by panic and rage. In the warm room, my body began to tremble. Yet from this confusion of heart arose a more urgent issue of passion.

"Becca," I whispered hoarsely. I could see over the curve of her body a wasp that had somehow gotten into the room. It circled and returned, circled and returned between the slats of the blind, buzzing and butting against the invisible barrier of glass.

Becca lay still.

"*Becca.*"

I needed a response from her silence.

Slowly against the pillow she relaxed the fingers of her cupped hand, her fingertips, one by one, lifting into a stripe of sunlight. Then she rolled lazily from her side onto her back, her legs flat against the tangled sheets. Sun and shade rippled over her body as she moved. Her far leg lay extended; the leg next to me lay on the bed in a triangle, her foot resting against the far knee. It was a posture of openness, her center open. Yet it was a posture of protection, her angled leg a barrier against me. Or was it an invitation, the barrier left there precisely to be overcome? *What was she feeling?*

Desire and despair, rising beyond my control, almost blinded me. I rolled over above her silent body, gently shifting it to receive me, and acted out my mastery and defeat.

4

Becca was taking her shower.

I could hear the water splashing and the mechanical hum of the ceiling fan from behind the bathroom door.

The face of the digital clock on the television set counted out the succession of seconds. A red 12:45 pierced the shadow.

My meeting with Cash was at one-thirty. But this knowledge did not have the bite of reality, and I didn't move.

I lay still naked on the disordered sheets. They were partially torn away from the mattress and bunched uncomfortably beneath one of my legs. The smell of our lovemaking rose from my body -- sweat, semen, *her* smell. It rose and surrounded me like a cloud. I was too tired to move. Still, the anxiety-driven current of my desire worked restlessly in my groin. I reached down and touched myself briefly. No, I wouldn't go find her. I might be able to start it, but I wouldn't be able to finish.

I drifted in reverie.

At the start of the affair, I prided myself on my ability to dovetail all my activities. The conferences with clients, the committee meetings, the network of responsibilities with political and cultural organizations in the community, the social obligations with Julia and the fresh adventures with Becca,. I dovetailed them all into the pattern of my life with what I delighted in as special deftness. I left no visible seams, no rough edges. The planning of our meetings, the designation of place, the stealing of time without disclosure—all this, apart from the ecstasy of the passion itself— contributed to the excitement of these adventures. To my excitement, and my sense of liberation. I had never felt so free.

Free from what? From all that my life had imposed upon me.

Or let me be rigorously honest: of all that I had imposed upon myself. For I had offered my wrists to these chains: this wife, this job, this position in society.

Why do we make it a virtue to remain faithful to the unseeing commitments of our youth? We mark the first stroke on the canvas before we can see the entire design, and when it unfolds, we've invested so much in it we become reluctant to revise it.

Or so it was for me and Julia.

For neither of us had known how to think beyond the imagined profits of the social investment we had in one another.

It was first of all out of my ambition that I married Julia. Not that she was its object. There were other girls more beautiful or well-connected than Judge Henderson's large-boned, thirtyish daughter. But she was my ambition's ally. I recognized instinctively her inclination to interpret the demands of her own intense ambition as moral imperatives. I saw, even in the lines of her posture, her unshakeable strength of will. I knew I could rely on the fact that she was stronger than I was. If I should falter, she would help me go on. She completed the process that began with my father's death: Julia rescued me from poetry.

This, then, was the tacit agenda for our lives together. In the complex fabric of our marriage, woven, to be fair, of need, affection and desire, of tenderness and even moments of sheer, giving love, the dominant element, the background so encompassing that I rarely recognized it as the foundation of the design, was our colleagueship in ambition.

Julia brought to her own sphere in the community intelligence and will that in a later decade could have directed a major business. Spontaneously sensitive to the patterns and levers of power—how I learned to trust those finely-tuned instincts in building my own career—she climbed the invisible ladder of an informal but powerful social bureaucracy. And her contribution was real. She enhanced culture and social welfare in increasing areas of Jackson, and then the state. A succession of governors drew with respect on her talent, knowledge, and network of contacts as these matured with her experience.

"Man and wife are one flesh."

During the years when we were building our joint career, whenever I heard these words, I genuinely felt that our marriage was our most successful act of obedience to God.

And God apparently blessed us. Together we presented a for- midable front to the community. The achievements of each en- hanced the achievements of the other. Where we were not liked,

19

we were at least taken into account. Yes, Julia Burden was George Burden's appropriate consort.

Yet as I write this I realize there was more. For Julia allowed me to feel companionship, even the regular satisfaction of desire, without asking the surrender of full passion. She allowed me to be dependent on her, without acknowledging it as dependency. We developed a code which imposed such constraints on awareness of feeling over the entire family. Burdens don't talk about their feelings. However they feel, Burdens always fulfill their obligations.

So my youthful instinct was right. Out of our life together, out of our common code, I did achieve my ambition. This position, this network of large responsibilities, of equal privileges and recognition: I owned these as truly as I own my house. And I was happy with the bargain.

Or I was happy until about two years ago when I turned fifty-three, and saw fifty-four and behind it fifty-five on the horizon.

Then, oh then, something in me that had been asleep, or perhaps had never been born, began to feel terror at the thought that this was all I would know until I died. That, I think, is what began it.

Talk had circulated around my name as a possible candidate since the last governor's race. Then it crystallized into informal support for my run for the office. This seemed a natural culmination of my career, of *our* career together. About two years before the next election, some of my political allies called a small meeting to discuss it with me formally. When I saw where the talk was leading, I suddenly felt a panic so intense I was hardly able to let them finish speaking. I thanked them, told them I'd think it over, and that evening reported the conversation to Julia. But the next day, without consulting her further, I telephoned and declined the offer. I told them I would be glad to take any role in Cash Sessums's campaign instead.

Poor Julia! As a result, she had to surrender a dream that she didn't find empty at all. When, that evening, I brought myself to report what I had done, her blue eyes hardened and the lines around her mouth drew tight. She must have felt it as a double betrayal. For it ignored our lifelong precedent of reaching such decisions together. And it rejected without explanation a goal I knew she'd coveted for a decade. I am sure she'd begun to envision her initial projects and staff as First Lady and to consider how we would shape an emergent campaign. But a Burden does not talk about her feelings. However she feels, a Burden always fulfills her obligations. So Julia remained a dutiful, but now a more distant, wife.

Throughout my withdrawal from ambition, and our mutual withdrawal from one another, my unforeseen panic persisted. I never knew when it would appear, the nameless feeling of dread, to which everything and nothing could attach itself, and whose sources were hidden.

My youngest son, Mark, and I have always been close. Perhaps because he came along so much after the others, and reminds me, as if it were a shared secret, of my own vulnerabilities when young, the family rules against feeling seem to relax between us. I sometimes sought him out, knocking with embarrassment at the door of his room and sitting amid his tangle of clothes and books and soccer equipment and tapes and posters, apparently for some point of family business, but really to find consolation in his presence and affection.

Last fall, when he left for Ole Miss and Julia and I were alone in that huge house, my panic worsened. For days at a time I felt such anguish that I could barely force myself to go into the office. I looked sick, and lived in dread my colleagues would ask about it.

It was during that fall that I really became aware of Becca. She worked in bookkeeping. I knew that she was divorced and had a five year old son. We met one Saturday morning in November when I had to take care of an especially painful family task. She was warm and fresh and at first she dissolved my anxieties. Maybe it had been part of the plan from the beginning, a part of the successful man's *cursus honorum,* which I had not desired earlier, but which I now felt I deserved.

So we drifted into an affair. The rediscovery, after my despair, of desire—or rather: the discovery, for the first time, of the possible meaning of desire—was like a new life. It had the force of a conversion, a delivery from death. I felt born again. Together we created a new world, foreign as Saturn, radiant as the sun, a deep, warm secret.

5

Why had that changed?

I lay alone with my arms and legs flung out across the sheets tangled and stained with love. The splash of the shower continued from the next room. The light and the shade from the half-closed blinds next to the bed printed stripes across my body.

My anxiety kept flickering in and out. Not like a strobe light, but like a film whose light source brightens or dims or breaks. And suddenly there bloomed in me an overwhelming apprehension. The walls telescoped to a great distance and then closed in. The room was the face of a shape-changing spirit or pieces of a kaleidoscope shifting.

From where I lay, the mirror on the facing bureau reflected only the top of the heavy gray headboard. On the reflected strip of wall half a painting hung. Blue and purple flowers. Blue and purple repeated itself endlessly, the gabbling speech of the room. Blue and purple drapes. Blue and purple bedspreads. The gray, phony-looking wood of the headboard, too, spilled from the mirror's frame, multiplied itself over and over, mocking from the bureau, mocking from the table by the window, mocking from the two thick-runged captains chairs shoved in beside it.

I wanted them to shut up, I didn't want to hear what they might be saying.

I turned my face away from the great eye of the window toward the more shadowed side of the room. My glance moved across the door of the bathroom and the dark, recessed hallway leading to the door of the room. Locked, the plastic covered card with the motel rules gleaming dully from it, chained against possible intruders. Yet closing me in.

The bathroom door stood ajar, creating a line of fluorescent light in the shadow. Behind it there was a sudden cessation of sound as Becca cut off the shower. She seemed sealed away from me an infinite distance.

My heart skipped a beat, skipped a beat and stopped. What was happening? My heart's silence pulsed in my ear. I tried to make it beat by power of will.

And then it started again, racing. It thrust and thrust like a jackhammer inside the hollow of my chest. I sweated dread.

Trying to muffle awareness, I turned and threw my feet to the floor. I lowered my head in my hands, ground my elbows against my knees, and stared at the blue blank of the carpet.

Let me get control!

My breath was coming too fast. I carefully counted the warm rush of air into and out of my lungs. My breath and then my heart began to slow. I raised my glance to the facing bed, neatly made except where I had pulled away one of the pillows to place under Becca's hips. I clung with my eyes to its inescapable solidity.

Becca elbowed open the bathroom door, her white skin rosy from the shower. She was pulling on her brassiere. She handled her breasts as if they were not attached to her, a gesture as impersonal as if she were slipping paper into the office copying machine. Becca donned always with her clothes a brisker, less compliant manner. This transformation, so familiar, once amused me, but this afternoon it obscurely fed my anxiety.

"George," she said. "I'm worried about Chris."

The fluorescent light from the bathroom door punctured the shadowy wall of the bedroom. She was standing between our world and some other. I struggled to look toward her. Her fluorescent halo appeared menacing, as if it carried a weight of fearful intention.

Pain, dull and intense, exploded beneath my left nipple. It pierced my chest like a spike driven through to my back.

God, I asked, *is this how it happens?*

Becca paused and glanced at me on the bed as she awkwardly fastened her brassiere-strap. As if my silence had been an acknowledgment of her words, she rushed into what she wanted and didn't want to say.

"Chris knows that Mrs. Marshall—I told you about her, the woman next door—Mrs. Marshall doesn't want him over there. She says he takes things."

Becca's strained concern was taking her away from me, removing her presence with each word to a greater and greater distance. I watched from the foxhole of my terror.

Under the pressure of her feeling, she sat at the end of the other bed, then lay back on one arm. She was struggling to find in what she believed was our intimacy the courage to talk about something she was afraid to look at.

"I know he sometimes takes things. But it isn't stealing, George. He just wants to play with them. I've talked with him about it, but..." She paused again, her voice trailing off. "I can't make him obey."

Now she glanced up directly at me.

Becca was asking for help and I couldn't give it. The shadow concealed the hazel of her eyes. The shadow was eating her up. I wanted to respond, but my throat closed over: I was afraid I was going to choke. The pain in my chest and the sweat in the air conditioned room made me begin to tremble.

I nodded.

Becca stood again, as if to move away from the truth she'd just confided. She vanished again into the recesses of fluorescent space, the vacant rectangle of brightness. Her voice, disembodied, coursed on against the rustle of her clothes, against the squeak of the faucet at the sink and the following splash of water. I was dying.

"She was waiting for me last night when I drove in. She had that look of excitement and pleasure she gets, mixed up with anger.

"As soon as I pulled up, she ran over to let me have it: 'Your damn *boy* took my daughter's two-wheeler and left it down the block! Do I have to call the police?'..."

I could hear the sound of Becca's voice, but could no longer make out her words' meaning.

I felt myself pulled into a momentary vision.

In it I was walking a tightrope hung between two small airplanes, gripping a rod for balance. Below me opened the eyes and mouths of a gaping crowd. I swayed, sweating, with the jolts and bumps of turbulence, swinging the balancing rod in concentrated attention. Breathing dread, I knew if I paid perfect attention, I could finish the performance in safety. But then I glanced to the right and saw the pilot slump as in slow motion forward over the instrument panel.

In a paralyzed instant I knew what must happen now. The nose of the plane veered down. The taut rope slackened beneath my feet. *Oh, God!* I was dancing insanely on nothing. I plunged in accelerating terror toward the earth as it rushed up to meet me.

Becca's voice was running confidingly on.

It was like one of those dreams where you are paralyzed and know you're asleep and struggle to wake up. I *strained* to pull myself free.

All at once I was on my feet.

As I rose from the bed, another George Burden rose in the mirror to meet me: naked as at birth, flesh sagging, gut bagged out, hair a white disorder around a mask of dismay.

I was moving through the shadow toward the bathroom door. Becca was dressed now. She stood in front of the sink, her purse open on the back of the toilet, holding a comb under the running water. I lifted my hand in front of my eyes against the confusing assault of light.

"*Forget* about last night, *forget* about Chris!" I cried. "*I* need you now. *Be here with me!*"

My voice overrode Becca's, harsh with fear and rage.

She looked up, startled.

"George!" Her voice was astonished and hurt.

Then her eyelids closed like shutters over her large hazel eyes and remained closed for a long moment.

"George," she finally said in a patient voice, "shouldn't you dress, if you don't want to be late for your meeting with the Governor?"

This was her habitual refuge. Whenever anger appeared, her manner denied to herself and to me that it had existed.

"No!" I yelled. "I need you to be really here, with me!"

A moment earlier I would have died before Becca in silence rather than confess my panic. Now I was enraged that she didn't penetrate my unspoken need and comfort me.

Becca grew still, like an animal whose one strategy for safety is to mimic death. She stood in the fluorescent glare as if paralyzed, her hands drawn back from the brightly streaming water.

"George," she said finally. She spoke as if in demand, but I could hear the fear beneath it. "We don't have time for this. I have to get back to work."

She pushed against my right arm which blocked her exit from the bathroom, expecting it to yield.

"Wait!" I screamed. "We're not through with this!"

Dear God, I sounded like my father.

Under pressure Becca fled into silence as I fled into words. Now I was hunting her down in that silence. Out of my fear I was trying to drive her out of that safety. Her eyes bloomed with reciprocal panic.

"George, let me go!" Her voice rose shrilly. "Don't be crazy!"

We had entered new territory. What was happening between us? I wanted only to be with her, but had made her fear me. Yes, *I*. But *she* wouldn't help me undo it. I loved her so much and needed her now, and she was distorting me into an enemy.

I couldn't bear the sight of her fear-glazed, distanced face, closed down against me. "Listen to me!" I choked.

As if a spring had been released, I grabbed her upper arm and pulled her roughly through the doorway. She turned her face away and flung her hand up before it, palm out, flinching, as if she expected me to hit her.

In my imagination I watched a red stain fade into her cheek, like a photograph darkening in developing solution; watched her crumple into herself, as if wounded beyond her grasp.

The framework of the world seemed instantly to alter: a moment before, all was anger, now all was guilt and shame. I saw myself through Beccca's eyes, and what I saw frightened me. Yet at the same time, I now recognized what I wanted.

I put my arms gently around Becca's trembling shoulders and drew her in against my love-stained body.

"Becca, I'm so sorry," I whispered, lowering my head toward her ear. "Becca, listen. I'm going to divorce Julia. I want you to marry me."

6

I drew Becca down onto the bed nearest the bathroom, to rest in the emotional exhaustion that settled over us. She did not consent or resist. She simply lay still in the shadowy recess of the room with her lids closed over her great eyes.

I ached with guilt and longing. I wanted, though the habit of years made it impossible, to cry. What was *she* feeling in her closed world of silence?

"Becca," I said. "Becca, I'm so sorry. Please don't make this the end."

A memory flowed into my mind of myself as a child, unremembered for a lifetime, a fragment, yet so vivid I knew it was real. I must have been under six, for my mother was still alive. Somehow I had been hurt and she held me on her lap. I saw my feet, in square brown shoes, resting against the side of the chair; I felt the soft curve of her breast, against which my cheek rested, hot and wet. She was rocking me—how vividly I recovered the rhythm, back-pause-and-forth, back-pause-and-forth—as her low voice, which vibrated with the heartbeat in her chest, floated above and around me. Again and again as we rocked, her hand stroked my hair.

"Hush," Becca whispered. "Don't apologize, George. *I'm* sorry." Effacing herself, she was building the magic circle to keep anger outside.

I paused, not wanting to throw us back into the pain we'd begun to escape from. But, oh, how I wanted Becca to understand what I now knew! I lay my hand, mapped with veins and fringed with gray, over her pale hand and spoke in a low voice, carefully erasing from my urgent words the intonation of urgency.

"Becca, I want you more than I've ever wanted anything in my life! When I'm with you—when I'm *away* from you -- it's as if my flesh pulls toward you. I *want*. I'm all want. I thought I wanted everything else I have *and* you. But I've been fooling myself. I don't want anything without you."

Her hand tensed in the embrace of my hand. I pitched my voice even lower.

"I'm serious about marriage," I said softly. "Only think about it. Then *you* bring it up when you're ready."

Becca raised herself on her elbow, tossing her head to move her black hair away from her face. Her hazel eyes were veiled and grave. They reflected a powerful emotion held in reserve, an emotion I couldn't read. Love? Anger? Grief?

"George," she said, "this is too sudden for me. I can't make you any large promises. Please. Let's go on as we are for a while. We'll see how things work out."

I accepted even this with gratitude. At least I hadn't destroyed everything by my display of rage. I'd never let it happen again. I'd persuade Becca to marry me.

The excitement of this certainty rose in me as my terror had earlier.

Come down to earth!

"It's one-fifteen," I said with deliberate matter-of-factness. "Let me call Cash's secretary and tell her I'll be a little late."

I released Becca's hand and rolled over, wheeling my feet to the floor. The slatted blinds met my eyes alive with the dazzle of the day outside. I picked up the phone from the gray night table and dialed the Governor's office, at the same time pulling my shoes from where they had lodged beneath the side of the other bed.

7

Becca waited while I dressed and then I opened the door and slipped into the hall. Of course, we never left together, and it had become our habit for me to leave first.

In the elevator, I felt a drift of anxiety returning. The floor numbers, lighting up lower and lower in sequence, brought me closer and closer to the lobby. The lobby was always an arena of exposure.

I had to enter the lobby in order to rent the room. And, when I was in a hurry, it was usually—this depended on the hotel—the quickest way back to my car. But when the elevator doors slid back, I never knew who might face me.

In fact, I had never met anyone I knew. And I'd rehearsed what I would say a hundred times. I would mention the out-of-town client I was seeing in one of the rooms. Or the business I was dropping in on which the building housed. Or the restaurant in the hotel where I liked to eat. But in recent weeks every leaving after our love-making had been an occasion of fear.

As the doors slid back, I made myself step out casually toward the hotel entrance. Apart from the clerk behind the desk who looked sleepy and bored, there were only two people in the lobby.

One, a plump, white-haired woman, was browsing through the half-filled rack of postcards. She wore a pink pantsuit which made her complexion doughy and outlined in two half moons the bite of her underwear into her thighs. She didn't look around.

Nearer to the door in one of a group of wing chairs sat a young man. His hair was black, his complexion deeply tanned as if he spent a lot of his time outdoors, his features noticeably handsome. Even sitting he had the all-of-a-piece, coordinated posture of a good golfer. His vitality charged the air around him with energy. I thought he looked vaguely familiar. Had I met him on the golf course?

He looked up, and his glance met and momentarily held mine.

Was he going to speak?

I lost my hold on my rehearsed explanations. I was afraid the panic, a glaring confession of guilt, showed in my face. I started to nod.

And then he turned back to the magazine he was reading. My hands were sweating as I grasped the handle of the door.

The noon heat engulfed me. The sky was so pale it was almost white, the sun in the haze a more radiant pallor. The air, dense with moisture, clung to the skin and made breathing an effort. After the air-conditioned lobby, the humidity and heat nauseated me. I focused on reaching the mobile oasis of cooler air, the car. How had we managed Mississippi summers without it?

Trembling, I pulled open the door of the Lincoln and slumped into the driver's seat. It was like an oven. Turning the key in the ignition, I adjusted the air conditioning. It filled the car with a faintly sour smell. A drift of cool air reached me.

I felt beaten by the emotional tumult of the preceding two hours. Perhaps I shouldn't try to handle the meeting at the Mansion. I could easily excuse myself by calling in sick and going home. Perhaps I *was* getting sick and that was the reason everything had so unstrung me. I was pressing my limit.

The cool air began to restore me. I reached under the passenger seat and pulled out the brown leather cassette case. I wanted to hear some Bach, something by Dinu Lipatti, that marvelously lucid pianist without darkness or flaw. The notes of *Jesu, Joy of Man's Desiring* began to fall, one after one, on the enclosed air. I lay back and closed my eyes.

Everything will be all right. I know I can make Becca marry me.

Did I doze? I wasn't sure. I jerked myself upright.

Opening my eyes, I reached forward to shift the transmission into drive.

Becca was walking across the parking lot. I watched her come marvelously into view, black hair, white summer dress with a small pattern of roses, unaware that I was watching her. She was as composed and neat, and at the same time as energetic as if it were early morning. Her step had its public, confident mixture of definition and vitality.

Becca's head was bent toward her breast, her dress flowing lightly around her legs as she walked. She was speaking with intense concentration to the young man I had seen in the lobby. His face was turned toward her, listening with a skeptical and somewhat amused expression that appeared inconsistent with her seriousness. His step had the confident sureness and elasticity of hers.

I wanted to hide myself in case they should lift their eyes. At the same time I wanted to catch every gesture of the scene playing out before the glass, as if it were a film in which the clear, sweet score played on, but the words were erased from the sound track.

What would make credible Becca meeting anyone here after being with me? *Had* he been waiting for her? Or was he perhaps a friend she had met by accident, whose suspicions she wanted to quiet?

I could ask her the next time we met. But did I dare? What that I could bear to hear would explain the intimacy of her confiding earnestness?

Three rows away, they turned and disappeared between the glinting cars, walking toward the street. When they reappeared, I could see only their backs.

The young man leaned over and placed his arm along Becca's shoulder, his muscles riding under his shirt with easy energy. An impudent look crossed his face as he said something into her ear.

She turned, as if annoyed at this counter to her earnestness. Then slowly she shook her head and unwillingly laughed. Without breaking step, Becca stretched up and kissed his lowered cheek.

How can I tell the effect that the scene I had witnessed had on me?

A number of years ago, while driving home, I passed through an intersection in which a major accident had just occurred. A car making a left turn had been broadsided by an on-coming truck. The intersection was a litter of glass, the car almost cut in two by the impact, like a wasp pinched at the waist. Reducing my speed, I felt the muted apprehension one always does as the accident slowly slid past my left window. Yes, and the sense of relief that it did not involve me.

Then a totally contextless thought materialized in my mind. *That car looks a lot like Brook's car.* Brook, my oldest son!

No, it can't be, an inner voice answered. But suddenly my arms and legs madly swerved my own car into the facing lane and rushed me back toward the accident. I saw two policemen pulling Brook from the driver's side of the automobile. His face was bloody and he was trembling, but he was trying to cooperate with them. I pulled up and ran toward him. Yet my consciousness remained in an oddly dissociated state, as if it were a scene from somebody else's life. Only when I was assured he was all right did I feel, like an unforeseen punch, the terror of losing a child.

So now, before this unbearable loss, this apparent betrayal, my mind hung suspended. Yet somewhere in my body there hammered fear.

I watched, straining. Distance and the sun's white glare among the cars swallowed Becca up, her hand resting familiarly on the arm of the black-haired young man. She was gone.

What was it that Martin had referred to that morning? My knack for sizing people up. Could I, who had achieved so much by my power to read the human heart, have misread Becca and the love between us so completely?

One of my professors in law school, lecturing on evidence, told a story about certainty. A man was afraid his wife was having an affair, so he hired a private detective. "I want you to follow my wife," the client said. "Find out whether she *is* having an affair. The uncertainty is killing me."

Several days later the detective called him back. "Yesterday," he reported, "I followed your wife to a hotel. There she met a man. They signed the register as 'Mr. and Mrs. Smith' and went upstairs."

"What happened next?" asked the man.

"I was able to find a window across the street that opened onto their window. Your wife and the man undressed and lay down together on the bed."

"And what happened then?" asked his client.

"I couldn't see," said the detective. "She reached up and closed the blinds."

"Couldn't see?" exclaimed his client. "Oh, this uncertainty is killing me!"

But *could* I truly know the meaning of what I had just seen?

My mind tried to take refuge in uncertainty. But my heart trusted my fear.

Dazed, I released the car into motion, paused at the exit to the lot, and turned into the stream of traffic.

Ordinarily, as I drove through a part of the city like this, its old functions bypassed by growth in other areas, my mind seized on the city as an unfinished problem. Extending its lines of development into the future, how could this area be turned again into a resource?

But today I barely saw it.

Fragmented memories of the afternoon dropped into my mind.

Please. Don't let this be the end.

Over and over again.

Wrenching Becca back into the shadowed room.

Over and over her face flinching in fear away.

I'm so sorry. I'm sorry. I'm sorry.

Marry me.

Shame like a tide flooded my most secret being; shame exposing my aged need; shame like the sting of salt on a naked wound. I was drowning.

I beat my hands against the steering wheel in despair.

Dear God! Help me!

8

The white brick structure of the Governor's Mansion loomed up to the right. I turned into the long driveway that led to the office wing at the rear. The old, black guard in the guardhouse next to the wrought iron gates, recognizing me, flashed a warm smile and waved me through. In this most public place, perhaps I'd find the inward privacy to resolve my confusion.

Steering the Lincoln into a space beside a car with a coast dealer's insignia on the tag, I parked. There were no trees protecting the parking area and at this hour each edging shrub sat above its own puddle of shadow. I pushed open the door and stepped out. The heat bouncing from the pavement flowed into the heat from the sky.

Still, here amid the neon dazzle of the watermelon-colored crape myrtles and the luminous green of the lawn, the wild heat had been made somehow civil. I glanced again at the car from the coast, a dark blue Cadillac. It was Harriet McEnloe's car.

The long white wall of the Mansion's office wing has only one door. I walked up the graveled walk and pushed the black button beside it. The security guard at the gate would already have signaled the mansion: I heard the click of the mechanism releasing and entered.

I nodded to the blue-uniformed guard at the desk.

"George Burden," I said.

"Yessir, Mr. Burden, I know who you are," the guard responded with detached friendliness. He had a youthful red face and a stiff blond mustache which made him look younger rather than older and more authoritative as he must have hoped. "The Governor is expecting you."

"Thank you. I can find my own way back."

The conference room was at the end of the corridor to the right. Light from the open door reached into the hallway. As I approached it, I began to make out familiar voices.

What was happening in this place had been the normal fabric of my life for thirty years. It was an arena whose rules and cues I knew perfectly. But my preoccupation with Becca didn't want to release me and I felt I was about to enter a world now alien. Gathering my will, I finally forced myself to step into the room.

If I had so chosen, this would have been the room where I was now conducting my business. It was long and narrow. The muted rust carpet richly set off the dark wood of the table and the deep blue leather of the chairs around it. At the far end of the room the single window rose behind the Governor's chair, framing it with a glimpse of crape myrtle and white outbuildings. On one of the pale beige side walls hung a massive medallion of the state's seal. Facing it, above the side tables and plants, were paintings and prints by present day Mississippi artists and acceptable images of the fantasies and visions that had haunted Mississippi's history.

Cash, a glance at the room told me, was not yet here. We were meeting at the Mansion, in any case, rather than in the Council for Economic Development offices, out of deference to his day's heavy schedule.

As I looked around, a figure detached itself from one of the conversing groups and made in my direction. Jim Gorman extended a well-shaped, carefully manicured hand, the color of creamed coffee. Jim, with his square, handsome face and now salt-and-pepper hair, was dressed, like Martin, noticeably well, in a style classic rather than idiosyncratic, which stressed position and role rather than the individual qualities of his person. He began to talk without further greeting.

"Well, the northern division is falling into place."

This was follow-up about a fundraising campaign he and I had discussed at the Chamber of Commerce meeting the week before. Jim was raising money in order to continue a program at Hawthorne, the black college which he serves as president, a program which readies underprepared high school students to handle college level work. He had spoken to me earlier because the chairman of his campaign's northern division was not being active, but was too influential to offend by asking him to step down. I suggested appointing a lieutenant who *would* work, while giving the chairman credit. We've all taken on publicly thankless positions like this at times, and I knew someone who was sympathetic enough to the drive's goals to work under these conditions. If he had the time to accept the responsibility, he would carry it out effectively.

"So Engel took it?" It was a statement framed as a question.

"Yes. And we discovered we have something further in common. We both graduated from Harvard, although in quite different years."

Gorman's ready reference to his Harvard career was perhaps not vanity, but a habitual reflex to remind people that he belonged where he was by right. His parents, who played a frequent part in his speeches and interviews, drilled into him the belief that he could achieve anything he wished, and that education was the key. Under their influence he had imitated the career of a number of his white peers, leaving the state for the connections and credentials of an Ivy League university. And it was a measure of his commitment that he returned to Hawthorne when so much else was open to him, first as a young teacher of sociology and finally as president.

However, he also discovered the limitation of his parents' optimistic advice. Education could do much, but it could not resolve the ambiguities of success in Jim's time and place. People respected his great competence, but even if he should become governor, he would never personally belong in just the way he had dreamed in the days of his youth. His manner was a mixture of competence and wariness, resilience and muted resentment.

"Engel's a good man," I forced myself to engage with the conversation.

"What are you saying about my friend Huston Engel?" broke in a hearty contralto voice. Harriet McEnloe's appearance was, as ever, imposing. The length of her face was emphasized by deep lines between nose and mouth, mouth and strong chin. In recent years she had developed a mild tremor, a side-effect, as I knew, of medication, and the soft, pink skin of her cheeks and throat shook slightly as she spoke. She simply accepted it, just as she had allowed her blonde hair to gray, wearing her age, like many a man, as a badge of competence. Her dress was candidly that of a wealthy woman, someone to be treated with respect. Harriet loved the possession and management of power. She handled her social and professional transactions as an experienced priest performs a mass, entirely secure in the rituals of her devotion.

"Hello George, hello Jim," she continued with a smile that was warm but business-like. "I hope you're going to help us with our proposal this afternoon?"

Jim turned and automatically held out to her a manicured hand. She shook it firmly and turned her long face with an acute, inquisitive gaze, toward me.

I was finding the conversation an effort and shrank inwardly from the gaze.

"Do you have any questions about the festival?" she asked me, noticing my discomfort and wrongly assessing its reason.

"Harriet," I said, falsely hearty, "I'm sure the festival has been so well considered that it's a shoo-in."

I sounded hollow even to myself.

"And I appreciate your support," she said, claiming my disinterest as approval. "We *know* what influence you have with the Governor."

My falseness had drawn forth a corresponding falseness in her. She heard it herself. Turning to Jim she said, "George is *never* moved, however I flatter him."

The misstep, recovered, had never been; she had lost nothing.

I felt a hundred miles away.

Harriet McEnloe, in her sixty-five years, has lived in and out of Mississippi. Charles, her husband, a second generation oil man with conservative political ambitions, has earned himself with his wealth and generosity a number of minor political appointments in Washington. Perhaps because of this early enlargement of horizon, Harriet has never defined herself as a volunteer. Like the men in the room, she has pursued a professional career and one with national reach.

Harriet is mistress of an effective blend of polished charm and, even now, of sexual flattery. Deference and admiration can, of course, be very powerful instruments of influence. But this has never been the principal element in Harriet's repertoire. Hers is ultimately the polish of the boardroom rather than of the actual or implied bedroom.

She moves easily back and forth between persons and the more abstract realities of principles and policy.

There is a story about a man from New York who was riding a train through Mississippi, reading *The New York Times.* A well dressed local woman sat down opposite him. He held out the sections he had completed and asked her if she would like to read the paper.

"Oh, no," she replied mystified, "I don't know a *soul* in New York City."

Harriet would have known everything that woman knew about the power of personal relationships, but she could have launched an informed assessment of the biases of the *Times* editorial pages as well. It would depend on what she considered in the interest of her stock of influence.

And this is her greatest weakness. She responds too immediately to the present possession of power. "If I want to know where my influence stands on any given day," I once said to Julia after a frustrating dinner with the McEnloes in Washington, "all I have to do is observe Harriet's manner toward me. She is a perfect barometer."

Harriet turns toward present power like a sunflower toward the sun, not taking into sufficient account that the young person sitting ignored across the table might be seeing more than she knows and might one day remember her public slight. Nor is she a prudent banker of influence with those whom the turning wheel has set out of present authority.

Today, I was important to her. She had placed her prestige behind this project, and she knew my closeness to Cash and several members of the Council. But she was prepared to respect my distance until she more fully understood it. I saw her shrewd eye watching me as she turned back to Jim. She placed her large, ringed hand on his sleeve above the wrist and let it rest there for a moment, as if she were taking his pulse.

"I hope there are ways we can involve some of your students, Jim, although it *is* some distance away. It's important to make clear to the national media how far we've come as blacks and whites since the early sixties."

Truly transactions of power are a condition for creativity in managing institutions. It is unceasing activity of this kind which weaves the pattern of civilization for human life. So Harriet, sleek with her expertly maintained satisfaction, and Jim, who could never fully erase his lingering frustration, fed themselves and each other; and both did the world's good.

But I felt I had entered a ship of fools. Or perhaps I was now the fool, for this had been the primary activity of my adulthood, my habitual and congenial home. Now it seemed drained of any meaning. I was reminded of the mental illness in which the ordinary words of one's language can still be heard, but the mind cannot assign them significance. Everyone the sufferer accosts smiles and gestures as if the language makes sense. But it seems to him only a fraud or malevolent joke, for what he hears is gibberish. I was forgetting the very rules of the game: I couldn't remember enough to keep my mask in place. If Harriet turned to speak to me now, I'd be dead.

9

There was a movement at the door.

As if at a signal, conversation fell and all heads turned in anticipation. Cash Sessums strode into the room. We had been friends since we were eight. We had roomed together at Harvard, two Southern exiles grinding our way through law school, yet finding time to sit on the steps of Widener and watch the girls crossing Harvard Yard. It had been a joke between us to ask which would become Mississippi's governor first.

Cash, I think, is the best governor of this state in my lifetime, a man who thinks a generation ahead, who begins to see and work out the solutions to problems before others have recognized that the problems exist. He knows on how few key decisions the outcome of any endeavor depends, and while attending efficiently to the daily business of the state, he has a small set of priorities which are the focus of his most intense activity. He also has the ability, indispensable in a leader, to reduce these issues to their essence and frame them to the various constituencies whose support will make a policy work.

Cash moved in my direction, smiling, nodding in greeting to those he passed. He recognized that since he had become governor, his greeting or lack of it had assumed for people a weight of meaning which it did not possess before. His face, in its squared outlines, reflected his strength; the fineness of his mouth and the warmth of his eyes reflected his intelligence and humanity; slightly premature white hair gave his appearance dignity.

He squeezed my shoulder.

"Let me see you when this is over," he said, his glance full of warmth. In this warmth I began to feel reconnected.

Cash walked on to the head of the table. As if awaiting a signal, everyone watched for him to take his seat in the chair framed by the tall window at the end of the room with the glimpses of crape myrtle and white outbuildings beyond them. As soon as he began to sit, they seated themselves.

The meeting was chaired by the Executive Director of the Council for Economic Development, Leonard Stein. Stein is a heavy-set, dark, personally somewhat untidy man in his mid-fifties. His manner is straightforward; like his accent, it reflects his origins in the Bronx. He had made his reputation in Albany and Mississippi had invested a large amount to bring him here. This afternoon he sat to the right of Cash, unkempt and with his perpetual appearance of five o'clock shadow.

Every meeting makes for Stein its demand on a patience which is not the natural expression of his temperament. He's in Mississippi because of his technical expertise, not because he was born in the community. The basis for any influence he has is his reputation for effective knowledge. But I had watched him discover that, although he had been hired to introduce innovation, his proposals were discounted if they departed very widely from the state's familiar practice. Yet he knew that if he were not effective, he would be fired. So with methodical tact, he pushed slowly forward.

"The major item on our agenda this afternoon," he began, nodding to Harriet and the other members of their group -- to Gerry Anderson, Director of the Coast Restaurant Association, Jack Parrish, the mayor of Ocean Springs, John Morse, the leading Ocean Springs banker—"is a proposal to help fund a performing arts festival on the coast.

"There are two or three smaller items, however, which we need to take care of first. None of them is private, I think." He paused and, his eyebrows rose in inquiry, surveyed the Council members, resting his glance particularly on the Governor. Then, seeing no objection, he continued, "Therefore I think you gentlemen - and lady," nodding to Harriet, "might as well stay while we run through them. We'll proceed as rapidly as we can."

I surrendered to this enforced repose. The purposeful but irrelevant background drone of voices, like the jingling of keys in a pocket, at once absorbed and released my attention.

My imagination slipped back to Becca.

Becca in the latticed light at noon, her black hair, spread across the pillow, shining lilac in the sun's fall.

Becca in so many lights, seen in the drift of a year.

At dinner on a weekend in New Orleans, candlelight tangled in the black, fine hair of her forearm as, leaning toward me, she pressed it softly against the table.

Becca lying on the front deck of my boat as it swayed at anchor off one of the channel islands, the pale white dazzle of deck-light, reflected, blurring the blue shadow beneath her breasts.

Her breasts beneath the hand of another man ...

I jerked myself back to the conference room. Harriet McEnloe had chosen the seat opposite me. Her long face held an abstracted expression, but I feared that with her inexplicable intuition she might turn at any moment and somehow penetrate my mind. I focused my attention on Stein's words.

But I found it impossible stay with them.

My mind drifted again, to the day Becca and I had met.

10

It began by accident. No image I then had of myself admitted the possibility of a mistress. Nor had I really noticed Becca until we met one Saturday morning while I was performing a grim, necessary family errand.

Our family owned an English sheepdog. One day when Mark was seven I asked him if he wanted to come with me while I drove out to a local kennel to look at the hunting dogs. He eagerly hopped in the car. The kennel was a rather large operation that sold several breeds. Mark, wandering around while I sat in the shade of an old sweet gum tree talking with the owner, came upon a pen full of sheepdog puppies. He squatted beside the fence and one of the pups waddled over to sniff him out. Soon they were in deep communion.

I could see them in the distance as I sat talking, like the memory of a boyhood experience I never had. When Mark begged me to buy her, my objections were only perfunctory. I soon said yes. I bought her as the family's dog, but everyone knew she especially belonged to Mark. Mark named her Daisy.

Daisy soon became a presence in the family. A ball of fur -- a muff walking, said one of Julia's friends—she waddled the floors with her nose down, eagerly following a scent, until she was distracted by a sound. Then she stilled into stiff attention until, the disturbance assessed, she melted again into motion.   Mark, who at times seemed hardly older than Daisy, took charge of her housebreaking. He did a good job, too, although there are still scars chewed by her teeth in the side of the grandfather clock, a fragment of that family history which gets written physically into the space where people live.

After Daisy was bred she became more subdued, and then even matronly. But she never completely lost the air of a teenager on a class trip, fond of the chaperones, but always ready to be led astray by excitement. She trotted into a room, her button eyes peering from behind the bangs that fell over them, her mouth open in a little terrier grin. She visited each person in turn, her hindquarters going like a motor, then flopped nearby, her head on her paws, her eyes following under her bangs when anyone moved, ready to scramble up and pursue any lead of interest.

Most often she accompanied Mark; she slept in his room. Mark loved Daisy as if she were human. Sometimes he treated her as a younger child who had to be patiently checked, sometimes as a joyous friend, sometimes as another parent whom he could depend on in any trouble for unlimited love. Perhaps she gave him something he could not easily find from the rest of the family. The Burdens did their duty more easily than they displayed their affection. As Mark grew older, his relationship with Daisy became more laid back, but they continued to share the same communion that had moved me when I watched him at seven squatting beside her cage and playing with her through the fence.

At eleven Daisy began to have a series of kidney infections which made her lose the ability to control her urine. No more visits to the family room: now she lived in the kitchen, shut in by a wooden gate. She flopped down on the linoleum floor, her head on her paws, watching under her bangs for someone to walk in, whining if she were left alone too long. Mark took her outside on a regular schedule. As the year progressed, Daisy's hips, too, weakened. When she tried to squat she collapsed. In order for her to relieve herself, one of us had to hold her belly in our hands as in a sling and lower her hindquarters toward the grass.

When Mark left for Ole Miss, we continued the routine, Ella Mae, our maid, Julia, or I regularly leading Daisy, slipping and scrambling, out to the yard and lowering her hindquarters. It was absurd in a way, a spontaneous tribute to Daisy's continuing joy of life and patience and the deeply-felt way human beings and family animals come to live in each other. But as Daisy entered her twelfth year, the infections caused her more pain and the medication helped less. However frequently we took her out, she more often lost control in the kitchen. We would find her whining and scrambling in the mess, trying to stand, looking up at us with a deep mixture of distress and trust.

One Friday evening after an especially harrowing episode I went into my study, picked up the phone, and called Mark. We talked over carefully what Daisy was suffering.

Saturday was one of those overcast November days when the air is as hot and thick as summer, the trees dropping their dry, brown leaves beneath a milky sky. I walked into the kitchen before breakfast. Daisy was sleeping, her head down on her paws, but when she heard me her stub of a tail began to move back and forth like a cloth polishing the floor. I jangled a leash, our familiar signal for a walk. Eagerly she scrambled to get her front legs under her and sat, her tail switching faster, waiting for me to attach the leash to her collar.

"Want to go for a ride?" I asked, in the confiding, hearty voice people use to engage children and animals. I could hardly bear my betrayal.

"Let me carry you, old girl." I hoisted her up in my arms, paused to cradle her hindquarters on the lawn, and hoisted her again into the back seat of the car.

Daisy rode balancing shakily on the seat, thrusting her nose forward into the slipstream through the opened window. Three children in the back of a passing pickup shouted to her and waved their arms in delight. She answered with a deep-throated volley of barks, and subsided onto the seat to rest.

Bob Stoddard, our veterinarian's office is a tan cinder-block building at the edge of town. A neat circular bed of yellow chrysanthemums grew in the middle of the gravel parking lot, in contrast to the weathered red and brown weeds that grew wildly everywhere else. I swung in at the billboard-like sign:

STODDARD VETERINARY CLINIC
Boarding and Grooming
We Love Animals

The tires crunched over the gravel and came to a stop next to a battered red pickup and a white Chevrolet. This, too, was a signal: Daisy raised herself to look out.

I again lifted her into my arms, as large as a seven or eight year old child wrapped in a fur coat, reached beneath her to grope for the knob of the door, and entered the waiting room. I was at the same time so agitated and so emotionally removed that the scene had the vividness and unreality of a dream.

The desk stood straight ahead. Above it on the wall hung the familiar framed decorations: a Norman Rockwell print, an old veterinarian caring for a cocker spaniel puppy, all coppery ears and liquid eyes, while a long-and freckle-faced boy with a missing front tooth looks worriedly on; next to it Stoddard's professional credentials. And credentials of a different kind, the most prominent an elaborate cross-stitched motto from a grateful client:

> *FOR DOCTOR ROBERT STODDARD,*
> *WHO TRULY LOVES ANIMALS,*
> *THERE IS A SPECIAL PLACE*
> *FOR MEN LIKE HIM*
> *IN HEAVEN*

I found this a little ostentatious, but perhaps it was only because clients rarely cross-stitch such testimonials for attorneys.

I had called Stoddard before setting out, but no one was behind the desk. I stood there vaguely aware, to my right, of the long waiting room, whose gathered calico curtains, pine paneling, and early American furniture were meant to give an impression of coziness, but felt to me now only cheap and ominous.

A raw-faced country woman in a print dress sat in one of the chairs, both her hands wrapped tightly around the bottom of a chain leash, while her pit bull terrier strained against her. She was speaking about her dog's gentleness to a young woman in white slacks and a daffodil blouse who sat opposite. "She'd never hurt a living soul!" she was saying in an injured, rising cadence, stopping the mouths of anticipated critics who might take it into their heads to malign her dog. "Why, I let her chase my little grandbaby around the yard!"

Her chanced confidante listened quietly, resting her hands on a carrying case from which an unpersuaded cat kept an eye on the struggling dog. The faint smell of antiseptic soured the air.

I set Daisy onto the floor and struck the bell. It rang sharply against the woman's continuing indignation. Daisy, familiar with the routine, began to whine in anticipation. Bob came bustling through the door from the dismissal corridor. When she saw him, Daisy let out a joyous yelp.

Bob Stoddard's about sixty, red-faced and white-haired. Although over-sensible of his professional dignity, he has a genuine love for animals. He nodded to me in a detached way and then turned his attention to Daisy.

"Hello, Daisy," he exclaimed warmly, "I've been waiting for you." His large hand reached over the counter to scratch her forehead where the fringe of bangs fell over her dark eyes. "What an old teddy bear."

Under the caress of this deep, warm voice with its emphatic and varied intonations, Daisy shut her eyes and her stub tail began to switch.

"Want to come behind and see me?"

As if they were having a private conversation, he reached out, lifted Daisy's leash from my hand, and guided her through the swinging door at the side of the counter. It sprang shut behind her. She was on the other side.

The event was over more quickly than I had imagined it. I stood alone and unsatisfied on my side of the counter, while Daisy sat waiting a further signal from Stoddard. Somehow I wanted more time to accustom myself to what was to happen. Or perhaps I wanted to be with her when she died. I wasn't sure what was possible and felt it awkward to ask.

"Is there anything else I can do?"

"No. I'll take care of it all."

"This won't hurt her?"

"It will be an injection. She'll simply go to sleep." Stoddard's voice was curt, as if Daisy belonged to him now and I were intruding.

"And the...the disposal...should I come back?"

"I'll take care of all that."

I wanted to ask him how Daisy's body would be treated, but his manner had become so withdrawn that I was afraid to say more. I felt helpless and ashamed before my unforeseen sense of bereavement.

"You'll bill us?"

"Yes."

He waved to indicate to the others waiting that he would be with them in a moment. I turned away.

47

On the wall beside the door my eyes met another decoration, a frame with a carved profile of a St. Bernard at its top and, beneath it, written in an amateur calligraphic hand,

The One Unselfish Friend
A Man Can Have In This Selfish World,
The One Who Never Proves
Treacherous or Ungrateful,
Is His Dog.

"Christ!" I whispered. I pulled open the door and hurried out into the hot, milky morning. As I stood there pulling myself together, I heard the door open again behind me.

"Mr. Burden?"

I turned. It was the young woman who had been holding the cat.

"The doctor took my cat back with him. I saw you come in and just wanted to say hello. I don't know if you remember me. I work in bookkeeping. My name is Becca Talbot."

That was how I met Becca.

11

I've been trying so hard to make clear my feelings about Becca that I haven't found words for what it meant to *see* her.

Becca was twenty-four when I met her. I had glimpsed her in the office, but bookkeeping was on a lower floor, and I'd only noticed in passing appreciation the way her black hair set off her pale complected features.

Now as we spoke I recognized that she was tall, as the Burdens are, but more lightly built, her figure at once elegant and full enough to be womanly. There was something about her both fresh and tranquil, energetic and stable. She stood as if especially connected with the ground. Even in those first moments, I not only appreciated her with my eye, but echoed her presence in my body, feeling with a faint ache of longing how well that height and shapeliness, that mixture of definition and vitality would lie into me length to length.

That day I began to learn her face, like a lesson never to be mastered. No catalogue of features describes a face as it is known to those who love it, but perhaps I can convey something of it. Becca swept her hair back across the tops of her ears into a black coil, showing up her white neck and the rose-pale lobes of her ears below. This gave her a classic, ballerina- or Madonna-like beauty, severe yet sensuous. The most noticeable of her features were her large, long-lashed, hazel eyes, set above rather prominent cheekbones. Her mouth, too, was large and full. Proportion made these strong features beautiful.

I don't know whether I loved her face more in its nakedness, its large features and pale color emphatic and unadorned, or muted, made civil, her eyes carefully made up, her mouth softened by the pale lipstick she wore.

But her appearance itself was less important than what I felt I read in it. Becca had a social ease and ability to sense and fit herself to any present atmosphere. Sometimes this warmth appeared almost anxiously attentive, at other times tranquil and as spontaneous as her breathing. Yet like the iridescence in a shell whose color and pattern shift with a shift of light, I sometimes caught in her eyes as well an absence, a constrained inwardness, as if she were regarding something cold or sorrowful that took her unreachably from me.

On that morning her presence drew me from my shadowy struggle with loss back into the public world. I saw only her warmth: it flooded the recesses of my need, made me feel less helpless.

"How is your dog?"

"Not well," I said, attempting a polite smile. Less seemed dishonest, more too intimate.

Her eyes modified with concern as if there were a change in the light, their hazel darkening toward brown.

"She looks like she's been in your family a long time," she said with quiet appreciation.

I wasn't ready to return to the house. There, I would be free neither to put the morning out of my mind nor to speak about it. Nor did I want to leave Becca. Impulsively, I asked, "I was going across the street to the doughnut shop for a cup of coffee. Will you join me?"

"Yes, I'd like a cup of coffee."

She smiled and reached for the waiting room door. "Let me make sure everything is taken care of for my cat. Then I'll be ready."

I waited in the gray, wilting air, aware in my returning anxiety of her absence. I wondered if Daisy were already dead.

Finally, the door reopened.

"I'm ready," Becca greeted me in her warm, composed voice. I smiled acknowledgment. Our silence was already so comfortable I didn't need or want to complicate it with chatter.

We started across the parking lot, the displaced gravel crunching beneath our feet, skirted the chrysanthemum bed, its lemon-yellow suns muted in the flat light, and made for the street. Becca's long-legged stride kept easy pace with mine. It was a pleasure to have this tall, beautiful woman walking beside me. There rose in me a sense of the freedom one feels when turning out of the driveway into a vacation.

Old North is a two-lane highway, half-town, half-country, patches of business interspersed with patches of scrub. The traffic was light this early on a Saturday, but in a spontaneous gesture of care I took Becca's elbow. It was the first time I touched her. I felt her flesh slide beneath the loose silkiness of her daffodil blouse. But what unfolded in me then was not desire, but a sense of rightness and familiarity so deep that it seemed to touch something timeless.

DoNuT
DiNeR

The neon letters, a pale snake of tubing in the daylight, floated in front of the red and green painted name. It was a local chain, the look and operation stamped from shop to shop as uniformly as the doughnuts. I knew the owner. He had kept the locally well-known name, while recently updating the decor into a trendy new version of a fifties diner. It had made his fading business competitive again.

I pushed open the door and Becca preceded me into the shop. Its surfaces gleamed, sparkled, shone: tile, glass, chrome, more neon over the register, green, sleek Formica tabletops and booths in silvery vinyl. The smell of hot sugar hung in the air, like the stale, sweet smell of cotton candy at the Fair. Beside us, in hypnotic rhythm, a conveyer belt lifted, row by row, rounds of flesh-pale dough, flipped them into sizzling oil, then carried them, puffed now and brown, through a drizzle of liquid sugar dripped from above to the place where a gloved girl agilely packed them in flat **DoNuT DiNeR** boxes.

"My little boy loves these places," Becca said.

"I can see why," I said. "What is his name?"

"Chris." The tempo and engagement of her voice quickened as she began to speak of him. "He's four—the Fearsome Fours," she said warmly. "I don't know why everyone told me about the Terrible Twos but not the Fearsome Fours. He wants his way in *everything*!"

She sounded as if she were announcing a particular distinction.

"Chris is with his daddy today," she said again. My glance must have drifted to her ring finger, for she added, "We've been divorced for two years. My husband—ex-husband, Mike—he

51

likes to have Chris, though his wife is pregnant. I hope it doesn't change anything. Chris needs a daddy."

She said this last with a certain passion, then faded off into the sad abstraction I was to come to know so well. It made me feel protective toward her.

"I'm sure things will work out," I said, gently but meaninglessly.

We were standing in front of the chrome and glass display counter. Rows of doughnuts sat in ranks on long, slanted trays with their names inscribed above: *Cinnamon, Powdered Sugar, Glazed, Raspberry, Lemon, Creme, Chocolate with Sprinkles, Chocolate Iced Glazed, Chocolate Iced Custard.* A teenage girl behind the counter turned to help us.

"What would you like?" I asked Becca, tapping the glass.

In a momentary childlike gesture of decision she pursed her mouth and crooked her index finger across her lips.

"Hmmm." She paused, then looked up at the waiting girl. "I'd like a Chocolate Iced Custard. And a cup of coffee, please."

"I'd better skip the doughnut," I said. "I'd like a cup of decaf, if you have it."

As the girl gathered our order onto the tray, Becca reached for her purse.

"No, no," I said. "You're doing me the favor of keeping me company. Let me pay."

She let her purse fall back to her side and I paid and picked up the tray. I led the way to one of the booths next to the window and set the tray down on the green Formica tabletop.

"Is this okay?"

"Yes. I'm glad we came here," Becca said as she squeezed onto the bench opposite me. The window looked out on the parking lot, almost empty, rows of white lines and grease-stained cement. Becca's daffodil blouse was soft and cheerful against the hard colors of the booth and the flat November day. "In my family we often came to a place like this to celebrate."

"How large was your family?" I asked. It was more than courtesy. I was eager to share something of her experience.

"Eight," she said. At my raised eyebrows, she laughed. "Well," she corrected, "six of us kids."

"What does your father do?"

"Daddy was a Methodist minister. He's retired now. We moved around a lot when I was growing up."

"Did you find that hard?"

"Sometimes. Then I got used to the fact that my relationships outside the family wouldn't last long. I expected it and that made it easier."

The plastic coffee cup bent slightly under my fingers as I picked it up and sipped the stale-tasting coffee. Becca hunched her shoulders and bent slightly over her plate, taking a generous bite of the Iced Chocolate Custard doughnut. Raising her head, she caught my eye merrily.

"Maybe I should have taken something easier to handle." She laughed confidently.

"And your brothers and sisters?" I continued.

"They're mostly older. Bobby and Tom, the first two, live up in the hills. They're almost forty. Then there are my sisters, Sandy and Pat. Sandy lives in Mississippi, in Tupelo. Pat's in Birmingham. Chris has a lot of cousins. I'm glad about that. My parents planned to stop with the four, but ten years later Frank and I came along. The twins. A double surprise, Daddy says."

"Well, a fortunate one," I smiled.

Becca again picked up her doughnut and managed another sumptuous bite.

"You know, you make that look so good," I said. "I couldn't eat a whole doughnut, but would you mind if I tasted it?"

"I'd be grateful!" she exclaimed, pushing it toward me on her napkin. "Take as much as you want."

I started to pinch off a corner of the chocolate covered dough.

"No, no! Take a real bite. You need to get some of the custard."

Gingerly I pulled off a chunk of the doughnut, held my left hand under it to catch the oozing filling, and stuffed it into my mouth. I licked the fingers of both hands.

"My verdict is messy, but good," I gravely announced through my fingers.

Becca's hazel eyes, flecked with gold, opened in feigned wonder and she laughed again.

"You must spend time in courtrooms!" she said playfully.

I wiped the remaining stickiness from my fingers with a coffee-stained napkin.

In the comfortable silence, a snatch of background music, a radio piped through the speakers, became audible, a singer with driving falsetto backup.

"I like this group," she said. "Cows on Acid. No, *really*," she added immediately, as if expecting my face to register disbelief. "Don't you know them?"

"Love them," I said, and broke into one of their songs. "But I pretend it's my son who likes them," I whispered, leaning forward.

Becca laughed and picked up her coffee. I watched her. Against the music drifted the conversation of the two young girls behind the counter, another world.

"Nothing wrong with dancing!" said one. "Singing, dancing, praising the Lord!"

"Well, when you're at a prom, you aren't praising the Lord."

"So her Mom and Dad never dance?"

"When you're married, it's different."

I leaned forward, returning to our conversation.

"And where did you say Frank lives?"

"I didn't. He lives in L.A."

"Married?"

"He was.

"But I really did want to hear about your dog."

It seemed natural now to talk about Daisy. And talking with Becca I came to understand why Daisy's death had so shaken me. In it something larger had slipped irretrievably into the past. Mark's going away to college, all the children away now, Daisy's death, these were the snap of a connection between the part of my life that had preceded and all that was to come. I'd just put to death a part of my own heart.

12

"George..."

I heard my name and fell back into the conference room. Still the tall window with its glimpse of watermelon-red blooms, bronze-green leaves and white outbuildings formed a luminous frame behind Cash Sessums's head. Still the state seal loomed from the wall. And still Stein's Bronx-accented voice commanded the meeting. He was apologizing to the representatives of the Coast project for the length of his preliminary business.

Then he picked up the xeroxed agenda again in his thick fingers and read out, "Three. Far East Trade Initiatives..." I glanced restlessly down at my watch.

My ordinary power to split life into compartments, to forget everything else under a pressing task at hand, was crumbling in this enforced unemployment, the protective levee engulfed by the flood of memory. My mind pitched back to those early months, infinitely distant now, infinitely desired.

And fragments of this noon's experience flowed into the memory current, as sharp to my consciousness as shards of glass. I sat in this public room, my hand raised against Becca. I heard the consonants and vowels of Stein's Bronx voice, watching Becca disappear into the glare with the young, dark man. I studied the watermelon-hued crape myrtle in the early afternoon heat and saw Becca now perhaps with him, now opening herself to him.

No!

I had to see Becca now.

I couldn't tell how long it would be before the coast project came up and my inner agitation made sitting still a torment.

Maybe I should try to call her.

My body decided for me. Spontaneously I found myself pushing back my chair. The legs scraped softly against the carpet, bringing a quizzical, alive glance from Harriet McEnloe. I held up my hand, its fingers curled, against my ear and tapped my watch.

Once in the hall, I walked rapidly back toward the security desk.

A new guard, a middle-aged black man whose uniform strained around his middle, had replaced the red-faced young guard with the mustache who had greeted me when I came in.

"Is there some place I can make a phone call?" I asked.

"You can use this phone," the guard said, pushing it toward me without leaning forward.

"Thank you," I said, "but is there a private phone?"

He gave me a blank look, as if unable to figure out how to help me.

"I'm sorry," I said apologetically. "The Governor asked me to check some data for our discussion." This lie was a little corruption, like the breaking of a single capillary beneath the skin.

The guard seemed to lean back even more passively against the wall.

"Well," he said finally, "I think Mrs. Sessum's secretary is with her in the other wing. You could use her office."

He gestured toward a door across the hall.

Claudia's desk was cluttered with newspaper clippings, invitations, correspondence. I wondered whether confidential matters were kept out of sight, where a random visitor could not come upon them. Surely other visitors, official and unofficial, made their way into this room.

Standing over the desk, I picked up the receiver and dialed out of the Mansion to my law offices.

The sun, beginning to slant through the tall west-facing windows, filled the room with heat, but it wasn't only the sun that made my hands sweat.

The telephone barely had time to ring before it was picked up.

"Burden, Cassel, Fairchild and White," the familiar voice of the operator announced. Somehow she always made the greeting sound fresh.

"Ms. Talbot please."

The telephone rang again and kept ringing. I took my handkerchief out of my pocket and wiped my forehead.

What had Becca said about her afternoon? I couldn't remember.

I listened into the silence. *God*! The pleading prayer was a reflex, like the spasm of a muscle. *Let her be there!*

My eye falling on the desk caught a memo pad with the scribbled word "president". What president? I wondered idly. Of the United States? Of the Jackson Garden Club?

The intermittent buzz, regular and relentless, continued.

Then there was a click at the end of the line.

"Becca," I said urgently, "This is George."

"I'm sorry, sir," said an unfamiliar voice. "Ms. Talbot has gone for the day. Would you like to leave a message?"

I slammed down the receiver. My legs shaking, I fell back into the chair, then, in the same movement leaned forward and picked up the receiver once more. I dialed Becca's home. Hopeless, hoping. The mechanical ring, laid down and laid down into the charged silence.

I caught a glimpse of my face in the mirror on the opposite wall, helpless with feeling, and closed my eyes against it.

"I can't sit through this meeting," I whispered. "It was foolish to come."

I forced myself to return to the conference room. Turning over the sheet of paper on which the agenda was xeroxed, I scratched a note:

"A small emergency has arisen. I must leave. Please speak in any way you wish regarding my whole-hearted support of this project. I will be glad to speak with any of the Council members at a later time if they so wish. Please make my apologies to Cash. George."

I pushed the piece of paper across the table to Harriet. She'd be disappointed, perhaps even annoyed.

I no longer cared.

13

I hurried into the parking area and made for the Lincoln, as if someone might pursue me from the conference room and demand an accounting for my departure.

The humid mid-afternoon air closed around me like water. I slid into the car and slammed the door. Easing the car into motion, I made my way down the Mansion driveway and into the anonymous embrace of the city traffic.

Safe from imagined pursuers, I reached for the air conditioner and flicked it on. A drift of cool air thinned the heat.

I needed to see Becca and I couldn't find her. The office would be intolerable. At least at home I could deal with my agitation alone.

I drove north, turning off the freeway at Eastcourt Drive, following the narrow, almost rural road along the lake into the subdivision. Two boys were fishing in the lake, a bowl of white light under the afternoon sky. Bicycles, yellow and red, lay beside them in the weeds. Across the road stood the small, ragged woods in which my own children, ten and twenty years ago, possessed the pleasures of summer: small, sour-sweet, yellow wild plums; purple blackberries, staining the hand and the mouth; honeysuckle, its nectar a brief gush of pleasure to the probing tongue. These and the quickening, subduing sun; the pine-fragrant noon tranced in the silence of birds and the wandering hum of the bees; and at dusk, the cold, green globes of fireflies drifting up through the darkening branches of sweet-gum as they had for me in another place as a boy.

I nosed the car around the final corner, into a short, dead-end lane. Three houses with large, park-like lawns, one on either side and one at the back, topped the low hills. I turned left and ascended the driveway, eased the car into the garage, and switched off the ignition.

Julia's car wasn't here.

I walked around to the flagstone patio, loosening my tie with my thumb, and sank into a white wrought-iron chair in the shadow of the patio umbrella. I looked at the pool, wondering whether a swim would wash the tension from me. But suddenly, I felt so engulfed by weariness that I wanted only to sleep.

Sleep. But I held onto my tension like a life raft. I dreaded, if I should relax, the feelings that might flood and overcome me.

My eye rested momentarily on the lacework of shadow laid down on the hot stone by one of the wrought-iron chairs. It suddenly occurred to me that I hadn't eaten any lunch. Perhaps food would help restore me, get my body back in order. But my stomach was so tense it rebelled at the thought of eating. What I really wanted was the anaesthetizing succor of a drink.

Pulling myself up, I unlocked the door of the garden room and crossed the tile floor to the bar. I tugged off my coat and dropped it across the counter. Then, pulling open the door of the bar refrigerator, I grabbed a handful of ice cubes, tossed them into a glass, and poured over them a large measure of vodka. I swirled the vodka in the glass, waiting briefly for its sharp edge to be softened by the melting ice. Then I raised the glass, threw back my head, and let the first sip flow down my throat.

The coolness was wonderful, married with it the unfolding warmth radiating into my chest, my stomach, my limbs. I rarely drink in the afternoon, so much of my life has been founded on not repeating the behaviors I hated in my father as a boy. But now I lifted the glass and drank the rest down, swilled it, feeling it lift and soften my weariness. It would keep the loneliness of the house from peopling itself with the images of noon.

But after the brief lift the vodka threw me into a more crippling fatigue. I could barely stand up. The drink was not sitting well on my stomach. I had drunk too much too fast and felt a pressing need to urinate.

Concentrating on quelling the rising nausea, I made my way to the bathroom. I leaned over the toilet, placing one arm against the wall to hold myself upright, and waited for the stream to begin. Finally, the flow started. A cloying odor of urine rose from the bowl and made me gag. I was afraid I might fall to the floor and have to vomit into the pool of urine. I fumbled, flushing the toilet to clear the bowl.

The effort of resisting the impulse to vomit brought sweat to my forehead. I closed my eyes, but my head spun so much I could hardly stand. I opened them again and this only increased my dizziness.

I forced myself to walk down the wheeling hallway toward the bedroom. Perhaps I could sleep it off. Now I only wanted to be unconscious. I tried to bend cautiously toward the bed, but, stumbling, struck my face against the headboard. In confusion I lowered myself onto the mattress, my right hand spread against my stomach, my left rubbing my aching face as I carefully laid it to one side. I wondered whether to close my eyes again or whether that would be the step that would finally make me vomit. *Another problem to solve!*

But before I had time to think further, I was asleep.

14

When I woke up, it was through a marvelous impression of ease. But almost before I opened my eyes, fragmented images from the day fell into my consciousness.

I heaved myself up to a sitting position.

The clock on my bedside table read almost eight. Was Julia home? She must have found me asleep and not disturbed me. The lawn outside the window was already in shadow, the trees silhouetted against a dying sunset. Soon it would be dark.

I switched on the light, rubbing my face.

Becca.

I glanced up. The light outside had faded further. Against the darkening day, the window became a mirror and threw back at me, hanging in the darkness in meticulous replication, my own face, the bed on which I sat, the embracing room. It was as if I were once more shut up in myself, couldn't break through.

But however I felt, I had to get up. I had to face Julia.

The fact that she had let me sleep established a small indebtedness, which in the present situation I unfairly resented. It was her rule, Julia liked to tell people, that no matter how busy she became, she was always home by six to put my dinner on the table. She would not believe my word that having my dinner served by her and at six was not particularly important to me.

I stood up. Bracing myself for the encounter, I headed out the door and down the hall.

Julia sat at a table in the garden room, a box of envelopes beside her. A many-paged list covered with names and addresses was folded in front of her. From the size and color of the envelopes, I imagined they were invitations. She was addressing them in her clear, strong hand.

Absorbed in this task on behalf of some community organization, lost in surrendered attention, she had the vulnerable air of someone come upon in sleep.

Hearing me, she looked up over her reading glasses, a look of fathomless familiarity and concern.

"I didn't expect to fall asleep," I said. "I came home early, feeling sick." Too late, I wondered whether she had smelled the vodka?

The attentive concern of her expression deepened. Poor Julia! I was the one who was wronging her, yet I resented her habitual love as if it were a wrong against me, an injustice when she touched the raw flesh of my guilt.

"I'm sure it's nothing serious," I went on. Julia removed her glasses. Her eyes, a pale blue that seemed to have no depth, remained unchanged in the face that had aged around them, the lines of purpose and attention become a habit of the flesh, the finer corruscation of the skin.

"Harriet called," she said.

The note I had written to Harriet returned sharply to my mind. The perpetual guardedness arising from the affair had become a task that could never be put away.

"What did she say?"

"She wanted to tell you that the Council granted the festival allocation. She also said she hoped you worked out your emergency."

Julia's words were a question.

"I became sick during the meeting and had to leave," I said. "I didn't want to worry anyone."

I thought Julia would ask about the weekend trip to the coast, which she had so insistently protected for my birthday, but she didn't. Only her silent look of concern remained.

"For Christ's sake, Julia," I snapped. "Don't be so damned solicitous!"

This had become my habit, the minor preemptive strike, blaming her in small, persistent ways in order to make her keep her distance.

She returned her glance to the desk and, with competent gestures, stacked the envelopes she had been addressing into a pile, fastened them with a large rubber band, and placed them neatly together with the folded computer printout in the box at her side. Everything would be ready to find when she resumed her task, with no wasted motion. She put my annoyance down to my unreal illness and it only increased her concern.

"I'd be glad to make you some dinner," she said as she finished.

I suddenly realized I was ravenous. "Yes, thank you," I said, a wave of guilt and gratitude washing me back into the established small dependencies of the marriage. "I hope I didn't inconvenience you."

"No, I had to get ahead with this addressing in any case. Can I get you anything in particular?"

"I don't want to make you cook a meal if you haven't already."

"Scrambled eggs?"

I consented. Julia rose and walked toward the far door that opened into the kitchen. Awkward in her young womanhood, as she had grown into the experienced competence of middle age, she had taken more graceful possession of her large-boned body. She carried herself with a certain rigidity around her shoulders, and despite her discipline was thickening about the waist and hips. But a man might still desire her.

But when I left her, she would not remarry.

I sank into a chair. It was too unfair to Julia not to tell her the truth. *Or did I know the truth?* A spasm of anxiety wrung my heart. What sense could I make of Becca's muted consent to stay with me? The dark young man rose up in my mind like an actor who has been waiting in the wings for his cue to step onto the stage. Had Becca been betraying me all along? How could I distrust what had seemed so genuinely the intimacy between us? My ability to read human problems was suddenly baffled by the impenetrability of my own situation. Being so much at a loss was more new territory, and I didn't know how to live in it.

I simply had to know the truth.

I wondered whether I dare call Becca. Or perhaps I should make an excuse to leave, drive to her house, and press on her again my need to resolve this now. Tomorrow morning Julia was intending to get into the car and drive with me to the coast for the celebration on Sunday of my fifty-fifth birthday. The time had been so set apart and guarded that I couldn't well change it. How was I going to talk with Becca? I couldn't wait until Monday.

My mind stopped, jammed by uncertainty and a wave of anxiety.

Julia, working through the twilight, had not closed the curtains over the glass doors onto the patio. One side of the large, empty room gaped onto a great darkness, screened by the reflected light which painted on the night the treacherous mimic of its solidity and safety. I recalled my thought on waking. Surrounded by reflections of myself, I couldn't break through! But suppose someone or something on the other side could break through to me? Who might be moving there? I suddenly felt the presence of some unknown figure, driven by who knew what motive, himself curtained behind the reflection but seeing me with perfect clarity boxed and bathed in light. Someone at that moment might be lifting a rifle to his eye, fixing me in its sights and beginning to squeeze the trigger, preparing to snap off my life, all feared or desired futures, all consequence and completeness, in an explosion of glass and blood.

This hallucinatory image filled me with dread. I wanted to close the curtains. But my habitual prudence—prudence now in the service of what reason told me was fantasy—warned me that if I moved I might invite a shot more quickly. I sat paralyzed, struggling to shake the fear off, ashamed of the empty, urgent deliberations through which my mind kept racing.

If I continue to sit, I make myself a target. Even while I'm deliberating, the trigger may be squeezed, a bullet released which by moving I could have escaped. And suppose I move?

Abruptly I rose and in constrained haste made my way across the room to the drawstrings, pressing my body sideways along the wall beside the doors as hand over hand I pulled the drapes shut. Only the repeated *shhhhh* of the swaying curtains broke the silence. It came into my mind that I didn't know whether the doors behind the curtains were locked. But surely they were! Julia and I had always been careful about that.

My paranoia seemed to be rising with my jealousy.

What is happening to me?

I walked over to the bar. After the experience of the afternoon I was afraid to drink, but I needed something to stop the ceaseless turning of my mind.

Yet what would Julia say if she found me drinking after telling her that I was sick?

Somehow in the past day the roots anchoring me to the taken-for-granted had been cut. I could no longer enter on any action with spontaneous trust in its rightness. I had to justify every step I took now to an imagined crowd of observers. I craved the return of peace. Only marrying Becca would do this: I knew it with the certainty of noon's sudden, violent conversion. But I was almost too exhausted by the effort of trying to hold together my real and desired worlds to be able to discern and take another step.

I poured out a glass of white wine. It did not warm me as much as the vodka, but it was not making me sick. I heard Julia returning. Quickly, I drank it down and poured another.

Julia was carrying a tray with two earthenware plates made by a potter we had come to know during a summer trip to North Carolina, each a swirl of melting blues. On each of them rested softly yellow scrambled eggs, slices of red midsummer tomatoes, thick pieces of toasted French bread and sweet butter. Two tall glasses were filled with iced coffee marbled at the top with freshly poured milk. Characteristically, Julia had made the unpretentious meal beautiful.

Yet there was a reserve in her manner which I could not immediately understand. The creases between her eyebrows were pinched, as often when she was readying herself to talk about something she found difficult. It was a signal familiar to me from the thirty years of our marriage. What was she harboring in her silence? I realized I had no clear idea what she might know or suspect.

Our sexual life had already become more episodic before my affair with Becca. At first, my rediscovery of desire had carried over into the bedroom at home, and, as a kind of ironic byproduct, created a temporary sexual renaissance with Julia.

But then the tension of the affair—its split loyalties, habitual hypocrisy and practical complexities—had made me withdraw into myself. Occasionally, I still made love to Julia from prudence or scruples. My moods of preoccupation or episodic withdrawal into work had always been part of the rhythm of our marriage. Julia simply accepted it. Julia, who so often joked with our friends that my work was my mistress, and she feared no other.

She set the tray on the sideboard and carried the plates to the small glass-topped table where we ate informally.

I left my wine at the bar and walked over to join her.

Julia looked up, the lines deep between her brows. I was alarmed by this new sign of concern and hesitation.

"Would you prefer to drink your wine?" she asked. "You don't have to drink the coffee."

"No thanks. I thought I might want it, but it bothers my stomach."

The lie was unnecessary, a thread in the fabric of unreality I had woven between us.

I could see that she was preparing to speak. She leaned forward over the table, her shoulders more rigid than ever, her fork poised over the plate. I waited for the possible blow.

"George, this isn't easy to say." My mind leapt ahead. *I know that you have been seeing a girl who works in your office. We can't go on without talking...*

But I was missing her words.

"Ellen called me today."

Ellen, our oldest daughter.

Was this about *her*?

"She said she's been having a...an affair. She's just told Jeff she wants to leave him."

15

I sat utterly still before Julia's waiting gaze.

My heart fled to Ellen. I felt visceral identification with the entangled pain and relief she must be experiencing, of the vastly increased burden of responsibility and complexity she must be bearing now she'd reached her decision to leave Jeff and made it public. And I felt for her what I couldn't feel for myself, that falling into an affair was weak and sordid and deserting her family a sin. It was a thing I knew she couldn't explain even to me in such a way that I could hear and accept it. I was angry at her, but I didn't want her to suffer.

Secrets! I thought angrily. Did we all have secrets? Would Mark call from school with a girl-friend pregnant? Would Julia confess a lover? I had sometimes wryly hoped it, as a medicine to ease my conscience. Had I understood what I was mockingly asking? Did I really know now what I was doing?

Julia still waited my reply. This had been one of the cords of our marriage, our alliance in responding to the problems of the children. I flinched from any conversation I could foresee: its subject made me feel exposed and endangered; to join Julia in indignation made me feel the liar I was.

"Julia, I don't know what to say."

"I didn't want to bring this up when you weren't feeling well," she said, "but I have to talk with you about it."

"Yes, of course you do," I said. "What else did Ellen say?"

"It was hard to discuss things on the phone. She feels terrible and Jeff feels worse. I don't think she'd really thought through all the consequences. She asked if I would come out for a few days, to help with the kids and let her get things straightened out in her own mind."

"When do they want you to come?"

"I've already made a reservation for tomorrow morning. George dear, I know this ruins our plans for the coast and leaves you alone on your birthday.

"I'm so sorry."

I reached across the table and took her hand.

"Don't worry about me, Julia," I said. "Ella Mae can feed me, or I can eat out. I might even drive down to the coast by myself."

Her expression began to relax. I leaned back in my chair.

"Although I hate the reason for it," she confessed, "I do look forward to seeing Ellen. It's been very lonely this summer with none of the children in the house."

A further surprise. She'd never mentioned her loneliness when I said how much I missed Mark. Stoically, she had disciplined herself to fill her mind with additional projects, as if to talk of her loneliness were only an incitement to further pain, an employment of energy and time that achieved no good.

She was living now in a deeper loneliness than she knew.

We returned to our meal in silence. After we had finished, Julia picked up the plates, placed them one on top of the other, arranged the two glasses side by side atop them, and laid the silverware neatly alongside the glasses.

"I'm going to pack as soon as I rinse these," she said. "And then I may do the rest of the addressing. It has to be finished. I hate to leave it for anyone else."

She carried the dishes toward the kitchen, her skirt moving about her hips as she walked with her competent, graceful carriage.

I pushed back my chair and stood up. I still felt restless, but also washed with relief. I was sorry for Ellen, Jeff and Julia, directly involved in this crisis. And I recognized it added a complicating factor to the way I would have to address my own situation with Julia. But the pressure of time that had been so tormenting me was lifted. Here was found time. At least I would be able to talk with Becca tomorrow morning.

I returned to the bar. The wine I'd poured myself earlier was warm. In any case, I no longer wanted wine. I opened the refrigerator door, pulled out a clutch of ice cubes, and dropped them in a small glass. Groping under the bar, I found the vodka and poured myself a healthy drink. I was feeling free now and wanted something to stabilize my relief. I swirled the glass to chill the vodka, then lifted it to my lips, and drank down its magical mix of coolness and unfolding warmth.

Often in the evening I read or did some extra work. But this evening, I wanted to indulge my freedom, wanted a distraction that would demand no effort. I sank into a chair, picked up the remote, and switched on the television.

A dot of light on the gray screen bloomed into the image of a local newscaster whom I knew well. I touched the remote again and switched the channel. Two boxers filled the screen. This caught me. Perhaps it matched an element in my own turbulent mood. Two lightweights, one Black, one Hispanic, were regarding each other with intense awareness, circling for an opening. The young Hispanic suddenly released a series of blows, fast, intelligent, and lethal, that hurt the Black fighter and sent him plunging to the canvas. The fallen boxer shifted, almost twitched his limbs laterally, but was unable, by no matter how concentrated an effort of dimming consciousness, to lift himself.

The referee rose from his crouch.

Seizing the wrist of the victorious Hispanic, he thrust his arm into the air. The camera closed in on his dark face. It was cut, beaded with sweat, but burning with the wild exultation of triumph.

I was caught up into his exultation, felt it ride the vodka and rise as a certainty of fulfillment in myself. And then, as if it were a haunting, suddenly the image of the fighter, the black hair, the dark complexion, the elastic, athletic stance transfigured itself into the image of the young man in the parking lot with Becca.

I didn't want him inside my mind! I cut off the television set and rose. Struggling to keep the image in abeyance, I returned to the bar. I'd re-top my drink: It would keep my feelings away.

I poured the additional vodka. As I drank, I restlessly paced the room, trying by my activity to keep my thoughts from drifting to the place I desperately wanted them not to go.

My glance fell on an early photograph of myself with Julia, which sat on a side table between a cascading tradescantia vine and an ashtray for guests who smoked. Ellen as a baby, tiny and perfect-featured, lay against Julia's breast. Julia's hands, strong and capable, almost covered her body. I stood beside Julia, my arm around her shoulder as if protecting them, our eyes resting together on Ellen. It was the morning of Ellen's baptism.

Could *I*, I wondered, still recover in memory what had lived behind the unbelievably young faces in the image, living on in separation from the inwardness of their long ago lives?

16

Julia and I married the year after I completed law school.

My decision to marry was partly a matter of convenience. Like an earlier lawyer, Thomas More, I found by the end of law school that I wasn't suited for celibacy, and the time and energy spent arranging impermanent liaisons took too much time away from my absorbing project, establishing my career.

And perhaps even more profoundly I wanted to be the creator of a flourishing and happy family.

After my mother's death my father never remarried. We were alone. Since he divided his time between working and drinking, really *I* was alone. Summers with my grandparents on the coast were a blessed reprieve, but since most of my grandparents' friends were as old as they were, it didn't allow me to learn much about how people my own age were supposed to behave. So when I finally left the isolation of home for Ole Miss, I studied my new friends more carefully than my classes. I struggled to learn the forms of a normal life as if they were a foreign language.

Only someone who's been in this situation could know how simple the things were that I had to watch and practice, sweating not to get them wrong. Once the parents of a dorm mate who were visiting the campus invited me along to eat with them. My conversation rose only to the answering of questions, careful, pedantically precise, but covertly evasive. After lunch I pulled out my wallet and began to remove what I calculated I owed. My dorm mate's father laughed and said, "Put your wallet away! Don't your friends' parents *usually* pay when they invite you out for lunch?"

I thanked him rather formally and slipped my wallet back in my pocket. He gave me a quizzical glance and turned back to his joshing conversation with his son.

The truth is that this was the first time a friend's parents had ever asked me to lunch, so I simply didn't know what to do. My spontaneity was frozen at the core by the shame and fear I felt in my ignorance. Yet I also felt a secret, fathomless desire to love and be loved. Learning to be normal seemed to me the key to earning that love.

As my undergraduate years went by, I learned this new language well enough to pass as a native and relaxed enough to have a number of real friendships.

But I dreaded the possibility of making a humiliating mistake with a girl and dropped any relationship that threatened to become serious. Finally, at Harvard, my fear began to feel unnecessary and simply faded out. I discovered how much I liked women and had several pleasurable, if still somewhat guarded, affairs.

I've said I married Julia first of all out of ambition. That's true, but it's not the entire truth. There was a further motive, less consciously acknowledged, but almost as urgent.

In the deepest fiber of my being, I wanted to avoid repeating with my own children what I had suffered as a boy. Or perhaps I should say I wanted to repeat it while making it right, creating a household full of cherished children and married love. As I became an adolescent, the fantasies of sexual pleasure which accompanied my drift to sleep always pictured their object as wife, as young mother, as co-creator of family happiness. The imagined thrust of pleasure was bound to the marital bed.

So on my return to Jackson, ready to build my career and family, I began to notice the available girls. With surprise I recognized, one evening at Judge Henderson's, that my heart had hiddenly made its own choice already.

Julia was five years older than I, and in the eyes of most of those who knew her had passed into the status of spinsterhood. She, too, had lost her mother as a child. But she was then twelve, and circumstance drew her to assume her mother's role, raising a brother and sister who were younger than she and, with a circle of responsibilities that extended as she grew older, managing the household for her father.

Had circumstance cheated her? Perhaps it had offered a welcome refuge. For Julia was large-boned and gawky, maturing early and continuing to grow into a large, awkward young woman.

Julia's size was no problem for me. I was so tall and large-boned myself that we might have been born of the same family. And I was drawn to her intelligent appreciation of my ambitions. But what also attracted me to her was that she appeared in the role of my dreams, presiding over her father's table, the foster mother of her younger brother and sister, a goddess of the household.

As Julia became aware that I accepted the invitations to the Henderson home not merely for the sake of her father, the judge, she allowed me to assume the conventional role of suitor. I was able to lavish on her—it is hard to believe this now—an ardent tenderness that had found no object during the solitary years of my childhood. She appeared enchanted. Who can tell now what was authentic, what conventional, as we played out those ready-made roles?

But this much was certain. Julia had a hunger for experience even while, with her characteristic discipline, she had schooled herself to be content with small expectations. She would have married almost anyone who asked her, as an avenue to larger experience. She wanted the knowledge of what it meant to be wife and mother. And she was herself ambitious to be a contributor to the good of the community in the fullest manner.

The earliest years of sensual intimacy, her pregnancy and the birth of Ellen, were a grace, an adventure, a satisfaction of deep desire for us both. But as the marriage settled, it restored us in some measure to our original selves. My habits had been those of solitude, my tenderness spending itself in fantasy rather than act. Julia had kept the younger Henderson children disciplined and successful, responsibilities assumed to serve a busy father. We fit each other. Each by our behavior encouraged the other in slipping away from intimacy into our familiar, separate roles.

My glance refocused on the photograph of that foreign young family in their already dying happiness. Yes, I had helped form Julia into what she was today: her just sense of propriety, her secret vulnerabilities, her readiness to sacrifice herself without martyrdom or self-righteousness, receiving her satisfaction in the feeling that she was doing her best to perform her duties properly as she expected others to perform theirs.

This is what I had chosen her for: as collaborator in creating the perfect family of my dreams and as my ambition's conscience. So, inevitably, we had grown distant.

17

I opened my eyes onto darkness. I could feel the presence of Julia beside me in bed. The room was too hot. I pulled myself with difficulty from the terror and desire of a fading dream.

I was ejaculating.

The warm fluid puddled against my skin, trickled down my crotch. Out of my body it grew cold. I felt the discomfort and the shame I knew when I wet the bed as a boy, a messy and public loss of control.

My heart was racing. I tried to slow it down. The chill against my skin was increasingly uncomfortable. I would have to go into the bathroom and clean myself off.

I heaved my legs over the side of the bed. Julia, tangled in the sheets beside me, stirred. Her hand brushed warmth against my arm as she turned.

"Are you all right?"

"Yes," I said softly. "Go back to sleep."

I stood up. My eyes strained in the deep darkness of the room. I could make out the faint, gray rectangles of the windows. I knew approximately, from habit, the locations and distances of the furniture. I groped toward the bathroom, my hands stretched out before me. They found the door frame, the knob of the bathroom door. At each step the patchy wetness of my pajamas rode up to meet my skin.

Inside, I leaned against the back of the door and clicked the lock. Alone. The dreamless darkness was like a gift.

What had I been dreaming? The mood remained, but the images that had created it had fled to whatever inward place they are shut away when one awakens. Then, as I rested there, one or two fragmentary images drifted back into my inner vision, as tenuous, as elusive as smoke. *Becca and I making love. Yes, and a third in the room, hiding in shadow.* I stood without breathing to see if more would disclose itself to my waiting attention. *Becca was stroking me. I felt choked with desire, but also afraid. What other was watching us?*

I struggled a double struggle, rehearsing the straining vigilance of my dream and laboring now to remember; but the watcher lay hidden behind the white door of amnesia. Then, suddenly, as if I had pulled on a string, all of the dream images, so quickly it was almost a single illumination, unfolded.

The face of the young Hispanic boxer, cut, beaded with sweat, wildly triumphant, his arm around Becca. Yet he watched as Becca caressed my straining flesh in the bed. Oh, I was overborne by the mounting waves of desire and the mounting dread of danger. Yet I couldn't draw back. I looked down at Becca's hand. She was pressing her long fingernails into my flesh stretched to accommodate her. I looked up with a fresh surge of horror. They were coupled now on the bed, she and the young boxer, grinding in love. I wanted to withdraw from her caressing, severing hand, but couldn't. I was already slipping over the edge. I glanced down in paralyzed dread and ejaculated an issue of blood.

Caught back up in the dream, I flooded with shame at its grotesque images of my humiliation. The darkness was charged with self-disgust and panic. I needed light!

My fingers groped along the wall, felt for, found the switch. The flicker and blaze of fluorescence over the sink momentarily confused my eyes. Then my image settled into focus in the mirror, my sleep-numbed face and white night's beard, whiter than my hair.

The dream: what truth did it tell?

I undid the buttons that lined the front of my shirt and threw it on the floor, then untied the drawstring of my stained pajama pants. I stepped out of them and kicked them to the side with my shirt. The light faintly picked out the viscous smears of semen on belly and thigh.

I leaned over the sink and twisted the tap, releasing a rush of hot water. Taking the washcloth, I held it under the steaming stream until I could hardly bear the heat, then wrung it out. Carefully, I drew the rough-textured warmth of the cloth over my smeared flesh. Cleansing myself of what? Of the terror of the dream? Of its revelation of weakness and shame?

I rinsed and wrung out the cloth again and held it against my groin, as if stanching the dreamed wound. The hair of belly and thigh lay matted where the washcloth had touched them. The soft

74

draft from the air vent above my head created a gentle coolness against the still damp skin.

I wadded up the washcloth, leaned over to pick up the pajamas, and thrust the bundle into the hamper, burying it under the towels that lay on top.   An unnecessary secrecy, like my earlier unnecessary lies.

I flicked off the light.

Engulfed again in darkness more profound after the fluorescent glare, I reached for the door knob, opened the door, and groped softly across the bedroom to my closet. Sliding open the folding door, I found my robe and slipped it over my body.

What time was it?

Over the curve of Julia's hip I could make out the illuminated face of the clock on the table beside the bed.

Four-thirty.

There was no point in trying to go back to sleep. I would find it difficult, and in any case I wanted nothing now but to see Becca.

My fingers searched blindly in my dresser for underwear, socks; gathered from my closet in the darkness shoes, a couple of shirts, a suit; grabbed three or four ties. Something in these should make an ensemble. I'd shave in the bathroom off my study.

Opening the door quietly, so as not to invite further questions from Julia, I padded down the carpeted hall from the bedroom wing to the central part of the house. Entering the garden room, I switched on a lamp. The scene of last night's conversation leapt into visibility as if newly created.

Before long Julia would waken into her preoccupation with Ellen and Jeff, and prepare to take the early plane to San Francisco. This would give me the weekend to make things work with Becca.

The shame and dread of the dream began to lift. Considered in the light, the dreamed images of betrayal melted like a mirage. It was clear what had inspired them: Becca's rejection of my proposal, the enigmatic glimpse of Becca walking through the sun-glare with the familiar-unfamiliar young man.   This didn't credential their truth.

I walked into the kitchen, flipped on the light switch, and splashed water into the coffee maker. My fingers tapped against the counter as I waited for the slow, insistent trickle of the coffee into the pot. The sharp fragrance lofted into the room.

I felt a mounting restlessness, a suppressed excitement. Even if Becca had another lover, even if my dream was not simply a projection onto what I had seen by my fear, I could fight for her. I had the resources for such a fight. I was more well-to-do than she'd ever dreamed of being, moved among the powerful, was more skilled at reading and managing human situations than any young adversary could be. My potency was not impaired. I loved Becca more than anything in my world, and would learn to love Chris, too, as the father he needed. I could even begin a second family, my age an illusion imprinted in the flesh, not my inner self.

When could I reasonably go to see her? It was now five, I could stop by her house at seven. *Two hours.* My mind, too restless to settle in particular images, fed on the confident general sense that I would have her.

There was a sound behind me. Julia stood by the sink, her aging, strong face still somewhat blurred by sleep, her nightgown falling in folds about her thickening hips. Through the soft material I could see in faint coloration the nipples and triangle of pubic hair of which she, lost in sleepiness and concern, was unconscious. She scratched the inside of her thigh. It was a gesture of taken for granted at-homeness.

"Good morning," she said. "I couldn't get back to sleep after I heard you wake up. Are you all right?" In offering comfort she was also seeking comfort for the anxious errand she was facing.

I felt the familiar impulse to wound her so she would withdraw. A word could make her feel that, however well-meaning her intrusion, she was in the wrong, could undermine that trusting freedom from self-consciousness which makes a place a home. But I felt immediately, too, how cruel it would be to attack her experience of safety in what, after all, was her home.

I answered gently.

"Yes, I'm quite well. Are you ready for your trip?"

Julia, too, I could see, did not wish to extend this conversation. Her thought was already in the future with Ellen and Jeff. Yet she felt a responsibility toward the larger situation, the fact that she was leaving me alone for an indeterminate period of days, among them my birthday. This responsibility she would have to discharge.

"I still have to do some packing. I told Ella Mae you might want her to adjust her schedule so she could give you dinner."

I felt annoyed by this solicitude.

"I can take care of all that," I said. "I'll be in my study until six-thirty. Then I need to go by Becca Talbot's to pick up some figures I asked for when I thought we'd be leaving for the coast."

What was behind this recklessness? I never mentioned Becca's name. Julia had only met her once, on an early fall evening at the State Fair, as we strolled along the fairway after I'd finished an official duty. Stopping to watch the children on the merry-go-round, I realized we were standing beside Becca and two of her girl friends. Becca looked up. After a momentary hesitation, she held out her hand to me and said, "Good evening, Mr. Burden, I'm Becca Talbot in book-keeping." I introduced her to Julia. Becca held out her hand and said gravely, "Good evening, Mrs. Burden." I could see Julia liked her.

I shook away the memory.

Walking over to where Julia stood, I put my hands on her upper arms, approaching but resisting a full embrace, and kissed her softly on the cheek. I felt her relax slightly toward me as if for reassurance, then recover and hold herself upright.

"I know you'll help the children, Julia," I said softly.

"I hope I can," she said, stepping back from the embrace. She turned down the shadowy hall toward the bedroom.

I poured myself some coffee and put the cup to my lips, savoring its rich, bitter taste. My senses seemed especially clear. My mind raced toward the day to come.

My study was directly off the garden room. I carried the coffee into it. Already at five-thirty I could hear the birds.

The upper sky was beginning to lighten, creating, I could see through the window, a world in silhouette, black against gray.

Soon the earth would turn at this place further toward the sun and its light descending would elicit color and volume from this world of black cut-outs. A solid world! Soon others whose business was with the day would waken into engagement like the singing birds.

I closed the massive, paneled door, which I had found on the coast when we were building this house and bought for its age and—the word seemed right—its nobility behind me. The mahogany desk, large but proportioned to the spacious dimensions of the study, had been my father's office desk. The painting on the wall behind it—a nightscape of the coast, the four warm, square yellow windows of a beach house contrasting with the cobalt, indigo-black objects which emerged from or submerged into the night -- was the work of my mother. There were mementoes of the children's growing up, pictures and gifts. And a photograph of Julia and me on our wedding day, two people tall, angular, and thin, our faces more naked of experience than we could then have recognized or understood.

All these were evidences of the factuality, the unalterable solidity, of the experience that had shaped this present. I did not want to be unjust to it, did not want to deny its claim to have fully and meaningfully existed. But neither did I wish to be coerced by it, locked into it, as if my life now could only have a shape already given, a blank defined by all the other pieces of a puzzle.

I opened my briefcase and removed a file; its code was neatly typed at the upper left hand corner. I placed it on the polished surface of the desk and opened a drawer, reaching for the compartment where I kept the black, fine-line pens which suit my small, rather regular handwriting.

Why was I working? Only because, I realized, the words had slipped from my tongue when speaking to Julia. I was keeping faith with my lie, fidelity in the service of betrayal. But I really felt too restless to write. Slamming shut the drawer of the desk, I stood up. I wanted to *act*. I walked over to the window and watched the thin, early morning sunlight deepen over the bowl of the sky. I slid up the window.

The air was still cool, but underneath I could already sense the massive hammer of heat which would strike later in the day. It spoke of a world beyond the subdued atmosphere of the house: tempered air, tempered voices, tempered passion. I had created this tempered world by an ardent process of will. And now, in a bitter irony, as in the growth habit of certain animals, it had grown into a thick exoskeleton which threatened to kill me.

I *had to* shatter it!

A prayer I could not intentionally speak from shame formed itself on my lips in spontaneous appeal.

Eternal Father, God, help me!

18

Father, I suppose this question is no longer avoidable: Where did I think God was in this story I am telling in such detail, but, I'm now obliged to confess, with the most important element left out?

Now that I've dared to ask the question, I'll try to be scrupulously honest in my answer.

Throughout my relationship with Becca, I did continue to attend Church, out of habit, out of belief, out of involvement in St. Monica's governing committees, out of my firm's dependence on me for its relationship with the Catholic community.

Every Sunday at ten-thirty Julia and I made our way down the aisle before mass, our progress choreographed by the hands and smiles that bobbed up before us, and took our customary seat. I couldn't resolve the conflicting loyalties of my experience, but neither could I abandon any of them. So I lived within them, praying for resolution.

To my dismay, I found that my mind had its own mechanisms to protect the passion that had begun to rule my life. Kneeling in St. Monica's, my eyes closed to secure the inner darkness in which without distraction I could raise myself to God, I found that while praying for Jesus' help, I would, in a simultaneous mental act, be vividly remembering my last encounter with Becca; could be pleading for the relationship to end, while on another level willing it to continue, not allowing myself to withdraw from its inner savoring. The two impulses seemed to move in the same mind at the same time in total independence of one another.

In those early days, there were times as I lay beside Becca in one of our interchangeable motel rooms, when I would think of Julia's trust and feel guilt as sharp as the touch of a probe on a raw nerve. Then, in double betrayal, while my hand followed the soft beating of Becca's heart, I would resolve to pull myself free from the passion which, in the quiet after love, seemed so distant from me. Yet, in the very act of visualizing in order to reject this pleasure as thick as honey, as intense as anguish, I was drawn back in.

The imperious penis has no conscience. Like a confidence man, it baffles, deceives, blinds the conscience, and sometimes teaches the conscience its own philosophy. So I came desperately to reevaluate old truths and found them no longer compelling. Was I really harming Julia? Might I not bring something back to the marriage that would renew it? If I were careful that she never know, how would it hurt her? And how could the affair do anything but enhance life for Becca?

But sometimes, eluding all desire's craft, I glimpsed the fuller truth of what I was doing.

Early in the affair, Julia and I were sitting in our customary pew midway down the aisle, where we could see the lines and feel the full body of the church rising around us: the focus toward the altar with the rose window soaring radiant above it and the smaller altars to Joseph and to Mary on either side; the stained glass windows floating in the walls with the terra-cotta stations of the cross resting solidly between them; the answering spaciousness of the rest of the church behind us, not seen, but felt from decades of familiarity.

I had often glanced at the stained glass window to the right of our pew with a casual appreciative appraisal: it is a portrayal of the Last Supper. Eleven of the disciples look toward Christ, their faces concentrated and calm, their hands relaxed or raised in attitudes of devotion. The haloes that glow around them are the spontaneous radiance of their hearts' candor. Christ rests in the center, one hand on the communal cup, the other blessing the loaf they are about to share. Judas sits at the front of the frame. His hand resting on the side of his face near his companions exposes to us what he hides from them. The others look toward Christ, Judas turns away, clutching his dark cloak with knotted hands. His expression is illumined by no halo, yet the artist compels the viewer to see it clearly. I had sometimes wondered what the artist knew that allowed him to find that expression for Judas' face? Isolation. Misery. His eyes cast down, self-blinded. Grief. And no intention of changing.

The great service went on around us. I was troubled by the intensity of my preoccupation with Becca. My glance drifted in distraction across Julia toward the window. The movement of my head must have registered in her peripheral vision, for she turned toward me to see if I were preparing to say something. She caught my expression of pain. Smiling at me with concern, she touched my arm in familiar consolation. Then she turned back to the mass. Anguished, I looked past her and found in the face of Judas my own eyes gazing back at me.

If this was seeing, this knowledge of my bankruptcy, this claiming of my sin, then seeing was so unbearable that I would choose to remain blind. And as my desire for Becca opened depth upon depth and became transformed by love, my fear of losing this woman who was the source of my new life increased my unwillingness to see anything that might urge me to leave her. So nailed up by guilt and desire, my unholy crucifixion, I gave up any further efforts to know or control the prayers that rose in me.

I supposed if I died now, I would go to Hell, but I couldn't make it seem real. What seemed real was that God must be present in my love for Becca. But I didn't examine this. I continued to go to church, but ceased to pray. I left God's response to God.

Yet sometimes, as this morning, I still spontaneously turned to God with the broken prayer of my desire: *God, I need Becca so much. What I am struggling for is life, my life, and a rich life for her, for Becca. I don't want to hurt others, help me not hurt them.* My eyes ranged toward the light-entangled treetops of the woods, the disclosed and concealed depths of light and darkness, the green-gold richness.

But somehow, dear God, give us your blessing.

I threw myself down again into my desk chair. Perhaps I could rest for a half hour. I leaned my head back against the leather headrest and tried to let go. I checked my muscles, down from my forehead, one by one, relaxing any tension I recognized, dropping my mouth, letting the tension flow down and out of my body. My mind was empty, except for its loose focus on my body, unaware of the outside world, wrapped in the dark inwardness. I could feel the exhilaration, not diminished, but, as it were, clarified and balanced. My mind flowed toward Becca, now detached from urgency. Yet the prayer of my desire returned. *God,* I prayed, *God...*

I drifted, abandoning consciousness for flickering moments, the images becoming more tenuous, more tangled, mingled with a greater darkness. Then I touched softness and surrendered altogether to sleep.

19

I woke to a sharp rap against the door.

"Mr. Burden!"

It was Ella Mae, her aged voice raised and slightly tremulous.

"Yes," I struggled into consciousness, trying to orient myself.

"I just want you to know I'm here."

The room came into definition around me; I was in my study sitting at the mahogany desk. The morning light outside my windows was now full.

"I was working, Ella Mae," I said, as if to be caught asleep was a weakness to be dissembled. "I must have forgotten the time." What time was it? I glanced uselessly at my wrist: I must have left my watch in the bedroom.

"What time is it, Ella Mae?"

"Almost seven o'clock, Mr. Burden. Mrs. Burden acks me to come early in case you need me to make you your breakfast."

"Has Mrs. Burden already gone?"

"Her car gone. I think she left already to see Miss Ellen."

"Thank you, Ella Mae. I won't have breakfast; I'm already late myself."

I took a swallow of the cold coffee remaining in the cup on my desk. If I scrambled, I could still shave and get to Becca's house before she left. I hurried through my routine, cutting myself in the haste with which I shaved and resenting the moment it took to repair the damage.

Returning to the garden room, I grabbed my briefcase and made for the door. Ella Mae was setting some freshly washed glasses on the shelf behind the bar. Sunlight flooded into the room and made them gleam.

"Mr. Burden."

Ella Mae is sixty-eight, her polished leather complexion lined with decades of worry and work in the service of Julia's families, first the motherless Hendersons and then ours. I knew she kept working so she could care for a fourth generation of her own family, three of her great-grandchildren, whose mother was lost in drugs. Ella Mae has a well-worn network of strategies and labors for her family's survival. I honor her courage and endurance and usually I surrender gladly to the slow and sometimes repetitive pattern of her conversation. But this morning I couldn't make myself wait.

"I'm late for an appointment, Ella Mae."

"Yessir. Mrs. Burden acks if you want me to get you dinner tonight."

"It's not necessary, Ella Mae. I can take care of myself, I think, this weekend."

"Thank you, Mr. Burden. I'll see you Monday, then. Mrs. Burden already paid me."

"Thank you, Ella Mae."

I found my keys in my suit pocket and passed through the side door into the garage. My watch read seven-ten. If I got there before seven-thirty, I would still find Becca in. With a rush, I felt certain that luck would be with me.

The slow, creaking rise of the garage door seemed to take forever. I turned the key in the ignition and hit the gas with a lurch.

Careful, careful.

I backed the car slowly down the sloping drive, then turned toward Eastcourt Drive and the highway. The lake, bordered by the woods along its east side, was still in partial shadow. I gave my attention to the road. The heavy traffic, work and school, had not started yet. I slipped a tape into the deck, the prismatic chromatisms and sculptured urgencies of Chopin, his inseparable longings for pleasure and pain. The music filled the space of the car.

Restaurants, motels, the shopping malls along the highway, floated in a brilliant clarity, as if the early morning sunlight elicited from them a greater fullness of being. They unrolled on either side of me scored to Chopin.

It was only seven-twenty, and the exit to Becca's rose on the horizon and sped toward me. Everything was cooperating.

Becca lived in an older residential neighborhood, whose houses were small and close together. It was shifting slowly from white to black. Cars stood in the driveways. Here and there the evidences of children -- bicycles, balls, baseball gloves -- lay where they had been dropped on walks or lawns the evening before. An old woman in a flannel bathrobe was tugging a garbage can to the front of her driveway to be sure to make the Friday morning pick-up.

I almost never visited Becca at home. In a town as small as Jackson there are too many connections between this part of the community and the part where I live and work. But I had found reasons for occasional trips. Becca's house was ahead, a small, yellow frame house. The foundation plantings had grown recklessly out of proportion around it.

Becca's old Chevy was still in the driveway.

I pulled up in front of the house and parked. Now that I was here, I hesitated. Becca did not know I was coming; and our last encounter had been so ambiguous that I didn't want to risk pushing her further away. But wise or not, I simply could not resist the compulsion of my desire to see her. Now. To force the questions that had tortured me awake and in sleep. I stepped out of the car into the already warm morning.

As I walked toward the door, my mind was busy rehearsing, not the words I was going to say, but, as in court, the emotional stance, the overall awareness of the situation, that would shape the right words and arguments as I spoke.

I pressed the doorbell and waited. Exhilaration and nerves! Why didn't she answer?

Becca *had* to be there, she couldn't have gone to work without her car. I pressed the bell again, and kept my finger on it. A black teenage girl carrying her schoolbooks came out of the house next door and glanced at me with casual curiosity as she drifted toward the street.

There she was! I heard Becca turn the lock with a scraping sound and the door pulled open.

"Becca," I began urgently. And then I stopped.

I was thrown back into my dream. Standing in the arc of morning sunlight, unmistakable against the shadowed hallway in the flood of front light, stood the young man I had seen with Becca the afternoon before outside our motel. Dark hair, tousled, fell about his sleep-crumpled face; his square, handsome jaw was unshaven. He wore wrinkled boxer shorts. Still pulling himself from sleep, he rubbed his palm across his broad chest and studied me through sleep-blurred eyes. He looked me over in taken-for-granted possession of his place, as one of my sons might stand at our door before an importunate stranger.

"Yes?"

I felt a shock and rage that made it impossible for me to respond.

"Where is Ms. Talbot?" I finally asked in a choked voice.

"Becca's getting ready for work." He looked at me, perplexed and beginning now to sound belligerent.

I heard down the hall a door open and the echoing flush of a toilet. Then Becca's heels clicked along the floor.

Stopping beside the young man, she pulled the door open further to see who it was. In the widening arc of sunlight, she looked radiant.

"George!" she said, puzzled. "What are you doing here?"

I couldn't grasp the meaning of her casual tone.

Then her features fell into their characteristic expression of competence and energy.

"Well," she said, "tell me in a minute. Now," she placed her hand familiarly on the stranger's arm, "George, I've mentioned my brother, Frank. Frank, I'd like you to meet my boss, George Burden."

20

The four of us were sitting around the breakfast table, Becca, Frank, Chris and I. The house was shaped as a long hall with rooms opening off to the right: the living room, then the kitchen, then, as I knew, a laundry room and bathroom and two bedrooms, Becca's first and the last, smaller bedroom for Chris. We had trooped in silence from the front door past the shabby living room into the oversized kitchen. A table pushed against the wall beside the door defined the breakfast area. Above it hung a souvenir plate from the coast and a cheap ceramic plaque of a little boy whose red-glazed shirt bore the name *Chris.*

My gaze kept returning to the now obvious likeness between Becca and Frank.

It had been in the service of a fiction that I suffered! A fiction I'd created out of our last conversation in the hotel room and my glimpsed vision of Becca and this young man walking across the parking lot the afternoon before!

For they were unmistakably twins. Frank had the same black hair and, I assumed, the same white skin as Becca, although Frank's bare chest was tanned. Their features, Becca's more delicate, Frank's stronger, were variations on a single theme. His eyes, like Becca's, were large and hazel. He even had, a connection I found faintly repulsive, the same large, coral-shadowed nipples that I knew so well on Becca's breasts. A stranger might have taken Chris as their son, or, given the degree of similarity between the twins, their little brother borrowed for a day out. This visible kinship and the shared history it attested made me feel alien.

Nor was it only appearance that made Frank resemble Becca. It was also the energy he brought into the room, Becca's energy, but in him almost manic.

His words tumbled forth in his soft Southern accent in an urgency to embrace and convey their subject. His hands, his body drew, almost danced an energetic embodiment of his words. As he spoke, he leaned forward, his vitality and candor inviting his partner to intimacy.

This invitation made me less rather than more relaxed. I hadn't given a reason for my visit. Somehow social habit had led us all spontaneously to conspire in my coming in to have a cup of coffee and meet Frank.

But more reserve between us would have made me feel safer. Did Frank know about me and Becca? How had he come to be in the hotel the day before? Becca had certainly seemed surprised.

I couldn't stop tracing and retracing the surface of the experience for signs of its inner meaning.

As the safest subject I turned the talk toward Frank and watched for an opportunity to speak with Becca alone.

"Becca and I were different," Frank was telling me. "She married Mike right out of high school and stayed here in Jackson. But I couldn't stand the South any longer."

He turned to embrace Becca in the conversation. His large hand pushed the imagined South aside as if it were a plate. "I just felt trapped!" He squeezed his hand to show how he felt, his muscles tensing with the action all the way up his arm.

"So you left," I said.

"Yessir. I got a great chance. I acted a lot in high school and the summer after graduation I worked crew at Jackson Auditorium. A musical came through," His strong finger traced a movement along the bare tabletop, "touring. I talked a lot with the actress who was starring in it." His face became less expressive. "When they left, she fixed it up so I could crew for the rest of the tour."

I thought about Frank five or six years earlier with his beauty, his energy, his soft Southern accent, more naïve than he could know, and on the make: it was easy to imagine she had found a way to take him with her.

A moment of silence followed.

Then Becca stood, picked up my empty cup and saucer, and carried them to the counter beside the coffee-maker. Her manner mixed the double detachment of employee and hostess, but the cup shook lightly in her hand. Frank sprawled back in his chair, relaxing at the pause in his story, enjoying, perhaps, the memory of his escape into freedom.

Chris slipped from his chair and climbed up onto his uncle's bare thigh. He seemed to sink into the thigh that supported him, with the unconscious trust that children extend to those, even those not often seen, who are family members.

And maybe, I thought, there was more.

With his mother's distraction and tiredness, with Mike's second wife now pregnant, it must be comforting to have this strong uncle who for the moment belonged only to him. Frank leaned forward and wrapped both large arms around the little boy, drawing him back against his chest.

"Is all this talk boring you, pardner?" he asked in a sudden cowboy voice, looking down at the top of Chris's head. Chris shook his head, *no*. Frank released his grip, leaving one large hand against the boy's leg, so he was supported but could get up when he wished.

I glanced up at Becca's face as she set the refilled coffee cup before me. She didn't turn away, but her face was snapped shut. She watched as I picked up my spoon, glanced around for some low calorie sweetener, found none, and settled for a spoonful of sugar which I stirred into my cup.

Then, turning her back, she returned to the counter and busied herself putting some jars and boxes into the cupboard above it.

Frank resumed his story. He leaned forward, his torso carrying with it the boy who was leaning against him, as if on a ride at the fair.

"So I stayed with the musical for two or three months. But I was still only doing crew work. What I really wanted was to act. So I went out to stay with another woman I met. She'd gone back to Hollywood to do a soap opera."

I couldn't pay attention to Frank anymore. He moved in too close, he clung; and his self-absorption seemed to heighten rather than distract from the intense feelings of the others which were building around him.

Becca was still standing at the sink, her back to us as she filled an empty coffee cup with water from the tap and attentively poured it while she slowly turned a flower pot that rested on the sill.

It was as if we were all enacting a ritual, which we didn't choose, and whose meaning partly eluded us.

"Excuse me, Frank," I interrupted, "Excuse me, Becca," my voice formal, pulling myself up in my chair and glancing at my watch. "I almost forgot why I stopped by. We need to discuss a few questions about the figures you sent up yesterday, so they can be typed. The report needs to go out by nine."

She stood immobile for a moment. The curve of her back, the shift of weight at her hips, the suggestion of her legs beneath the soft fall of her dress filled me with satisfaction and longing.

Then she turned toward me with a look of despair, the expression of a dog that recognizes she has been run into a corner and waits an inevitable beating.

"Can we speak in here?" she asked, her voice flat.

"Some of this is confidential," I said.

In the gesture I knew so well, her eyelids closed over her eyes and remained there, as if moment by moment removing her from this laborious present; as if, before she had to open them again, time might mercifully stop.

"No, no. Stay here!" Frank's accommodating voice broke in. "No problem, Sis. I've got to get dressed anyway."

He turned to Chris. "Keep me company?" He picked Chris up under the belly with his right hand and carried him, kicking and laughing, out of the room.

I stood and walked across the kitchen. I didn't want Becca to be able to take refuge in the familiarity of her home territory. I wanted to close the distance between us.

"Becca." I put my hand on her arm. She pulled away. "Please, Dearest. I know I took you by surprise yesterday and this morning. I moved too fast. But if you really do love me, why can't you forgive that and say yes?"

Her gaze that now met mine was deep and complex with suffering. I couldn't grasp where it came from.

"George, I'm so grateful to you." She put up a hand to stop me from interrupting. "Yes, don't speak, I *love* you. But for me to marry you, so many people would be involved and so many changes. Let me have time to get used to the idea, let me think it through."

Her voice began to take on its impersonal professional surface. "I have to take Chris to daycare now and get to the office. I'll already have to find an excuse to explain why I'm late."

"Be sick," I said spontaneously. "Don't go in. Julia is away for a few days. We can drive down to the coast and you can think about it where you won't have everything else on your mind."

A flush of anger rose and rode her pale skin. "Drop everything, Becca! Julia's gone! Great!

"Oh, but wait. Chris is here. And Frank's here, I forgot! Maybe Becca can't just leave. "

She was shaking.

"Shhhhhhh," I said softly, as to a distressed child. "We can work that kind of problem out. What did you say to Frank?"

"Only a little about us," she said finally in a low, resistant voice. "Not," looking up, "your question yesterday."

She held her body stiff with intent. "It's none of his business! Not any of my family's!"

There were tears under her voice, sharply disciplined.

"Becca," I whispered. "This is painful now. But we can't just pick up the affair in the old way. We *have* to talk about it."

"But not now," she pled, "not while Frank's still here!"

She was a negotiator who having given everything else away held out for one concession.

There was a sound at the door.

Turning, I saw Frank, shaven now, blue jeans pulled over his shorts, bare-chested, bare-footed. He showed no cognizance he was intruding. Was this unawareness or tact or some other thing?

I felt a surge of hatred for his presence; it rose huge and spontaneous from my gut and rode through the rest of my body like drink.

He smiled.

"I left my shirt on the back of the chair." He gestured at it with his large hand and padded over to us. I could hear Chris in the next room singing a commercial to himself.

Frank drew the tee shirt over his head. His tousled black hair, hazel eyes, large smile emerged successively from the neck as his blunt fingers pulled the shirt down across his torso. "Can't go where, Sis?" The air around him carried a morning smell of aftershave and toothpaste. Apparently fragments of our conversation had drifted down the hall. It took me a moment to register the import of his words.

And suddenly I had an inspiration. I could *use* Frank's presence. My conversation with Becca was like a business deal that's moving in the right direction but stuck. I could use Frank for a little external pressure to move it forward. Turning, I addressed myself to him.

"I was asking if your sister, and you, too, if you like, would enjoy driving down to the coast this weekend.

"There are a few things I need to discuss with Becca alone. But there's plenty to do. I'm sure we can get in some swimming and take out the boat."

Frank looked toward Becca, as if for a signal. She refused to answer his glance.

"I haven't been back to the coast since I was seventeen," he said finally. "My buddies and I used to drive down there to get into trouble," he added in a mock confiding manner, which appreciated, yet distanced him from that teenage self. "Sis?"

Becca raised her head. How alike their profiles were, but her face was a mask, her voice exhausted, as if it was too much now to resist both of us.

"Okay," she whispered at last. "If you're both set on it, I'll go."

I had won! Not for myself against Becca, but for both of us against her hesitation. And in this victory, my mind spontaneously read its ultimate outcome, not, indeed, the physical scene (Would Julia keep the present house?), but the human figuration.

I saw Becca and myself ten years hence, now with our own long past, the pain of this period faded or forgotten; Chris would be in high school, thinking about colleges. Becca and our children loved by Ellen and Brook, Elizabeth and Mark.

And an older Frank, married, with children of his own, Chris's cousins, and Becca's remaining brothers and sisters, by the decision of this marriage destined to be members of my family.

Now they were faceless, potential presences, but then they would be well-known, embraced or borne, a source of comfort or concern.

If I had to cause Becca a bit of pain in the short run in order to shape this, I'd accept the responsibility.

Becca was speaking, her voice flat, looking at neither of us.

"I'm supposed to take Chris to Mike's this evening. I'll have to let Mike know I'm going, so if something happens to Chris, he can get me." She added, lower, as if figuring something out in herself, "I don't know what I'll say."

I wanted to reach out and touch her. But I knew anger would make her pull away, and I felt awkward about displaying our intimacy before Frank. There continued a long silence, as if each of us were waiting for another to speak.

"Would you like me to stay," I asked finally, "and drive you down?"

"No. You go ahead. I'll meet you there."

"It's at least three hours. Do you want Frank to drive down with you?"

I turned to include him in my question.

"Let him go with you," a surge of suppressed anger colored her flat voice. Frank, by his affiliation with me, had also betrayed her. "In case there's any problem, I'd prefer not to be tied to someone else's schedule."

She turned away and called, "Chris!"

Chris appeared in the kitchen doorway.

"Time to go, sweetheart," she said, her voice gentle.

There was a flurry of gathering his lunch box and putting into his hands his favorite car toy.

Frank knelt down and opened his arms. "Hey, young man, how about a hug for your uncle?" Chris accepted the invitation, his face as open as Frank's. Frank's large arms closed around the tumbling body and lifted it up. "What a big guy," he said. "Almost too big to do this"—he lifted Chris until the boy's hand could touch the ceiling—"or this"—he tossed him in the air, caught him and dropped him gently to the floor.

"Frank, come outside," Chris shouted, grasping Frank's right hand in both of his and tugging on it.

"Yes, go ahead," Becca said from the table, where she was digging into her purse to see if she had her keys. "I'll be out in a minute."

Finding them, she walked over to the doorway where I was waiting and with an air of sadness placed her hand on my arm. "You're right," she said in sudden decision. "It all needs to be worked out now."

I followed as she walked through the shadowed hallway toward the front door. She pulled it open, and stepped out into the day beyond. I lingered as she locked up behind her. Two outsized gardenia bushes, their glossy leaves dimmed by a film of dust, encroached on the steps. The light and heat were already draining the energy from the day.

Frank was leaning against the side of the blue Chevrolet compact. Chris had already set his lunch-box, decorated with brilliantly colored space figures, on the front seat. He was standing beside the open door showing Frank that he could remove and reinsert the wheels of a little orange truck.

Frank looked up. With a tanned hand he shaded his hazel eyes against the glare. "All set?" he asked, smiling.

"Yes," Becca said shortly. "You and George are on your own now. I'll see you this evening."

She leaned down, planting a kiss on Chris's cheek which lifted in readiness to receive it, and patted the rear end of his jeans.

"Get in the car now," she said. "Josh and Scott and Jacob will be waiting for you and you can show the truck to Katie."

"Katie an' Matthew's seen it," Chris said, but he scrambled into the front seat, shifting aside the lunch box and his toy car. He set about fastening his seat belt, his face and small fingers a brief study in concentration.

Becca slammed his door and walked around to the driver's side of the car. Her white, sleeveless dress glowed against the brown and faded green of the yard. She had brushed her hair in the usual way, swept back across the top of her ears into a black coil above her white neck and the rose-pale lobes of her ears. The air of self-possession, which she seemed always able to don in public, shaped her lovely, self-possessed carriage. She was already apart, moving toward the office.

Keys in hand, Becca opened her own door, slid into the front seat, and slammed the door behind her. I stood watching as the engine turned over; watched as Becca, her expression distant in its absorbed attention, backed the car out of the driveway and disappeared toward the freeway. I felt a sick sense of loss out of all proportion to the brief, real separation between us.

Turning, I found Frank was gazing at me. "Are you all right?"

"Fine. I was sick last night," I grabbed at the social lie as at a life-preserver. "I'm still a little shakey."

"Yessir." His tone was compliant but concerned. "Still want to try for the coast this morning?"

I looked around at the tiny house, the unkempt yard, the cramped neighborhood: the familiar boundaries of Becca's life, perhaps the only life she knew enough to imagine.

"Yes," I said sharply, simply abandoning the dreamed-up report I'd been so urgent about earlier. "I'm ready to leave at any time. I have whatever I'll need there. How long will it take you to get ready?"

21

Once we were on the road, I felt paradoxically less that I was leaving than approaching Becca: we were moving now in the right direction. The road was familiar to me from hundreds of trips, the landmarks, the road signs, the patches of town, the turns and problems of the drive. Handling the car took little attention and offered the pleasant sense of mastery one knows at the wheel.

Frank sat beside me, his arm stretched along the back of my seat, his hand dropping relaxed behind it.

We passed through the outer edge of Jackson. Within my memory, this had been a string of small towns: to visit one of them was a country outing. Now they merged into one another, distinguished only by white signs marking jurisdictional divisions in a continuous stretch of commercial outskirts.

A strip of untrimmed grass and weeds separated the highway from the graveled frontage road. Along it auto repair shops, industrial plants, discount houses, run-down motels and quick-stop stores with two or three self-service gas pumps in front of them alternated in dreary repetition. At the intersections fast food restaurants piled up. They might have been anywhere.

Then came a break. The roadside activity fell away, the road extended through a heat-fatigued green emptiness.

Frank's voice, his accent soft, a slight bitterness slipping into his tone, broke the silence.

"This is as different from California as I remembered."

"How do you mean?"

He seemed to be trying but unable to constrain the tone of bitterness. "It's *nowhere*. I hated it when I left and it's still the same. Somehow, I knew it would be and forgot it at the same time."

"You mean Mississippi in general?"

"Yes. Well, I mean this," he drew his arm across the view. "In California, even in a place like this, there'd be hills or the mountains or the desert." His large, dancing hands sculpted the hills and the flat desert in the air before the dashboard. "Something big, something interesting, something, well, *more*."

"So that's really home now?"

"No. No, that's Oz. You change planes at the Dallas airport and all at once you're stepping into technicolor. Well, into more than this sort of run-down, choking green. This is Kansas. It *is* home."

"But it feels like a foreign country?" I asked.

His voice again took on that muted tone, as of a personal grievance.

"Maybe they're all foreign," he said.

"Why did you come back?" I asked. I recognized in his longing an ache similar to my own, was touched in him by a shadow of myself.

He turned his head, and as our eyes met he seemed to bring himself into focus and at the same time to let something go. The grin I had come to know so well took over his broad, handsome face.

"I had to work something out," he said in a quiet voice and returned his attention to the road.

Ahead, in the steaming shade of some trees, appeared a battered van with its side-doors pulled open and a hand-written sign on the roof. **FRUIET, BOILED PEANUTS**. An old black man in overalls sat sideways on the front seat, the front door open, his legs hanging down, ready to climb out into the sun if anyone stopped. He was fanning himself with a folded newspaper.

I couldn't remember how many years this van, and before that an old pick-up truck, had stood at this spot. All my children had waited for it to appear and rush toward us along the road, a sacred station, a necessary stop. Now there was no reason for me to stop. Perhaps it was that very sense of something gone that caused me to slow and pull off to the side of the road.

The old man climbed carefully from the front seat and walked stiffly toward us. I pressed the window button: *down*.

His face opened as he recognized me. We had known one another, if only in this setting, for over a quarter of a century.

"Haven't seen you this summer," he said warmly.

"No, we've been too busy to get to the coast. How are you?"

"The Lord's takin' care of me. Want some peaches this morning?"

"Are they good?"

"The best."

This conversation never varied. It was like a ritual or the words of a familiar children's story that must always be repeated in the same way.

"I'll take three pounds," I said, reaching behind me into the back seat for my suit coat with my wallet. The old man turned and made his way slowly back to the van beneath the trees. Picking up from a stack several used paper bags, he examined them deliberately until he found the right size and emptied three one pound baskets of peaches into it. His dark face shone with sweat.

He returned to the car.

"Your grandson isn't helping you this summer?" I asked.

"Workin' in town," he said.

I handed him the money. As he passed the bag in through the window he stooped and peered into the shadowy car.

"This your son?" he asked warmly, gesturing toward Frank.

"No," I said. "They're all away now."

"Couldn't tell. Know last summer the young one was almost a man." He counted out change from the pocket of his overalls and placed it in my hand. "You'll like these," he said. "The best."

I thanked him and nosed the car back onto the highway. Frank reached into the offered bag, took a peach, and bit through the furred skin into meat the color of fire. The sweet juice dribbled down his chin onto his chest and lap. He wiped his chin with the back of his hand and his hand along his jeans.

"Do I look like your son?" He asked through the mouthful.

"No," I said, "not really." The emphasis on the distance of age between us felt, stupidly, embarrassing.

"You do look a little like my father."

The road seemed to be winding up, like a metal tape; to be drawing the car, like a pulley. *Going down, going down, going down home.*

Frank put his hands together, lifted them over his head, and stretched out, yawning. Then he readjusted himself in the seat and turned toward me, smiling.

"Your father," I said. "Becca tells me he was a Methodist minister?" I wanted to show my interest in him. I wanted him to like me, to tell *Becca* he liked me.

"Yes," he said. "I was a minister's brat." He spoke emphatically, but his tone put the phrase in quotes.

"Was it hard?" I asked.

"Sometimes. Daddy had to move around. The older ones seemed to be used to it. I remember how much it hurt *me* to make friends and have to leave them. I made them promise to keep in touch, but it never lasted for more than a letter or two. Finally, I got used to it, too. I got good at making friends with anyone, but not deep, so it wouldn't hurt when I had to leave."

"Was your family close?"

"Becca and I came along so late that my brothers and sisters were beginning to go out on their own by the time I was old enough to remember. So mainly it was Becca and me and my parents. Of course, whoever was there was close in one way: we all had to be together at the services and at Sunday School and the church socials."

"Becca mentioned that sitting through all those services as a little girl was pretty boring," I said, laughing.

"I hated it!" His right hand curled into a fist on his lap. "No matter what else I wanted to do, I had to get dressed up and Mom was always telling me to sit up and listen because everyone was watching us."

His hand relaxing, he turned to me with a look that seemed elusively challenging.

"But things changed a little when I became a teenager," he said. "I had to do what people wanted on the outside, but I could do whatever I wanted on the inside. I'd sit there beside Mom with the hymn book on my lap and imagine having sex with every female in the congregation."

"You probably weren't the only one to do something like that," I said. "And not only among the teenagers."

He glanced at me as if wondering if my remark was meant as a personal confession: a gesture of camaraderie, or even of competition.

"I'd imagine it every way," he continued. "With the old ladies. With the babies. Whether they wanted it. Whether they were afraid." His fingers drummed lightly against the leather at the back of my seat. "Pretty sick," he said.

I couldn't tell if he was speaking the truth or now inventing, perhaps trying to shock me.

"I think it sounds as if it got you through the services," I said mildly.

He laughed and fell silent. My thoughts went to Becca, following her in imagination around the office. I could see why she had been reluctant to discuss our situation in front of Frank. Whatever his experience, it hadn't matured him! I wondered whether whatever he had to work out would keep him in Jackson.

"Will you be visiting Becca long?" I asked, following the thought.

"Sis? I don't know."

"Do you have a job in Hollywood?"

Frank seemed to rise from his own silent thoughts, sitting up in the seat, shaking his head like a diver breaking the surface. I wondered what those thoughts had been.

"If I want to go back to it. I've got a job in a health club. It pays okay and it keeps me in good shape." He patted his taut stomach.

"Given up acting?"

"I do a film from time to time."

"Anything I might have seen?"

His grin widened. "I doubt it."

The road continued on apparently endlessly, the earth sometimes folded, sometimes flat, but unrelievedly green. Shacks flashed past and old trailers with rusting, dismantled cars crowded around them, like metal offspring seeking mechanical teats. A restaurant bar appeared, out in the middle of nowhere, drawing its clientele from God knows where.

Frank leaned against the door-frame and fell asleep.

Twenty minutes later we slowed to pass through Hattiesburg. Frank pulled himself from sleep. "I'm going to need to make a pit stop," he said, yawning and rubbing his face.

"Good. I need to stop for gas, anyway."

I turned into a large Chevron station, its entrance decorated with a bed of plastic gardenias.

It was only ten-thirty, but the heat cut like a knife. By the time Frank returned with a sweating can of Dr. Pepper in his hand I had paid for the gas and was eager to get back on the road.

100

"An hour and a half to go," I said. *Halfway there*!

"Would you like me to drive?" Frank asked.

"No," I said. "I'll do the driving. I'll drive the rest of the way."

Now the land was barer, scrubbier. The pines were asymmetrical from wind and the chance fall of light. They rose out of red earth, their branches all at the top or to one side, their needles sparse, their cones like tumors stiffly attached. Sometimes kudzu choked them, smothering definition. A lumber truck pulling across the highway from a side road with a load of freshly cut logs spread a momentary rich fragrance through the air vents.

I glanced at Frank, briefly tracing the contours of Becca's face in his, trying to find a contact that would allow me to interpret what was going on beneath his now withdrawn silence.

Feeling my glance, Frank turned to me.

"Do you spend a lot of time on the coast?"

"Less than when my children were young. My..." I started spontaneously and then almost choked. To say either 'Julia' or 'my wife' seemed to make her too real to say comfortably all I might want to say before Frank. "My wife," I hurried on, "doesn't find a great deal there to amuse her."

"But you said you have a house?"

"Yes. On the bay. The original house belonged to my mother's family. We enlarged it." How could a few words make clear to this boy all that the house was and meant to me? "I suppose I'm doing what you said you were doing," I added.

"What is that?"

"Returning to where I was a child. Except that I was happy there. For a while it was the happiest time of my life."

"Yes, but you go back all the time. You never had to leave it."

The conversation spun on within. *Yes. I had to leave it. Why did I feel that now I might be allowed to go back?*

Across my mind swept a blinding wash of memory. Myself as a boy walking up from the dock, the boards warm and rough under my feet, surrounded by the flashing water-dazzle. Then the gentle green rise toward the house between the tamed magnolia, pine and honeysuckle. And my mother watching in the doorway, remembered or known from her photographs, twenty years younger than I am now, her blue eyes alight, her waiting smile only for me.

"Look out!" Frank cried abruptly. Ahead, a flashing yellow light marked a cross-road. A battered gray pick-up was edging into the faster stream of traffic on the highway. I swerved away and passed it.

"Thanks," I said, and became absorbed in the driving. Now green, even rows of soybeans unrolled behind the vine-choked barbed wire fences that marked the fields. The scattered houses were flat, rangy, built not to be insulated from cold, but shaded from heat.

A buzzard, black, plump, matron-bosomed, dropped to the road ahead. Strutting officiously, it pulled at the still bloody corpse of an armadillo, its round shell partially intact, on the side of the road. The bird rose at the approach of the car. Then it fluttered down and strutted on about its task.

"That," Frank said, as if picking up the earlier conversation—he gestured behind us at the receding scene on the road—"That's what *I* had here."

I didn't know what more to say to him and my own feelings were becoming more urgent as our descent approached its end. We fell silent.

The land flattened now into the coastal plain. The roadsides filled up. Billboards: **UNDERSEA FANTASY, BAYOU ALLIGA-TOR FARM, HOLIDAY INN, HOWARD JOHNSON, RAMADA SEASIDE,** *50% off for children under eighteen, golfers welcome, fishermen welcome*. And the first beach souvenir shops, hills of conch shells in wire cages, vinyl rafts, red, blue, silver, orange, vinyl flags strung between palm trees, neon road-signs blinking solicitations. A landscape for tourists, for pleasure-seekers.

Yet here, too, there was a world behind this world, sunk in time, sunk almost beyond time in the permanent regions which memory possesses.

We crested the bridge, crossing the waterway that threads the bayous and descended toward the heart of downtown. Frank's pleasure crackled in the air like ozone. He drew his body up and leaned forward, resting his forearms along the dash, his chin on his forearms.

"Energy!" he said, as we pulled to a stop where the highway intersected with the beach road. His eye followed the progress of a well-tanned girl with honey blonde hair in a pale green bikini.

We turned along the strip.

"Here's where we used to cruise," he said exuberantly, with a quick sidelong glance toward me. His hazel eyes were glittering.

It was a street shaped by needs, not only the needs of Frank and his friends, but all the needs of wildly diverse buyers who had money and sellers who were eager to take it. We rode past the dilapidated amusement park:

R   R   R
I   I   I
D   D   D
E   E   E
S   S   S

The ferris wheel, its girded frame a peeling white and yellow, slowly rotated, its cars lifting and dropping, red and white, white and orange, blue and gray. Bumper Cars. Flying Saucers. A red and white circus wagon shouted in ornate gold letters: ***Cotton Candy! Popcorn! Candy Apples!*** Children darted among the rides while their parents hugged any offered shade in the hammering heat.

The brightness of the gaudiest signs labored to shine against the bleaching sun.

SOUVENIR CITY
EIGHT DOLLAR BIKINI
T-SHIRTS SHELLS JEWELRY BEER ART

In the gaps between the shops, the downtown motels, the amusement areas, one could glimpse a scrubby beach and bare sky. The good beach lay beyond the strip. Here were other entertainments:

DALLAS GIRLS ARE THE GREATEST
WHAT DO YOU SAY?
8 P.M.
THE DALLAS ROOM
GIRLS GIRLS GIRLS
THE FINEST ON THE BEACH

And just next door:

GOOFY GOLF

Intent families on vacation poised over their clubs as above them a tyrannosaurus slowly rotated its head from side to side, jostling a golden Buddha and grinning sphinx.

Variations on a theme of need, one following another. **NEVADA CLUB. CHANDELIER CLUB. STAR DUST. THE SILVER SLIPPER.** Only the places to eat competed with the girly shows in variety: fish houses, donut shops, waffle houses, Chinese restaurants, hamburger stands, old and new, formal, drive-in.

"Wait!" cried Frank suddenly. He thrust his index finger toward a sign:

RENO PALACE
EXOTIC DANCERS
NEW ACTS NITELY

On the rim of a tilted champagne glass in which two lines of neon bulbs represented a sparkle of rising bubbles perched a pair of neon girls, one brunette, one blonde, wearing thin bikinis and conspicuous high heels.

"Did you want me to stop?" I asked, puzzled.

"No, no," his voice dropped and he sat back. "I just remembered. I know a girl who works here."

"Someone from high school?"

"No, I knew her in Hollywood. A dancer. She came back when her mom got sick. We worked together once. Maybe I'll look her up."

"You'll have the time," I said.

The strip fell behind. A curve of white sand receded to a vanishing point in the distance. Along it, vendors rented rainbow-sailed boats, blue umbrellas, beach chairs. Waders and swimmers played at the edge of the great expanse of water under the bleached high noon sky.

I had often returned to the house. But Frank was wrong. I had not come home. Home was what was now winding up the road, pulling the car, bringing me toward rather than away from Becca; home *was* Becca.

Will I come home now?

We'll see, my mind said; but my body, as if it had run on ahead and made its own reading of the future, was relaxing with the anticipated consummation, my nerves, my muscles reaching forward in trust, already unclamping from need.

I turned to Frank, smiling.

"Almost home."

22

I turned off the main road into Ocean Springs and entered a realm where the fall of time, the changing configurations of family and work and place dissolving down the years from one to another, was layered in the timeless space of memory. Past and present were present, co-embedded: the white brick **ARTIST'S QUARTER** which loomed ahead was itself, was still in memory the original grimy railway warehouse I passed with my father as a boy, was still **HOWARD'S ICE CREAM PARLOR**, where I treated my children on the steamy, gnat-ridden evenings of summer weekends.

Frank, his hazel eyes still mirroring the excitement of the strip, glanced out at Ocean Springs with only casual interest.

"Are we almost there?" he asked.

"Almost."

The streets now were so familiar to me that, without thinking, my hands on the wheel knew their way. I drove past the small, frame, downtown houses, hardly more than cottages, brilliant in the noon sun, with their neat lawns, leggy annuals and reddening tomatoes; descended past the more formal homes nearer the bay; and dipped down the hill toward the inlet, excitement swelling in my chest.

Brown docks reached into browner water, muddy and iridescent where oil rode the softly gathering and collapsing waves. My eye embraced the commercial fishing boats, embraced the dazzling ivory of the cabin cruisers under the sun, and the sailboats whose jungle of bobbing masts traced and retraced narrow circles against the sky.

The Lincoln lifted over the little bridge that spanned the inlet. Frank pulled himself up in his seat and studied the scene with renewed interest, following the sweep of the inlet out beyond the reticulation of docks and boats to the open expanse of the bay.

"Boats on water!" he said with excitement in his voice. His hands, moving outward, opened an ocean between them. "I wish I could get out and smell the air!"

I laughed. "It's not really fresh right here, too much oil and fish. But you can walk back later and see."

"Walk back?"

We were over the bridge. On the right stood a row of estates, the houses far back from the road facing the water. There were no walls and gates. The estates were large and carefully tended, but shared the welcoming air of the rest of the town.

"Yes," I said, braking as we began to pass a low, split-rail fence along which grew a sprawl of small, pink roses. "We're here." I pointed to the black mailbox. In neat, gold letters it read: **BURDEN**.

I turned in along a driveway paved with crushed oyster shells between the large live oaks which had been forts and jungle houses for generations of Thibodeaux and then Burden children and rounded the curve which brought into view the house.

This house after fifty-five years was almost as familiar to me as my own body, was an extension of the space of my body. Its shape makes a "U." The long, older section parallels the water; at each end two shorter, more recently added arms reach forward toward the road, creating the courtyard and parking area into which we now pulled up.

A pair of bicycles rested along a wood pile stacked beside the door against the house.

"Don't you lock the bicycles up?" Frank asked, lifting his eyebrows in surprise.

"No," I said. "This is a very safe place."

Smiling at him, I opened the car door. Frank, waiting for the cue, followed. He stretched and looked around. The energy that ordinarily flowed from him seemed to drop like calm in a wind.

"You must be rich," he said to me quietly over the top of the car.

"Not quite rich," I smiled again. The day was hot and windless. A faint odor of salt touched the air, as if it had labored up from the bay by its own effort. A film of sweat had already gathered on Frank's forehead; my shirt was beginning to cling in patches around me.

"Let's get inside," I said. "This is usually a time for naps anyway, unless you're at the water."

"Want me to get the luggage?"

"Yes, we might as well bring it in."

I tossed the keys to Frank, who closed his large hand over them. His manner still seemed, I couldn't quite read it, abashed or wary. Perhaps Becca hadn't spoken of me at any length. I stepped into the shade of the overhanging porch.

"We do lock the house," I said to him. "It may keep out casual intruders; in any case, it's our practice. Let me show you where we keep the key."

I reached up above the wind chimes which hung from the eaves along the wing of the house to my left. A piece of two-by-four several inches long was nailed into the underside of the eave as if providing a mount for the chimes.

"It's behind here," I said.

I reached behind the block of wood and pulled out a small, battered metal box which rested on a hidden ledge; sliding back the top, I shook the front door key out into my palm and held it up to show him.

"This has been the test of the adulthood for Burdens over the years," I joked. "By the time they can reach the key, they've grown up."

"I'd have found a way to get in anyway!" Frank said sharply.

"Yes?" I acknowledged.

Frank didn't continue. I walked back to the open car trunk to pick up my briefcase and coat. Everything else I needed was already in the house.

Following, Frank heaved his suitcase from the trunk and explosively slammed the door.

Then all at once, as if to deny the moment of annoyance, he relaxed into a contraposto stance and shaded his hazel eyes with his great hand, the lift of his arm pulling his shirt from his jeans over a strip of tanned belly. His stance and smile fell into place like a transparency of boyish contrition and candor.

"Sorry," he said in a subdued voice. "Some things press my buttons."

The truth is, I was feeling such a sweet urgency of homecoming that I couldn't care about Frank and his immaturity. Nodding, I carried my briefcase and coat into the shade of the overhang and pulled open the screen-door. Frank held it as I turned the key and pushed the heavy oak door open before me.

I was in the center of my own life.

"This is quite a place!" Frank said, setting down the suitcase and looking appraisingly around him.

Frank and I were, I suddenly realized, confronting two different places, one so familiar to me, another entirely strange to him. This central room of the house, the room fronting the bay, was the old house of my childhood. Julia and I opened it up when we added the east and west wings, making one huge room with a great fireplace along the landside wall and glass doors flanked by rows of heavy casement windows, a wall of glass and white pickled wood, on the bay side. The floor was red tile on which children in bathing suits could drip without damage.

A double couch and armchairs, wheat-colored, faced the fireplace. Together they could embrace a dozen people and were strong enough to survive any young rough-housing. Burden treasures and Burden junk which had become treasure from its association with moments of family happiness overflowed the bookcases, cabinets and tables around the room.

Frank continued to look over the room and out the glass doors toward the patio and the long slope to the dock and flashing sea. Even in the shadowed room he seemed to gather the available light about himself.

What was he seeing?

Not the history which for me made the large space so intimate. But (he had said it himself) a mixture of grandeur and comfort beyond his world. Perhaps it had been a better idea than I knew to bring Frank here. Perhaps, I thought, half-ashamed of myself, if I let him taste what it was like to live here, I could make him a more interested ally than I had foreseen. He would share this if Becca married me.

"Let me show you to your room," I said.

I led Frank across the red tile floor, shadowed except where the early afternoon sun shining through the casement windows created a brilliant border, and turned right down the hallway into the east wing. Here, too, massive casement windows let in light. Doors opened off the opposite wall into the bedrooms.

I stopped at the first room, at a set of glass-paneled double doors covered by chintz curtains. Throwing them open, I waved Frank in before me.

He stood inside looking around him. The room was shadowed. The light from the hallway did not extend this far, and the tall, narrow windows that covered the opposite wall opened onto a stand of pines which filtered the sun.

"The shade keeps this room somewhat cool," I said. "But you'll want extra light." I reached beside the door and flipped on the switch.

"Most recently this was my youngest daughter's room," I continued. "That explains the chintz and roses." I gestured at the four-poster double bed that stretched out from the far wall toward the center of the room. "But the bed is really comfortable, and it's easy to get to the family room and outside. Also"—I strode across the room and opened the door in the right wall—"you have your own bathroom."

"This is great," Frank said, but I still felt in his manner a hint of the wariness I sensed earlier.

"I'll be down at the end of the hall," I said, pointing. "After I've changed, we'll have some lunch."

I paused, torn between my desire to be alone, as if, by throwing all my attention into waiting, I could make Becca arrive faster, and my desire to guarantee Frank a pleasant time.

"Let me know if you want anything else," I added. "I really want you to have a good time this weekend, Frank."

I sounded like a salesman. I heard it. I couldn't tell from his expression whether Frank heard it too.

23

I changed into my old khaki shorts, a navy knit sport shirt, and my brown deck shoes, feeling, if possible, even more released in these clothes. Frank's door was shut as I passed it on my way into the kitchen, which is continuous with the family room in the west wing. The kitchen is the second largest room in the house, the source and the scene of many a celebration, formal parties and spontaneous family celebrations of fresh sausage from New Orleans or crabs caught by children around the dock.

I heard the muffled flush of a toilet from the other side of the house. While I waited for Frank, I pulled a bag of potato chips from the cupboard, opened two cans of chili, shook their contents into a skillet on top of the big double stove, and stirred them with a wooden spoon which I pulled from the adjacent drawer. Julia's kitchen could be counted on to be well stocked and arranged. When the chili began to bubble - the smell made me realize how hungry I was! - I turned it down and set two plates and bowls on the bar, a white oval island in the middle of the kitchen surrounded by red-topped stools.

"Frank!"

I reached into the nearest refrigerator for two cans of Bud.

"Lunch!"

Setting them on the bar beside the plates, I started across the family room to see what was holding Frank up. He appeared around the corner holding a framed photograph in his large hand.

"Sorry," he said with an apologetic grin. "I was looking around. This was on your daughter's bureau." He waved the photograph. "Is one of them her?"

I took the photograph and looked at it. It was taken at the dock a couple of years ago during a family gathering. We were all dressed in swimsuits; we squinted as we gazed toward the remorseless sun. Beth, my youngest daughter, stood in the middle. I was on one side with my arm around her shoulder. Julia stood on the other side with her arms folded beneath her breast. Mark stood beside Julia in turn, smiling happily, reaching out and touching her arm with one hand. On either end were Ellen and Brook with their spouses. Brook's son and Ellen's daughter stood proudly in front of their parents' legs. Ellen's second rested in his mother's arms. Everyone but Mark and the grandchildren looked patiently uncomfortable.

Gazing at the photograph while Frank stood, a little too close, at my shoulder, I suddenly felt vulnerable, vulnerable for the whole pictured family.

"This," I pointed, "this is Beth."

Frank leaned forward and touched her image with his large finger, as if he were wiping away a film so he could see her more closely.

"She's very good looking," he said appreciatively. "Married?"

"No."

"How old is she?"

"Twenty-five," I said.

"I'd like to meet her." He caught my eye and, unbelievably, winked. I flushed and said nothing. Frank returned his gaze to the photograph. "Who are the rest of these people?" he asked, running his finger across them. They looked naked and exposed standing in their swim-wear squinting back at Frank's scrutiny.

"Let's talk about it later," I said, turning the picture over and lowering it against the side of my leg. "Lunch is ready."

We sat across from each other, hunching over the bar. The house depends, in the old way, on high ceilings and shading trees for coolness. The windows were open on two sides, but no breeze created a draft. A fan hanging from the ceiling stirred the air, but did not add any appreciable coolness.

Frank ripped the top from the potato chip bag and placed a large handful on his plate while I spooned out the chili into the bowls and set the skillet back on the stove. Frank began eating greedily.

I still wasn't certain just how to approach Frank, but if Becca was going to be there that evening, I thought I should find out beforehand how much Frank knew. I took a spoonful of the hot, redolent chili and washed it down with a mouthful of cold, bittersweet beer.

"Has your sister talked about us?" I asked finally.

Frank, bent over his lunch, paused. He lowered a spoonful of chili, halfway to his mouth, back into the bowl.

"Some," he said cautiously.

"I love your sister, Frank."

He ran a hand through his black hair and looked at me with Becca's hazel eyes.

"Why tell me?"

"I don't know what she's said to you. We've been together eight months now: it's not casual for me."

Frank began to eat again slowly, glancing over the lifting spoon as he listened to me. I was losing my way among competing impulses about how to proceed. I moved off toward making a case rather than asking a question.

"You said I must be rich, Frank. I'm not rich, but I am well-to-do. I can do things to make her happy that another man isn't able to."

He thrust his head forward lightly, attentive.

"I'm not sure I'm following this, George." It was the first time he'd used my first name.

I was very aware of the whirling fan. Until I actually spoke the fact, what response could he make, what help could he give me? I laid down my spoon. In the intense silence it seemed to meet the plate with a loud clang.

"Yesterday I asked Becca something. Did she tell you?"

Something in his expression suddenly made me think of a child. He shook his head slightly.

"No."

"I asked her to marry me."

"*Marry* you?"

His glance fell on the turned-over family photograph, flashed quickly to my face, and then went blank. He lowered his hand and rapped the spoon in a quick staccato against the bar-top. My anxiety was too great to bear his silence. I veered back to making a case.

"I know you care about your sister, Frank. You must feel what a hard time she's had. She's had to live alone, she's had to raise Chris without his father. She deserves more."

I gestured toward the living room and the doors onto the lawn. "I can give her this. I love her and I'm sure she loves me." But my voice betrayed me on the word "sure" and took on an almost pleading quality.

"I want her to be my wife, Frank. I want Chris to be my son."

"No, she didn't tell me," Frank said, answering my earlier question. He returned to his chili. I spooned up a mouthful of my own chili, now crusted and lukewarm; it stuck in my throat and I took a swallow of beer.

"What did she say?" Frank asked finally, cautiously matter-of-fact, as if uncertain how to speak to me.

"She wouldn't answer me." The act of confession carried me along in a rush of confidence. "We had a kind of fight about it. I'm sorry. I just can't just let her leave me."

Frank reached over and placed his large hand around the sweating Bud can. Lifting it, he chugged down the rest of his beer.

"That's why Becca's driving down here this evening," I continued. "I'm sure she'll talk with you. I hope you'll be able to say you think it's the right thing."

He wiped his mouth with the back of his hand, listening.

"If she marries me, you'll be a member of my family, too. I'd like that, Frank. And I'd like to be able to help you."

Stop talking!

Frank's face seemed to lose shape. He picked up his empty beer can, crumpled it, and threw it explosively at the floor.

"I don't need help!" He pushed his hands under his thighs as if trying to control them. "Even if I did, why should you think I'd be your fucking pimp for Sis? You *sick son*uva*bitch*!"

I stood up.

"I'm sorry," I said urgently. "That's not what I meant to say."

Frank raised his head and gazed at me with furious disbelief.

"I don't know why I said that," I hurried on. "Love can make you say crazy things. Surely you know what it's like to be really in love."

And then I saw another of those amazing transformations I had seen in him before. His large shoulders relaxed, he sat back on the stool, and his face opened in an abashed grin.

"Forget it," he said softly. "We'll *both* forget it. You're right. I do know what it's like to be in love. I know it can make you crazy."

24

The two of us cleaned up the disorder from cooking and eating, working together in the kitchen as partners. It was like working with one of my sons. I still felt bruised and wary from my loss of control at lunch and Frank's explosive response. And below scattered attention as I cleaned up and talked with Frank, my mind was focused toward Becca.

I turned to Frank.

"I need to do a couple of pieces of work," I said. "Do you have something you can do this afternoon?"

Frank threw the sponge with which he had been cleaning the counter to the back of the sink.

"Did you say I could use the car?" he asked. "It's been five or six years since I've been here. I'd like to look over the strip and the beach."

"Not a problem," I said. I reached into my pocket and pulled out the keys. "Take the whole afternoon. When Becca gets here, we'll all go out to dinner."

Frank closed his hand around the offered keys.

"I'll just get my trunks," he said. "Can I take a towel from the bathroom?"

"Of course."

"I hope your work goes well," he said, making for his room with a parting wave of his large hand. His whole body seemed charged with the energy of anticipation.

I opened another beer, picked up a pad and pen for work, and grabbed a Simenon novel I'd begun the last time I was here: not a Maigret but *The Clockmaker*, one of his brief transparencies of doomed lives.

Then I stepped out a French door into the heat.

The Gulf heat closed around me like an embrace. I let my eyes rest on the broad lawn; the bordering sweep of magnolias, sweet-gums and pines; the hammock, far off by the water in the shade of a little pine grove; and the fringe of marsh grass and reeds, life of the zone of approach to the sea, beyond which shone patches of sun-dazzled water, partially screened by the bright reach of the dock. I felt a lift of rightness. It was like the swell of desire.

I strolled lazily across the lawn toward the break in the curtain of green that led to the dock. The air was dense with the smell of pine and a faint aroma from the bay. I walked into the widening pungency of salt. As the lawn fell away behind me, the water itself broke upon my eye.

This is the place I had always come for peace.

The slatted dock stretched above its own rippling reflection to join with the smaller cross-pier at the end. That far planked pier had been to me what the tree forts had been to my children, a separate world whose meaning I could define by my heart's imagination.

I stepped onto the dock. The boards, weathered gray, lighter where new boards had been put in, trembled slightly under my feet. I was enclosed in a womb of light. The tidal ripple gathered light to the surface of the water and shot it back: light and heat together, indivisible.

The only cold thing in the world was the beer in my hand. I lifted the sweating can to my mouth. The bitter liquid washed roughly down my throat.

I reached the pier.

When I was a boy, I would lay my back along the pier's hot wood, carefully, slowly letting it cool, then move my arms and legs to fresh heat and let it cool in turn.

I drained the beer. As a gesture of freedom on behalf of that over-conscientious child, I threw the can toward the water, watching it, empty and pillowed by air, flash and turn like a spinner, then land and bob in the waves.

The chairs were stored in a chest at one edge of the pier. The chest, which Brook and I had built when he was a boy, was of weathered plywood, now beginning to warp apart. The rusty hinges, pulling loose, made the lid hard to manage. As I pushed it up, an enlarging angle of light veneered the interior. It flowed over floats, over orange life jackets of various sizes, over an American flag folded away for the Fourth of July and reached a tangle of collapsed chairs and chaises, almost none of which matched one another.

I pulled at a canvas chaise longue, trying to disentangle it from the impediments which held it. The beer and the heat made me impatient. Shoving and tugging blindly, I worked it free and tumbled it over the lip of the chest to the dock.

The effort left me breathless and dizzy. I closed the chest and leaned heavily against it. Beads of sweat hung in my lashes, crimping the world. With the heel of my hand, I rubbed back clarity.

I shouldn't find it so hard!

My shirt clung to me in patches, mottling the tan fabric as if I had bled into it. I fumbled my fingers under the lower edge of my shirt and peeled it off. Maybe I *was* denying the attritions of age. It would be ironic if I ended my life out here, in the midst of my plans, of a heart attack caused by my own impatient exertion.

I straightened the chaise lounge, placed it so I could look out along the twisting estuary to the bay, and crumpled into it.

Beer and heat.

My consciousness fled into my senses. I watched the motorboats spinning at a distance with tiny skiers behind them. Sounds came to me: the chuff of the boats; the hum and horns of the traffic from the bridge; the slap of the water against the dock, proposing and eluding regularity. The impressions almost failed to assemble, as if the boats might break to the left, their sounds to the right, fragmentary messages, signs broken free of meaning: boat, glare, horn randomly pasted on the enclosing walls of light.

I fled down the drift.

Anticipating Becca's journey. She'd get off at five. She could pick up Chris and carry him to his father's by five-thirty. Then she'd be on the highway…

But I was forgetting, she'd have to pack.

She'd pack and put her suitcase in the trunk of the dusty Chevrolet, repeating our journey of the morning.

The stages of the journey flicker through my memory…

Her car traveling the long highway south, crossing the bridge into town, nearing, pulling into the driveway, *here*.

But no, I'm doing it too quickly. I need to start again at the beginning, do it right, *earn* her presence.

Finally, she pulls slowly into the drive, her face a bright blur in the summer dusk.

Or try it another way, lances of light from the headlights pierce the darkness, approach, slide up the side of the house.

Perhaps by eight-thirty...no later than nine or ten...

Not even if she takes it slowly, not even if she stops along the way...

I could feel I was beginning to burn. The sun had brought out a red speckling, like a rash, along my white belly. I ought to turn over or put on a shirt or go in.

I heaved myself up and pulled my shirt, hot from the dock, over me.

Then I settled back, gazing out from the dock, my eyes halfway closed.

Out of the luminous blank of the distance, space faintly modeled by vague forms of energy, the melting planes of color of sea and sky, flew, pale but definite, the figure of a gull. It flew toward me, laboring across the immense distance, emerging into full clarity; took the sunlight on its wings and vanished from my vision into the unseen world behind me.

The gulls, masters, like souls, of the alien element of air. I had watched them from this dock since I was a boy, watching and waiting.

Waiting that day for my mother.

25

That was another hot summer afternoon.

When I woke up that morning, my mother did not come to dress me. I lay looking through the pines which shaded the house at the pale blue sky touched here and there with the faintest clouds, smelling the fragrant mix of pine and salt in the warm air and happily letting the world be just what it was. My mother and I had been at her parents' summer house in Ocean Springs for a month. Father drove down from Jackson each weekend to be with us.

I couldn't hear my mother or my grandmother, Grandmere, as she asked to be called, for so she had called her own grandmother in New Orleans long ago. Disregarding her sense of propriety, my grandfather insisted on being called Papaw, the name by which he had known his warmly loved grandfather in the north Mississippi timber town where he grew up. Often the two women's voices floated into my bedroom as I was waking, my mother's warm and cheerful, Grandmere's somehow disappointed, but both part of the fabric of my happiness.

But this morning the house was silent.

After a while I began to get restless. I threw back the covers, slid off the side of the bed, and made my way into the bathroom. Standing at the great bowl, I relieved myself, then reached up and pulled down the handle with both hands, releasing the familiar but still somewhat frightening flush that swallowed a part of me down the toilet's growling throat.

Then I wandered out into the rest of the house. I found it empty. I climbed up on chairs by the front and back windows to see if anyone was outside. I was alone.

I felt disoriented by this strangeness and ill at ease. Going back into my bedroom, I climbed into my bed, and gave my whole attention to waiting. Later, hungry, I wandered into the kitchen and poured myself a glass of milk. Then I went back to bed, as if the day's mis-beginning must be corrected from there, and then the day would continue right.

I don't know how long I actually waited, fearing and trusting and drowsing. In memory the time has become stretched out in the manner of a dream. But suddenly I heard the front door open and close and keys fall on a table and Addie, our maid, bustled breathless into my room.

Addie had a flow of feeling, a kind of open-heartedness, in which I was able to relax, and I liked this. Grandmere didn't have it. Papa didn't have it and he didn't always like it, although he softened before it in Mama. Papaw had it, and I knew how much he and Addie liked to joke with one another.

Mama always had it. She would sing one of the French songs she loved so much as she gathered my clothes, then swoop me up from bed and hold me against the warmth of her body and the lily-of-the-valley fragrance, which I thought was the smell of her skin and later knew belonged to her favorite perfume.

I was glad to see Addie, but my fear at finding myself abandoned became vivid now that I was safe, and I filled up with anger. Addie looked concerned, but also excited and even more merry than usual. My curiosity dispelled my anger.

"Where's Mama, Addie? Where are Mama and Grandmere?"

Her dark face spread in a broad grin. I sat up.

"You'll soon be findin' out, George, honey."

Her laugh was a rich, warm sound.

"Is it a secret? Tell me."

"No, not a secret. You remember lying on the couch with your face against your Mama's belly, feeling that baby move inside."

"The baby! It's here?"

I climbed over and slid off the side of the bed.

"Not yet, honey. Won't be here for a while. But it's sure a surprise baby, wants to get into this world early. Your Papa called me in the middle of the night to come down from town so he and your Grandmere could drive your Mama to the hospital. You were still asleep, George, and they didn't want to wake you up."

"I *was* awake," I said. Somehow I felt this must be so. It was their fault that they had made the mistake and left me, and I wanted this grievance acknowledged.

"I'm sorry, George, honey," Addie said. "But you don't need to worry, lamb. Your Mama and Papa would never leave you really alone. They love you too much, more than anything in the world."

120

Addie turned from the old oak dresser that had my treasures on it, shells from the tidal strip beside the dock, blue jay and gull feathers, a sand dollar I'd bought in town and a small model of Jean Lafitte and his pirate ship that Papaw had brought me from New Orleans. She bore back my morning's clothes in her broad hand and settled herself heavily on the edge of my bed.

"Stand here, baby," she said, pointing to the floor in front of the fat rounds of her knees.

I hurried over and faced her, trying to endure the dressing patiently, my glance passing from Addie to the window and the bright day outside. I was possessed by an urgent anticipation, which divided itself between my desire to play and my desire to have Mama and the new baby come home.

Addie pulled off my pajamas and held out the white underpants. I held onto her arms for balance and stepped into them. Automatically, I raised my hands over my head, waiting for her to gather the sleeves of my shirt, poke my hands through them, and pull the shirt down in a single gesture over my arms and head. She gathered the sleeves with a practiced skill that I liked to watch. The backs of her hands were luminous black, the palms a warm pink.

The shirt came over my eyes, then the world came back. Addie's hand reached up to brush back my disarrayed hair.

"How many children do you have, Addie?" I knew the answer, but I wanted to hear it again, just as I never tired of hearing certain bedtime stories told again and again in the same way, their repetition making the world secure.

"Seven, George, honey. Four boys like you," she held out my shorts which I stepped into, leaning my small white hands on her great brown arms, "and three girls. But they're almost all grown up, now."

She reached for my socks and shoes, and I automatically sprawled on the floor, my hands back on the rug to support myself, holding up one foot.

Addie gathered the sock as she had the shirt, and leaning over heavily, pulled it over my foot. She tugged the shoe around my heel and tied the laces. I held up the other foot for her attention.

"What time *is* Mama coming home?"

"Oh, it will be awhile." Addie was sliding on the second shoe. "About a week. But you'll get to see her before that. And that new sister or brother."

Addie held out her arms, pulling me up from the floor.

"A house needs lots of children," she said, drawing me to her warm bosom. "Lots of children. But you know, you'll always be special, George. You'll always be your Mama and Papa's first."

She released me from her embrace.

"Now, come into the kitchen and let me fix you some breakfast. I know you want to get outside."

At noon, when I came in and settled myself at the dining room table, my feet hooked behind the middle rung of the chair, Addie's attention seemed distracted. She set my lunch, a bowl of Campbell's tomato soup which I had watched her open and heat, and a sandwich made from last night's ham, on the table before me.

"Addie," I exclaimed, "you forgot something! You forgot to ask me if I'd washed my hands." I grinned and held them out before me to show her they were clean.

She took one of my displayed hands in her large hand and, smiling, examined it. "You surely did wash these hands!" she said.

"Yes!"

I turned to my soup and began to tell her what I'd done during the morning.

Usually in the afternoon I stayed indoors. In the heat of the summer my grandparents took up the rugs, the intricate Turkish carpets that were already so old and belonged so much to the house that they didn't seem foreign, and stored them away. The bare hardwood floors were left to gather whatever coolness they could. When it was hot, the dogs lay on the floor under the turning fans to capture the coolness above and below.

After eating, I went into the living room and curled up along the back of Papaw's old setter, resting my head on his shoulder. He lifted his muzzle slightly, then dropped back into his heavy slumber.

Addie was in the kitchen. I could hear her washing up the lunch dishes at the sink. "Addie," I called. "I'm going out again."

I could hear the water still splashing in the sink. But as if Addie had been removed into some separate world, she didn't answer me.

I raised my voice to make her hear me.

"Addie! I'm leaving now!"

The sound of the water stopped, and I heard her heavy tread approach the doorway. Suddenly she stood framed there, wiping her hands on a dish towel, her love a palpable current which filled the room with safety. I jumped up and ran over to her.

"Addie," I said, holding up my arms. "Pick me up."

"George, honey," she laughed, "I don't think I *can* pick you up anymore. But I can sure give you a hug!" I buried myself against her legs and felt her warm arms around me, then reemerged, laughing myself.

"Addie, can I go back to the dock?"

"Well," she considered. "If you come in, if you get too hot. Here, I'll get you a Coca-Cola to take with you."

The tidal area, the shifting verge not land or sea, was my paradise. Above it was definitely land: wild hibiscus, cream-colored blossoms with glowing, ruby-magenta hearts and long pistils, into which I watched bees climb with their great legs; a thicket of loblolly pines shading a sweet- smelling mimosa; several magnolias which grew wild, huge flamboyant weeds; behind them black-eyed susans with yellow petals, water oak, live oak, yaupon, a planted row of oleanders edging the lawn.

Here the growth was simpler. A band of black rush, stiff sheaves of husks dead-brown to the eye, gave way to pliant marsh grass, light green, almost buttery in places, undulating in the tides of water and air. Below, at low tide, emerged the narrow beach, black mud soft with the detritus of decaying vegetation and patches of fawn sand. An old rowboat rested in the growth just above the waterline.

I stopped and examined the black rush. Along the slender swords clung small, gray snails. Sometimes I watched a shell pull away from the stalk as the snail resettled itself, like a cat seeking comfort before a fire. Then I could see a gleaming, dark brown bit of snail, like a snail's eye.

Today, the snails were less interesting than the stalks themselves. I broke off a large rush and clambered in and out of the rowboat being Jean Lafitte. Then, when I tired of that, I threw my sword away and went down to the beach.

The roots of the marsh grass held the brown earth in their web. Here each tide undermined the grass: exposed roots hung down, clots of root, as resistant as the gristle of a chicken leg when I tried to pull them apart. Fallen grass lay in the miniature pools left by the outgoing tide like a soup of tea leaves, decaying and adding to the boggy muck which, as I stepped in it, squished up hot and liquid between my toes. The flats, glistening and pocked, bubbled in the baking sun, flecked with pale brown foam.

This was the world of the fiddler crabs. As I approached, they tumbled out of my way, brown and light, like windblown cicada shells. But I knelt, looking for something else. Ignoring the flat oyster shells, I picked up any whorled shells, snail shells, tan and brown, or purple whelks covered with barnacles and green sea algae: houses whose original inhabitants were gone, occupied now by the squatters of the beach, the hermit crabs. As I picked up the shells, the claws of the crabs waved in indignant surprise and then they shrank back into the inner recesses for safety.

I ran back to the rowboat and reached under the seat. I'd brought a cardboard carton from the house and abandoned it there on an earlier expedition. Now, squatting again on the beach, I turned over shell after shell, tossing the empty ones back onto the mud, piling the inhabited ones into the carton. After I had gathered several, I cupped a little water into the carton with one hand, and carried it onto the dock.

Gingerly, then, because of the heat, I lay down on my stomach along the weathered gray planks and lined up the shells in a row. First one adventurous crab, then others, bearing their shells on their backs, crawled forward along the board. Their brown, curved legs reached and pulled; felt at the cracks for the next board and lifted their houses over the dizzying empty spaces. If I moved too quickly, they clamped down, like a dozen eyes shutting. I made it a race, choosing a nail three boards away to mark the finish line. The crabs scattered in too many directions to be good racers. I rescued those who approached the edge of the dock and I reversed those who tried to go backward. When the first shell was carried over the line, I gathered all the crabs again into the box and carried them back to the beach.

I was getting thirsty. I sat down on the back seat of the rowboat and pulled out the blue-green bottle of Coca Cola and the silvery, hooked bottle opener that I kept beneath the seat. I would sooner drink warm Coke than go back to the uneasy emptiness of the house. But I was also beginning to feel lonely.

Finishing my drink, I scrambled back up onto the dock. The water near the shore was green and threaded with ripples like shot silk. I knelt and looked down. Beneath the brown surface, I could see the fronds of submerged marsh grass swaying like the hair of a drowned woman. I felt restless.

I returned to the task of the morning. Wire crab cages hung by weathered ropes from the side of the pier. I walked to the nearest one. Pulling hand over hand against the soft resistance of the water, I watched it loom up from the still depths, hoping to make out in it the ghostly shapes of trapped crabs. I struggled to haul the cage up to the dock. Water gushed brilliantly from its hundreds of holes as it broke above the surface. With effort I tugged it over the rim of the dock and sat beside it. The crabs scuttled around their wire prison above the water-darkened wood of the pier. The crabs had colors you could only see if you looked close up: purple and blue shading the red and orange and ivory. I wasn't able yet to handle these crabs by myself. After a while, I lowered the cage back to the water until one of the adults could come down to collect the crabs for the kitchen.

When I saw Addie coming to the dock, I thought she must be on such an errand. Then it struck me that perhaps the baby had been born! I felt a breath of a sensation that I later felt more fully as I said my wedding vows and at the birth of my own children: as if I were swept up and could only endure my part in some decisive transformation which altered the whole universe. I almost ran to meet her in my impatience to find out.

But as she approached, I could see she looked graver than she had at lunch. She leaned her heavy weight against a piling, her face seamed with sweat.

"George," she said. Her voice was full of kindness, but of a different quality than I had heard before: a frightening kindness.

"Addie?"

"Come up to the house with me, baby. I got to talk with you." Her face looked as if she had been hit.

Suddenly I felt she had come from the adult world to destroy my place of safety on the pier. After she spoke, there would be no safety anywhere.

"Get off the pier, Addie!" I cried. "Get off the pier!"

She didn't correct me. A silence lengthened between us.

"Come back up to the kitchen and let me get you something cold, honey," she said, finally. "We can talk then." She held out her dark hand. I knew there was no use resisting and took it. We walked up to the house without further words.

Addie pulled open the screen door and we walked into the kitchen. I climbed up on the stool by the sink and sat there in my short pants and bare feet while Addie clinked some ice cubes into a glass and splashed water over them from the faucet. I swilled it down—whatever else was happening I was thirsty—and set the glass on the tile counter.

Addie lifted me down from the stool and walked me over to her chair in the corner of the kitchen. The window beside her was open and I could hear the ordinary sounds of the day beyond. She sat down with a sigh, the rounds of her knees protruding from her flowered dress, and pulled me lightly against her.

"Your Papa is home," she said slowly. "He came home to talk with you, but he needs to be by himself for a time." She might have added that he needed to be with a bottle of the bourbon that he used in his attempt to keep himself anaesthetized for the rest of his life.

"He said to tell you now, honey, or I wouldn't be the one telling you this." Muted grief and indignation stirred in her voice.

I remained silent. Where were Grandmere and Papaw? Why had Papa come on alone? Was one of *them* sick now? Or was the baby sick? Another thought came to me in this new strangeness. Maybe because of the baby they were going to send me away. What I heard almost relieved me.

"The baby is dead," Addie said. "He died being born."

It was a brother. How often have I thought of him, and with what rage for him and at him, at the milestones of the ghost life he has lived beside me since, every birthday, every family holiday, as real to me, if more elusive than, the loved presences I could see and hear.

I waited now for Addie to let me go. But her hands held me tighter, as if she were momentarily drawing support from me instead of offering it. She seemed to be having some trouble making her features work right.

126

"Addie," I said, twisting my arms in her hands. "You're hurting me."

She let go, then put her warm, dark hands gently on my shoulders.

"I have to tell you something more, George." She tugged the words up against a terrible resistance. I waited for what even now I couldn't foresee and couldn't fully grasp even when Addie was able to make herself say it.

"What, Addie?" I asked in voice so low it was hardly more than silence.

"It's your Mama, George. Your Mama. God took her, too, with the baby."

Then she stopped, as if completely spent after a great labor, looking at me with that suffering, grief-distorted, loving face.

"But she told me that she would come back," I objected. "She told me."

"Lamb, you got to believe me."

26

I can remember the day to that point as if it were still present. What followed I remember only in impressions and fragments.

Fragments, for example, of my father's shattering, counted over so often in memory that their outlines have blurred and simplified like the images on old coins, and I no longer know whether I am remembering the incidents themselves or memories of memories, a distorted residue of experience.

My father simply withdrew from the household. I almost never saw him: he didn't even come to meals. I flash on a queer still-life, the bathroom in the dull glow of the nightlight, the house silent all around, a half-empty bottle of bourbon left on the tile floor beside the toilet. Or a glimpse of my father at the cracked door of his study talking to Papaw, turning his face away when he saw me. I don't know when or by what process he came to acknowledge me again, for at that time he turned me over to Addie and my grandparents and shut me out from his grief.

I was afraid my father might die too; or might drive away back to Jackson and leave me forever. I had never felt as knit into Papa's bodily presence as into Mama's. But now my desire that he pick me up and hold me to him was a constant ache in my chest.

Or more, it was as if with Mama's death and Papa avoiding me my chest had somehow been ripped open and only in resting against him, my small body feeding on the safety of his large body, would my flesh know how to heal. Grandmere, Papaw, and Addie couldn't fully do this for me.

I sometimes saw my father drunk; or silently passing, his aloofness an unpierceable armor. But he never cried before me and he shrank from the grief of others. Grandmere and Papaw couldn't control their tears. They offered me wet embraces I wouldn't accept. Their grief terrified me. For what would happen if my father found me weeping among them? In my fear that I'd lose him completely, I became his Stoic mirror.

And this too: if I cried, I'd be admitting that Mama was irrecoverably gone.

The adults decided that I was too upset to go to the funeral. Papaw and Grandmere sat me down on the big couch and spoke to me about it, with many hesitations and glances over my head as they tried to find a way to help me with something which, after all, had to be suffered.

I heard again what I already knew, that when people died, they buried them. How could they put Mama with her radiant smile, her quick movements, her French songs, in the ground?

On the morning of the funeral, Papa, Grandmere and Papaw dressed up carefully as if they were going to church or to a party. Papaw's face looked even worse than Papa's. They said goodbye to me and, talking in low voices among themselves, went out the door, got in the car, and drove off.

I was left in the kitchen with Addie. I nagged her about something that had sharpened itself into a worry I could not put away. What would happen if in burying Mama they made a mistake, and she woke up in the dark ground away from us and couldn't get out?

Addie told me they couldn't make such mistakes, I would understand when I got older.

And she told me that although their bodies were in the ground, the souls of Mama and my brother were in Heaven with God. Mama could see me and hear me from Heaven; she would always be loving me; and when I got old and died, I would go and be there with her.

I spent hours alone thinking about this over and over, trying to believe what I couldn't understand. Why would God take her and my brother to heaven and leave me so desperately abandoned? But I knew from the way the adults talked that I wasn't supposed to get angry at God. So fear and anger, stored away as in a bank, and eventually hopelessness grew into the fabric of my soul, sinking so deep I forgot they were there.

This forgetting was my happiness.

In the days after the funeral, I came to avoid the sad house. I spent my time in *my* world, the world of the dock and the pier. I prayed to God that he'd let Mama come back, and waited hopefully for her to appear. I talked to her, up there beside God, still loving me and smiling down at me. I trusted that she loved me, but it didn't heal my loneliness.

And slowly my hope faded. I was later taken to see the two new stones, shinier than those surrounding them, in the family plot. I found it hard to associate them with Mama or the baby brother whose movements I had felt and heard when I pressed my ear against her belly. They were in Heaven; *he* was with Mama; I had been left behind.

The adults around me stopped talking about it. Sometimes I felt there might be some secret about what had happened that they were hiding from me or that some other unforeseen tragedy might happen. I became habitually attentive to the enigmatic signs of their adult knowledge and feeling, a persistent interpreter of what I could not understand.

Especially did I watch for every sign of his moods that I could read in my father's often drunken silence. Sometimes I felt angry at him for leaving me so much alone, sometimes I wondered if he believed I shared some blame for what happened to my mother.

But I showed none of this. Behind my apparent aloofness was not only a listening ear and a watchful eye, but a heart that tried to comply with my father's every guessed mood, wary to ward off further loss or loneliness.

The sun's hands pressed me down. I rode the drift in a part of my mind that collapsed time.

My glance fell on my hands, which rested along the sides of the chaise above the hot boards of the pier: the fingers edged by their whitening fleece of hair, the raised veins on the back of my hands, flowing rivers of life, running up my arm to my heart.

Who had whitening hair and hands with raised veins like Grandmere's? I was too tired to think.

It was a stranger.

27

I spent the day in the shelter of the pier. There was no possibility that Becca would arrive before well into the evening and the house felt haunted by loneliness.

The shadows lengthened over the lawn, joined, pursued the withdrawing light up the sides of the house and the tree trunks. The light briefly lingered, an amber entanglement, among the upper branches, and fled to the upper air. Dusk drowned the yard. A few fireflies appeared, floating eerily upward.

A calligraphy of stakes and piers stood against the dimming blank of water and sky, defining the immensity of the emptiness. The space took on a faint red hue, the water reflecting the rose of the fading light. In the distance, three fishermen in a boat, a penciled smudge, rested in what might have been an eternal stillness. The only sounds were the voices of the marsh, the rising whirr and hum of the night creatures.

Suddenly, at a signal of fading light, a flight of purple martins exploded from the marsh and pine woods of the nearby bayou. Like bats startled from a cave, the birds filled the sky, rapidly beating the air, then glided flittingly downward to skim the bay. Their chittering, called and recalled, loomed a net of sound over the water.

Now all was melting into one gray dark. The first faint lights appeared, yellow in the dusk, and the blinking orange eye of the channel marker.

A relieving wind ruffled my hair. It must be almost nine. Becca could have been here already.

In this enclosing dark the beat of my anxiety returned with the insistence of a metronome. Appalling images swam up into consciousness, as compulsive as the unbidden processions of erotic fantasy, appearing everywhere, like a swarm of bees. A ghostly lumber truck, entering too fast at a crossing, not seeing Becca's approaching car; a covey of police cars, their urgent, staticy radios carrying loud in the night; in their turning red lights, orange-vested silhouettes waving the gaping, indifferent passersby around the site...

No, no, no!

I stood up and ran across the dark lawn to the house as if someone were following me. With a desperate tug, I slid open the patio door, and locked it behind me, then stumbled across the dark room to the light switch by the front door and flipped it on. The room leapt into garish, confusing brightness and assembled in every window, its partial, disembodied counterpart hung upon the darkness.

It was only the night before that I had sat in the garden room in the city with Julia, enclosed by other images hung upon darkness. All my careful thinking had brought me round tonight to exactly the same point. Perhaps I had been wrong to try to bring Becca to this house: I seemed to be living in a storm of present, past, and future simultaneously.

"More lights."

My husky, whispered voice aloud in the room startled me. I flipped on the light in the carport. It returned the glass to transparency, made the carport an extension of the house in a community of light.

I wanted a drink, but did not want to be drunk when Becca came. Looking around, I found the *TV Guide*, thumbed the pages, and ran my finger down the columns for Friday evening. I realized I didn't know what time it was and glanced at my watch.

Ten minutes after nine.

Again my heart constricted.

"For God's sake, that's not late," I answered myself. "There's no reason she should be here yet." I spoke aloud, the sound a dam against the flooding images of my imagination.

I sank back into the soft cushions of the couch and picked up the remote control unit from the table, flipping through the channels like so many pages. I plunged my thumb down on the control button, setting in motion a ripple of channels. I stopped, *Friday the 13th*; better the horrors without than the horrors within. I surrendered to it so deeply that at first I did not hear the car.

No, there was no mistake: the approaching growl of an engine, tires grinding over the oyster shells in the drive. I pulled myself up from the couch and rushed to the heavy front door.

Becca!

As I tugged it open, looming into the light of the carport materialized, not Becca's Chevy, but my Lincoln. My disappointment was so sharp that my face buckled toward tears. I had lured Frank to accompany me as an ally in my campaign for Becca. And now, in his intrusive presence, I hated him as if he were an adversary.

I prayed he didn't feel it.

The car pulled to a halt. I struggled to regain mastery of my features as Frank's glance lifted and caught mine. His young face, alive with exhilaration, smiled warmly over the steering wheel. He turned off the engine and in the suddenly restored noises of night, pushed open the door and bounced out. He was high, his energy flowed around him. He was wearing jeans, his shirt and swim trunks wadded up with his towel in his right hand, his scuffed deck shoes hanging from two large fingers.

"Sis not here yet?" His glance took in the carport. He smiled the same warm smile toward my blank expression.

"No," I made myself speak. "She may have had some things to take care of before she could start. I'm sure she'll be here."

Who was I trying to reassure? Even to my own ear I was exposing the deep run of my anxiety.

I fell silent. I kept my gaze on the shadow-rippled oyster shells, feeling Frank's eyes on me, as if he were waiting for something I had yet to say.

"How was your afternoon?" I asked finally, looking up to meet his unchanged smile.

"Great." Frank set down his bundle on the hood of the car and dug into his pocket. "Thanks for the car," he said, pulling out the keys and tossing them to me. "I went to the beach for a couple of hours. Then I called Brandi, the dancer I mentioned."

I nodded, finding it hard even to pretend interest. Frank didn't notice or didn't care.

"We had dinner and a few drinks," he continued on in his soft voice like an overexcited child. "Then we went to her place and caught up for a while." All at once he seemed to run down. "I thought you might want the car, so I came back."

No, I didn't want Frank here and I ached to have Becca with me. But I recognized that the situation was not Frank's fault.

133

"Come on in," I said. "There's not much going on here. But there's beer, if you want it, and the T.V."

When I next looked down at my watch, a half hour had passed.

"Sis should be here soon," Frank commented, noticing my gesture.

We watched through the ten o'clock news. The local weather girl read off a tornado watch and predicted possible severe thunderstorms, multiplying the scenarios of my anxiety. Frank sprawled on the couch, an empty beer can and depleted bag of potato chips on the floor beside him.

I'd settled in an armchair next to the telephone and nearer to the door.

I could no longer pretend to myself that anything was on my mind but Becca's arrival. I heard everything, every creak of the house, Frank's shifting as he reached for the beer or rustled the potato chip bag, listening for any sound of the approaching car.

About ten-twenty it began to rain. Even over the sound of the television, I could hear the wind pick up. It tossed, then flailed, the branches. Low thunder growled far off, muttered closer. Then all at once the sky opened up in flash after flash of lightning and wind-whipped sheets of rain.

The storm absorbed any other sounds within it. It was foolish to listen now for the approaching car.

The bland, secure voice of the weather girl repeated the tornado watch and prediction of possible thunderstorms. *Possible*! Wasn't it storming around the station?

Maybe Becca had run into a storm on the road. But why would that have made her this late? And why wouldn't she have called?

With a sudden, emphatic movement, Frank sat up and threw his bare feet on the floor. He stretched and stood up, tugging down and brushing the legs of his jeans.

""If you don't need me," his voice turned into a yawn, "I think I'll turn in."

"Go on to bed," I said. "You know where everything is. I'm going to stay up a while."

I turned my eyes down to my hands resting in my lap, resting so still that they seemed to exist in another dimension of reality. Frank fell away into that abyss of detached reality even before he had left the room. I barely heard him walk down the hall and close his door.

Ten-forty. I can't handle this any more!

Being alone seemed to give my agitation permission to expand. It flooded my body, poured through my limbs. Shaking, I leapt from my chair, as if by movement I could escape from it.

Try to call her!

I hurried across the red-tiled floor of the family room into the kitchen and grabbbed the telephone from the wall beside the pantry.

One...one...five...nine...

My fingers fumbled on the buttons.

...six...three...zero...six.

I heard the click of the connection and the harsh beep of a busy signal.

Perhaps I'd dialed the wrong number! Resisting my urgency, I slowly dialed again.

One...One...five...nine...

The number as familiar as my own...

...six...three...zero...six...

Busy! So she was still at home!

My mind leapt in disbelieving anger.

Why hadn't she called me? She must know how worried I'd be.

Or perhaps she was trying to call me now. Abruptly, I hung up the receiver and waited. But I knew our calls hadn't crossed. She wasn't going to call.

I had to do something to calm myself; I wished Frank was not in the house!

And then, in one of those odd fluctuations of feeling, thinking of him gone, I realized how much more absolute my loneliness would be without him. Even his unseen presence was an anchor to sense and reality. I felt sudden gratitude for his unwitting custody, like the irrationally grateful yielding of a hostage to his familiar captor.

I hadn't eaten. I had been waiting for Becca, intending to eat with her. Perhaps it would be better to eat now and try to restore my balance.

Digging into the refrigerator, I pulled out eggs, bread, and tomatoes. Ten minutes later, I was sitting before a drift of scrambled eggs and new tomatoes, captured by the oddly morning pungence of toast and coffee. It was the same meal Julia had fixed for me the night before.

I hadn't thought about her visit to Ellen. She was there now. They were eating or talking, taking comfort in one another's presence. In the morning I had to call.

I hadn't realized how hungry I'd become. The food, the light, the warmth were one, loosening my muscles from the tension of the evening and letting me feel too how exhausted I was.

My body longed for bed and the further surrender of sleep. If Becca was truly in Jackson, she wouldn't be here tonight.

I glanced down at my watch. *Eleven-ten.* Half an hour. Surely Becca would have finished her call by now. I'd try her just once more. Then, whatever the outcome, I'd go to bed. My hands had already picked up the receiver and punched in her number. Perhaps because of the storm I could hear a faint ghost from another conversation, a reedy woman's voice saying, "But, Mother, they..." Then it was lost.

My imagination travelled ahead through the complexities of this mechanism by which I was trying to reach Becca: travelled the sequence of telephone lines, relays, switches, personnel: network and connection, a complex maze of intersecting mechanisms and acts, stretching over an interminable space. Becca seemed to dwindle to vanishing across this distance, to be swallowed up by it.

Then there was a click of connection.

But the harsh pulse of the busy signal again stung my ear.

My mind was an immense field, in some far corner of which, with a muffled sound, mines seemed to start exploding. I touched my hand to my chest, as if I were oddly about to say the pledge of allegiance. My heart. I couldn't handle this casually and risk losing what I so longed for. Even the hope was the most precious thing ever to happen to me. I *had* to reach her now.

Trembling, I called the operator.

"Yes?" The anonymous voice.

"Hello, my name is George Burden, operator. I'm hoping you can help me." My inner ears monitoring, my inner voices hissing instructions aside. *Keep it polite: charm this nameless woman! Keep it official: suggest authority! Let the urgency be heard!*

"I've been trying to call my daughter, who has been ill, for more than an hour now, and her telephone is always busy. Could you check whether the line is all right? Or break in on the call? Her mother and I are very worried." *Good, be plausible: no time for shame.*

Her voice took on a color of sympathy.

"I'll see what I can find out, sir. Please hold on."

The silence opened onto a darkness, like standing at night on the edge of a river I could not see across. I bent over, as if my stomach were cramping.

Then the voice of the operator broke the silence.

"I'm sorry, sir, but the telephone receiver seems to be off the hook."

"Off the hook?" I paused and spontaneously completed the lie. "Well, thank you, operator. We'll see if we can get in touch with a neighbor."

Off the hook! The words seemed incredible. Yet at the back of my mind, in my nerves, in the fibers of my muscles, they moved by themselves with the other pieces of my experience to complete a certainty.

Had Becca taken the phone off the hook to avoid me? Had her promise been an evasion, a lying game?

Everywhere now the mines were exploding: flooding, I howled with rage and sent the telephone receiver flying across the room. It cracked against the refrigerator and spun in pieces across the tile.

Grief and rage poured through me like an open current.

Simultaneously my habits of propriety drove to me repair what I had just done. I fell to my knees and reached for the nearest piece of the phone. Cupping it in my left hand, I crawled to the next piece, picked it up with my right hand, transferred it to the left, and crawled to a third, a fragment of the plastic shell like half a cracked egg. Intently, I picked it up and tried to transfer it, too, to my left hand. But the bulk of the three pieces was too large for me to close my hand around them and crawl on.

I sat back on my heels and stared at them in my hand. My mind simply could not think out how to overcome this obstacle.

I felt tears rising to my eyes, dropped the three pieces of the smashed receiver back onto the tile, covered my face with my hands, and wept convulsively.

"George." The low voice frightened me.

Frank!

I pulled my hands from my eyes. He was standing beside me, too close, his bare feet were about two inches from me. I could smell his skin.

I looked up. He had made himself ready for bed by tossing aside his jeans. To my vision he momentarily merged with the young Hispanic boxer, possessed by the brazen exultation of his victory, who had struck my attention the night before. He loomed like a figure in a dream, a threat, or maybe a part of myself that I had lost or never allowed to live.

Frank knelt down on his right knee, his left knee so close that it brushed my chest, and placed his large right hand on my forearm. I tried to pull away, somehow menaced by this intimacy, but his hand seemed to hold me in place. He leaned forward and moved his lips to my ear.

"George," he whispered, "Let me help you."

I could feel his warm breath against my skin.

"No," I cried, pulling away. He raised his left arm from his thigh where it had been resting and placed his left hand on my other arm.

"Don't," I gabbled. "I don't need help!"

He drew his mouth back from my ear and searched my face with a concerned expression. Whenever I made an effort to pull away, his grip on both my arms tightened; as soon as I relaxed, it loosened. I felt unbearably threatened.

At last, suddenly and fluidly, he stood up, pulling me up with him, and slowly released his grip. I stepped urgently back.

"Please," I rasped, "Let me alone now."

He still watched me, attentive.

"You don't have to be ashamed, George," he said finally in his soft voice. "Promise you'll call, if you need help."

I felt myself shrinking under his bland concern.

"Yes," I whispered. "I'll call. I promise."

But I had no intention of being there to call on him. Maybe Becca was playing a cruel game with me, maybe she wasn't. I wouldn't let her behavior go unconfronted. I was running on empty, barely kept going by my last nervous energy, but that only made it more urgent that I get back to Jackson and see her. My system would not bear the endless night hours of uncertainty.

28

The rain was still pounding on the roof, swirling down the French doors as if the glass on the other side had become molten. I hurried into my bedroom, put on a fresh shirt, stepped into my deck shoes, and grabbed my wallet; I didn't stop to look for an umbrella. Fumbling, I tugged open the massive front door which led to the carport.

On the iron roof of the porch the rain clattered like rivets. Even here in the doorway, the air was so wet that it seemed to clot in the lungs.

I stepped into the downpour, lowering my head to protect my eyes against the rain's onslaught. The oyster shells shifted beneath my feet, at each step creating a pool to soak them. Dancing in the assaulting wetness, I pulled the handle. *Locked.*

My hand fumbled in my pocket, searching for the key. The rain swirled down my arm as down a funnel, soaking the thin cloth that lined the pocket, wetting the skin; down the neck of my shirt; into my shoes. The fall was so heavy it was hard to see. Finding the key, I blindly felt for the lock with my thumb.

By the time I swung open the door, I was as wet as if I had fallen from the pier. My clothes stuck in patches to my skin, tearing away from it as I moved, then sticking again. I could feel the water moving in my shoes. Every discomfort felt magnified.

Sliding into my seat, I turned the key in the ignition. The air conditioning started up, Frank hadn't turned it off. The chill blast made me tremble. I found the switch and shut it, meanwhile backing wildly into the turn-around. In a moment the car was splashing down the driveway toward the street.

The streets were eerily empty. It was like driving through a ghost town or a deserted movie set. The clouds reflected the city's lights, creating a kind of garish dome, low and lit as by a fire. Beneath it the familiar landmarks, the Exxon station, the bank, stood in the diffuse glow like children's blocks, the rain melting their outlines. It was a dissolving world. Out on the highway there were a few cars and the whirr of trucks constant to their long-distance labors.

The storm ebbed and returned.

Sometimes I thought I had driven out of it, but five minutes later it was beating at the car windows, overwhelming the struggling windshield wipers. It was hard to feel in the wash of water whether I was moving or standing still. The car was not the center of a determinate landscape, but of swirling energies, indefinite and violent; held, rocked in the assaulting storm. I pressed my foot on the accelerator and plunged ahead into the darkness.

My mind rehearsed the encounter.

Holding back my anger, the intimacy to come.

The imagination of it rose and rode in my body. I imagined myself slipping into Becca, the movement of separation renewing the conditions for return; ambiguous flesh which I can never tear away. Not her, now: one. One in the ironic climax: forever and fading, delivered back then to our separate selves, to the realm of need and rage.

"Why?"

The long blast of a truck horn jerked my attention back to the road. A fierce corruscation of light gathered on the rainy windshield, illuminating the interior of the car. Confused, I could not tell where it was coming from. A flash of orange markers. I was in a construction zone. Instinctively, I pulled the wheel to the right and felt the tires spin onto wet clay and slide; then they again gripped the road. Looking up, I saw the angry face of the truck driver, pale as a moon, loom in the cab of the truck above me. Then it vanished.

My skin prickled with fear and shame. Bending forward, I made my eyes try to pierce the rain which gathered and dispersed, gathered and dispersed on the windshield under the rhythmic action of the wipers.

Exhaustion settled compulsively over me; my eyes stung with it. I pressed down my foot and fled toward Jackson and Becca.

29

Ten minutes outside Jackson, I left the rain behind.

The sky remained heavily overcast and, as the city neared, became another bowl of dull fire, glowing with the reflected lights of the capital. The low skyline, emerging from the denser darkness of the surrounding countryside, took on misty definition. I seemed to be moving without moving in a landscape two-dimensional and unreal.

Sleepiness settled more compulsively over me. I rubbed my hand across my chin. It was rough with new beard. I needed to clean up and pull myself together.

I drove beyond the empty downtown and took the exit toward the house: past the dark lake, around the corner, then the habitual swing into the driveway. Lights shone onto the lawn. They were part of the security system which automatically switched lights on or off, filling the house with a ghostly image of family life to keep out potential despoilers.

Turning the key in the front lock, I stepped inside, walked rapidly into the next room, and switched off the alarm. In the embrace of the familiar setting, home and not home, my body sagged with weariness.

Pushing myself, I made my way down the hall into the bedroom and flipped on the light. It was sleep that I really needed. The clock read almost three, and I had been up since four-thirty the morning before. But if I yielded to sleep for a moment, I'd be lost.

I walked into the bathroom and splashed water on my face. In the mirror the skin beneath my eyes was dark, as if it had been smeared with a thumbed line of greasepaint. I toweled away the water and reached for my electric razor. In the mirror I followed the motion of the razor, lifting my chin, turning my cheek, watching the civil, if weary, appearance emerge from beneath the stubble. Splashing aftershave into my hands, I rubbed it over my face, hoping the familiar morning ritual would help me wake up. Its smell suffused the bathroom, nauseatingly sweet.

Three-fifteen. I had to get to Becca's.

I drove through the night toward Becca's house with the window down. The moist, warmcool air blowing in my face carried a mingled odor of earth and the tarry, mechanical smell of the street. It magnified the sounds of the sparse traffic and laid down a fine mist on the windshield, so that from time to time I had to switch on the wipers.

My attention was all on Becca, but I couldn't allow myself to *think* about her: attention was a barely contained energy of my body.

Becca's block was silent, dark except in the light of street lamps purple-haloed in the mist. No houses showed light; there were no elaborate systems of protection for these shabby homes, although they were no less vulnerable than the homes in Eastpointe. In the early morning stillness I felt illicit and conspicuous. But there would be no policemen patrolling these streets either.

Becca's old Chevy loomed into sight in the driveway, resting as if in mechanical sleep. The house was dark, like an underexposed photograph in which one could barely distinguish the varying shades of dark and light. She must be asleep. A world in hiatus, not expecting a knock at the door at this hour.

The ragged lawn met the street curbless. I pulled up before the front walk and turned off the engine. The silence seemed to press me back into the seat like a palpable force. I felt light-headed and was overwhelmingly aware of my sleeplessness. Through the body of my fatigue washed unbidden implosions of tenderness and longing. Yet somewhere beneath it all, as if not joined to myself, beat a counterpoint of rage at Becca for making me endure this ordeal.

I concentrated on setting myself into motion as in a dream that one knows is a dream but from which one cannot wake oneself. With a jerk my hand reached the handle and shoved open the door. I got out and walked toward the shadowy porch. *I must be afraid*, I thought, for my palms were sweating; but all I could feel was a dulled anxiety. I wiped my hands against my slacks and knocked lightly at the door.

It would be hard to hear from her bedroom. I waited a moment and knocked more heavily. Had she not heard? Or was someone else there? Punished by fatigue and fear, my mind could find no purchase on secure reality and spun and spun in a panic of uncertainty.

And what was there to tell me I should *not* trust what could appear to be paranoia? I leaned forward against the bell, hearing the echo of its continuous alarm like a far-off siren.

After a moment I heard movement inside. The porch light clicked on, isolating me from the anonymous darkness.

Becca could not see the porch from the hallway. "Who's there?" she called in the firm, poised voice of the office.

"Becca," I whispered, my answering voice sounded old to my ear. "It's me. George."

I heard the lock click and she pulled open the door.

It was dark inside. Behind Becca I could just make out the thin figure of Chris, white-faced and moon-eyed. He held a stuffed bear in one hand whose worn arm scuffed the floor.

"Who is it, Mama?" he asked in a stuffy voice. His large eyes were frightened.

Becca turned toward him. The curve of her throat in the porch light, her look of confidence and love, took away my breath.

"It's okay, honey," she said softly. "Mr. Burden has brought Mama some papers she has to work on this weekend. You go back to bed, I'll be in in a minute."

Chris glanced up at me, not completely reassured. A thin trail of mucous had slid down to his lip. He unconsciously licked it away with the tip of his tongue and wiped his nose on his pajama sleeve. Becca touched his thin shoulder. "Teddy will keep you company," she said. "I'll be there as soon as we've finished."

He turned and walked toward the end of the dark hallway.

30

Becca turned back to me, drawing her thin robe close across her breasts and touching her hand to her neck as if the summer night were cold. Her hazel eyes poised uncertainly between suspicion and concern.

"George, I thought you were on the coast," she said. She looked down at her bare wrist and then back to me. "I'm sorry, I don't know what time it is. Why are you here?"

She yawned sleepily. I could smell the faint, familiar musk of her night-time breath.

"Let me in."

Becca glanced toward the car standing in front of her house, and then toward the other houses.

"Yes," she said finally. "Of course."

She moved aside.

I stepped past her and we stood in the hallway, too close for strangers, too distant for lovers.

"Are you going to let me sit down?" I asked her.

"Of course," she said again. She switched on the light in the front room. "Can I get you something to drink?"

"No. I want to talk."

I could see a familiar weariness begin to settle over her face. The phrase was so often a signal that what I really wanted was to vent my hurt and anger against her. Her glance slid to and away from the old grandfather clock that stood in the corner. It read four o'clock.

"You're awake very early," she said.

We sat down, I on the frayed, square-built brown and white checked couch, she on the brown vinyl recliner that faced it at an angle nearby.

"No," I said. "I'm awake late."

"Awake late?" Her tone was tentative, a careful exploration. I couldn't tell whether she was really trying to make sense of my presence (how could that be?) or understood it all too well and was playing a game with me.

145

"Do you seriously not know why I'm here? I waited all day for you in Goddamn Ocean Springs and you never came!" My voice strangled into a falsetto confusion and I stopped to recover myself.

I was *demanding* love in rage and grief. But I couldn't control it. It was as if a lifetime of grief were pouring through me.

Becca's hair, unbound for night, flowed against her white face, making her complexion more pale. Her lids closed over the large, hazel eyes and rested there for a long while. Then they slowly lifted. She sat on the edge of the recliner, her hands resting in her lap, with the stillness that was always her response to anger.

"Becca!" I choked. "I promise I won't be angry. But help me understand."

She looked down, down at her still hands, and began to speak rapidly in a low, colorless voice.

"I did try to call you, George. I tried to call you all afternoon from work. Then I tried to call you after supper to tell you that Chris was sick. I must have called you a dozen times. You never answered."

I pictured myself at the dock, waiting. It had never occurred to me to stay by the telephone. Had she tried to call me? How else could she know I wasn't there?

"Then why did you take your phone off the hook?" My voice was sharp with the urgency of doubt.

"I waited until nine, George. Then I decided that if this was really important to you, you wouldn't be away from the phone all day." Her voice took on an inflection of despair. "I'm tired after this week! Chris has been demanding, Frank has been demanding, you've been demanding. Everybody needs something special from me. Where were *you* all day? When you didn't answer by nine, I decided to go to sleep and try to reach you this morning."

I was having trouble grasping her words as bearers of meaning.

A vision filled my mind of Becca and myself, not as lovers but as partners in a game, at once allies and adversaries, enacting and reenacting ambiguous actions out of rules that no longer served us. Desire and fear held us in our positions.

"George," she raised her hand in a weary gesture that might be rejection or surrender. "George, please go now." Her voice came from a place of infinite fatigue. "Come back in the morning. Or trust me to come to the coast. If Chris is still sick, I'll get a sitter.

I'll do whatever you want. But I'm so tired. Don't make me deal with this now."

Tears were running down her face, although they did not sound in her voice. It was as if they were an independent plea of the hidden sorrow I sometimes sensed in her, as if her eyes were crying by themselves.

I got up from the couch and knelt beside the brown vinyl recliner. I reached across its arm and gently laid my hand on Becca's.

"Let me be with you," I said softly. "Please let me help you."

I turned her face and kissed her. Her body began to relax. I drew my hand tenderly along the familiar swell of her breast. Was this more than compliance after anger? Her nipples under her nightgown were erect.

I was stirred by her response and the damp warmth of her breath.

"Not here," she whispered urgently, "not when Chris is in the house. Come into the bedroom."

I helped her rise and taking her hand led her down the hallway like a bridegroom. My eyes were blurred with desire. I stood aside for her to enter the room and closed the door behind her. And turning I pulled her into my arms. My hands slipped down her sides and lifted away her nightdress. In the dark I could follow the white blur of its progress over her knees, thighs, hips, the curve of her belly, her breasts. I gathered the material as she stood there and lifted it over her head.

My tongue sought her mouth in out-of-control hunger as I held her to me, my palms caressing the familiar curve of her back. My heart knew this was worth any suffering.

"Get into bed," I whispered. "Wait for me."

I undressed hurriedly. The fantasy that had almost brought me to grief on the drive returned as if to drown me. Now dispossessed of the dividing self and flesh, we would be caught up anew in oneness. I was urgently erect. I touched myself briefly, as if for reassurance, my gaze grasping and not grasping the white blur of her body as she lay back against the pillow waiting. Her elusiveness for the eye excited me.

It was the first time we would make love in her bed.

I lay down heavily beside her, unseen in the darkness, wishing *I* could be seen by her. In the moment, I *was* this straining desire, wholly this suffusing feeling of power. Becca's love, Becca's desirous yes to me, created the sense of self that in the climax of self I gave back to her in ecstatic surrender.

The sheet was caught between us. I pulled it away.

She waited in the way that had always moved me. My fingertips explored the contours of her face, the curve of her neck, the delicate elongated V created by her collarbone. My hand flattened then to take in the swell of her breast. My flesh began to tremble with the float of premonitory spasms.

Not out here; in her.

"It's going too fast," I whispered. "Let me cool down."

I moved my body away from her and stretched up in the still darkness to kiss her cheek. My lips tasted the salty wetness of tears. Becca lay beside me in the dark, silently crying the same welling tears that had flowed down her cheeks in the living room.

"Becca, what is it?"

I leaned over her and dug my hands into her shoulders, as if I could pull her back from the place where she lay withdrawn.

"Answer me."

Slowly she turned her head. I could hear it move against the pillow. "I'm sorry, I'm sorry," she said, as if dragging the words from a distance. She reached down and wearily took my now relaxing self in her hand. I pressed my lips to her mouth as if to reach to the hidden skull beneath the skin.

Becca, where are you?

The erection began to soften in the warm sheath of her hand; blood receding drew it toward the harbor of the body. Now it hung like a piece of leather tacked or taped to my groin. She kept her hand around the limp flesh; squeezed and tugged; squeezed and tugged.

Rage and shame welled up in me. With a cry, I pulled loose her locked fingers and brought my palm down heavily against her cheek. She shuddered.

"Stop!" she screamed. "Oh, please stop!"

She rolled away and sat at the side of the bed, her elbows on her knees, her face in her hands, weeping now not privately, but publicly and without constraint.

I, too, pulled myself away, huddled against the pillow, my knees drawn up, my head bent down upon them, paralyzed by terror and self-hatred.

I moved only when I heard the doorknob turn. Chris! He turned the knob fumblingly and pushed against the door. I had locked it.

"Mama!" His light voice was urgent with fear.

Becca spoke slowly against the tears, the racking spasms.

"Mama's all right, sweetheart. I had a bad dream."

"You didn't come tuck me in."

"I thought you were asleep, honey. I'm coming."

Becca glanced toward me as if she thought I might prevent her from rising to care for Chris. She grabbed a corner of the sheet and wiped it across her face.

"I'll be there in a minute, sweetheart, to tuck you in. Go get ready."

Chris's feet scampered down the hall.

Becca stood up abruptly and switched on the bedside lamp. She stood naked: more truly naked than I had ever seen her, for now she was stripped of some fundamental sense of safety. Her face was red where I had hit her, her eyes large and alert with fear.

"Becca, I didn't mean it! I'm so sorry. I'll never do it again."

Her eyes didn't close, but held mine in disbelief and contempt. I buried my face in my hands to shut out the vision of what I'd just done.

"Don't tell, Becca," I whispered." Please. Don't tell."

31

There was a sound which I knew was important but which I had to search to place. It took me a moment to understand that it was the telephone; but who would be calling in the middle of the night?

But it was not the middle of the night; it was morning and I was back in Ocean Springs.

The second ring? The third? I reached my hand toward the bedside table and tried to force my eyes open to the day.

The bedroom, blurred but solid, sprang up around me. My head was swimming as if from a hangover. How many hours had I slept?

As my hand approached the phone the rhythm established by the ringing abruptly stopped. Had the caller hung up? Then I remembered that Frank was also in the house. I picked up the receiver.

Becca's voice was speaking with some emphasis. "I *have* to..."

I pulled myself up against the headboard, suddenly fully awake. The bedroom opened on a screen porch, built, as a respite from the heat, out into a pine grove. The shadowed green, the warm pine fragrance, the clatter of a jay sharpened into focus.

"Hello," I broke in. I waited to hear whether Frank had hung up, but there was no audible click and the silence was broken by Becca.

"Hello, George," she said gravely, out of a region more intimate than her customary detachment. "I want you to know that I *am* driving down this evening. Chris can go to his father's even if he's sick."

The scene of my violence a few hours before and Becca's desperate weeping appeared before my mind, as if someone had switched on an inner television screen.

"Becca."

"Not now," she broke in. "We'll talk when I get there. I think it'll be about seven, not much later." She paused and spoke with the quiet deliberateness one might use with children or the crazy.

"George, I'll be in and out most of the day. If I have any problem about getting there, I'll call you after six."

"You *will* call."

"Yes," she said and hung up the receiver. Was Frank still on the line? I waited for another click and heard nothing. Finally I set my receiver back on its cradle.

"Dear God," I whispered, "Don't let anyone else know about last night." A blasphemous prayer: What did it mean but: *Before anything else, save me from anyone else knowing my terrible shame!*

I pulled myself from the bed. Not yet nine. I'd slept for only an hour.

Dressed in pajamas and without slippers I padded down the hall to the front of the house. This was the weekend Julia had made me promise to save for us. In the ordinary way of things I willed to believe that life was predictable. Yet tomorrow I'd be celebrating my birthday in this house with Becca. At midnight my fifty-fourth year would come to an end and a new year would begin.

Help me make it work out as I need it to be.

I rounded the corner from the hallway into the family room. Frank stood in the sunlight that poured through the French doors before him, looking over the morning lawn. He had one of the large green towels from the guest bathroom wrapped around his waist. I noted the flat, reflective wetness which darkened the red tile floor beside the telephone table and the increasingly spare footprints that led to the window where he now stood.

Did they tell me how long he might have been at the phone? I could read nothing from them.

He turned. A few beads of water dripped from his black hair onto his shoulders.

"Phone wake you up?" he asked, bending his head forward and brushing his thick fingers through his hair to push out some of the water. A dark spatter fell on the sunlit floor.

"Yes," I said, walking over and looking out beside him. "Did you talk with Becca?" I tried to conceal the urgency with which I wanted to know.

"Sis didn't have time to talk," Frank grinned. In his relaxation my tension cautiously faded.

Outside, it was a paradisial morning.

The lawn fell away from the house as soft as a carpet. The descending morning light washed the eastern sides of the pines with brightness. Their plated, coppery trunks, leaning across one another in a random pattern of angles, rose through the dense lower growth raising green-and-rust brushes of foliage into the brilliance above. Below the pines, to the right, the leaves of deciduous oaks were as yellow as butter or pale green against the dark, glossy magnolia. I'd loved to climb the magnolia as a boy in the green, fragrant shade of summer dusks and watch the slow float of fireflies in the branches.

Above the fringe of trees hung a huge bowl of sky, pastel blue rubbed with paler pastel clouds. On the mirroring slate-blue water which glittered between the trees moved boats brilliant as jewels, their speed made slow by distance.

I could hear the soft mewing of a catbird unseen on the patio.

I glanced at Frank. He, too, was absorbed in the radiant morning.

Everything's still okay, I thought.

At breakfast Frank and I discussed the day.

The sunlight fell through the casement windows of the breakfast nook onto the jars of strawberry jam and marmalade, the silver toaster, and the dark, polished wood of the refectory table. It seemed not to plate them from without, but to draw forth a more intimate glow from within.

"It would be a shame to waste a day like this," I said, lifting the fragrant coffee to my lips. The surface of the liquid, tilting in the cup, sent a white reflection dancing along the wall.

Frank was silent.

"Do you like getting out on the water?"

Frank's shoulders shrugged beneath his shirt as he lowered his spoon to the gleaming cereal bowl.

"Sometimes," he said, his voice polite but noncommittal.

"You mean it would be a problem today?"

"Well, I did tell Brandi I'd spend the day with her." Frank held out his large hands, palms up, fingers spread. The gesture was almost Italian.

"Bring her along." Despite, or perhaps because of, the lack of sleep for two days, I was feeling unlimitedly expansive. "We can take my boat out to the barrier islands and swim. She'd enjoy that, wouldn't she?"

"I don't know," Frank said, hesitating. His inward glance of reflection, as unguarded as most of his other gestures, had the paradoxical effect of suggesting slyness.

"Come along," I insisted. I didn't want to spend the day alone. And I wanted Frank to see without my having to say it the further richness I would offer him through Becca. "Becca won't be here until six or seven. This way the three of us can enjoy the day."

Frank's green eyes began to shift away toward a look of intractable stubbornness, hesitated, and then came back to me in acquiescence. It was the purest expression I've ever seen of someone coming to an inward decision.

"All right," he said, rising from the sunlit table. "I'll go call her."

It took less than half an hour to clean up and drive to the strip.

32

Brandi emerged from the side door of a rundown two-story brick apartment building a block from the beach. Part of the first floor was occupied by a club and its overflowing garbage cans weighted the salt air with the smell of stale alcohol and rotting food.

She walked across the alley to the place where I had pulled up at Frank's direction and honked the horn.

When she appeared, I had trouble picturing her as an exotic dancer. She was about five-five, with a long waist and very small, round breasts, making her look more like a budding girl than a full-grown woman. Something in her face, too, plain and uncertain in repose, made her look not completely adult, yet no longer young.

Frank opened the door and stepped out, allowing Brandi to squeeze in between us. Her cheerfulness hung around her like a garment that fails to fit, her manner confident on the surface, but as vigilantly appeasing as a distrustful child's beneath. It gave her an air of effort, as if her watchfulness cost her more energy than her body could fund.

She gave Frank a quick kiss on the cheek. Then turning, she smiled and put out her small hand to me. She held my hand a moment too long before she relinquished it and caught my eye with a glancing look of sexual awareness that seemed to question, offer and withdraw at the same time.

"I'm glad to meet you, Brandi," I said, looking down, and then away so I wouldn't seem to be glancing at her breasts. I wanted to be a well-wishing bystander to her relationship with Frank. At all costs I wanted to avoid the appearance of trying to move in on him as if I wished to be his competitor.

"*I'm* pleased to meet *you*," she said. Her voice was hoarse but cheerful. "Frank's told me all about you."

Brandi plunged her hand into her purse. She kept talking, but paid close attention to her hunting.

"It was nice of you to let Frank use this car yesterday, it's a beauty. We had a real heap in L.A."

Frank hadn't mentioned that they once lived together in Los Angeles.

Brandi found what she had been hunting for in her purse.

"I'm trying to stop smoking," she said ruefully, pulling a pack of cigarettes from its depths. Without further explanation, she shrugged out a cigarette and put it between her lips, dropping the rest of the pack back into the bag. Her fingers found the car lighter. I noticed her fingernails were longer than any real fingernails could be and a dark red, the first sign that she took care of her appearance as a dancer. She pushed in the lighter, tapped a flutter of red against the dash as she waited, then drew the glowing tip to the cigarette and lit it with a deep drag.

The social exchange over, she leaned back with a blank expression on her face and silently smoked.

We drove along the beach to the yacht harbor. The coast has been a mecca for tourists as long as I can remember. When I was a boy, well-to-do Chicagoans came by train to vacation at the few and elegant hotels. Now the strip along the beach was more democratic and more crowded. We drove past the same mix of motels, souvenir shops, miniature golf courses, water slides, amusement parks, restaurants, and nightclubs that we had passed coming in.

I glanced up and addressed Brandi's reflection in the rearview mirror.

"Do you work along here?"

"At the Reno Palace," she said. Her personality switched on at my renewed attention. I wondered what her manner was when she was by herself.

"You lived in Los Angeles?"

"Yes, LA, Frank and I found out we were both from the South. Of course, with Frank you could tell a mile away. But I grew up in New Orleans" -- she said, "New *Aw*-lee-uns," drawing it out. "In the Irish Channel. I sounded like I was from Brooklyn."

She laughed, a surprisingly unguarded laugh.

"How did you meet?"

Brandi glanced at Frank's unmoving profile, as if looking for some sign of what she should or shouldn't say.

155

"We did a couple of movies together," she said in a flat voice, as if she were warily listening for Frank more than she was speaking.

"Really?" I said. "What movies were you in?"

"This and that," Frank said. "You wouldn't have seen them."

Brandi lapsed back into her air of weary diminishment.

The marina appeared on our left. The flat spaciousness of its lawn and its long, approaching drive gave it an out-of-time look of wealthy grandeur, as isolated as a ghetto from the carnival that had encroached on both sides. We drove slowly down the oleander-lined drive, past the Harbor Master's house, which was landscaped with a few hardy palms, dark green juniper, and gleaming white gravel. Three kids in white shorts and bright shirts dodged in front of us shouting on their way to the soft drink machine. Well-kept men and women worked on their well-kept boats, cleaning trim, touching up paint, their faces bright in the sun, intent in their labor. The gray, contained water, an arm of the great bay, seemed only a painted backdrop, carefully color-coordinated for its position in this artificial paradise.

With a familiar turn of my arm I pulled the car alongside the dock in front of the covered slip where *George's Dream* bobbed between its lines on the shadowed water. I opened my door and stepped out with a spring of anticipation onto the white oyster-shell drive. Frank and Brandi uncoiled more slowly from the car.

"Here she is," I gestured with pride and pleasure. "I renamed her when I bought her. Her true name. I dreamed about owning a boat for a long time before I found her."

"It's beautiful," Brandi said, her voice a bit wary, as if this were foreign territory. She kept close behind Frank as he followed me across the weathered planking of the dock, already hot in the morning sun.

This boat, more than any other *place*, had been the site of my happiness. She was older and more singular than anything I'd had in mind when I started looking. She'd been built by a sailboat maker, Patrick Hunt, as a sea-air rescue craft as long ago as World War II. The boat was designed for speed and the ability to run out from land for relatively long distances. That meant her bow had a V-shape and she'd had two powerful engines and larger than normal fuel and water tanks on either side. She was forty-two feet long.

I loved her noble history and her lines and the interior was commodious and well appointed. It could handle the family. The rear cabin made roomy sleeping quarters for Julia and me. The head was not cramped and had a shower. Beyond the bridge and the galley the forward cabin had bunks for two kids. Usually the girls had the bunks and the boys unrolled sleeping-bags on the floor of the bridge. By the time I bought her the large engines had been replaced and she cruised at a sedate nine knots an hour, fine for the family.

She'd been built of white fir, the only lumber available for the purpose at the time, so the planking was subject to rotting and sometimes required work. I'd spent hours working on her myself, work I could have hired out. I knew her every line and contour, not only with my eyes, but with my hands, as a trainer might know a beautiful horse he's repeatedly worked with and groomed.

I stepped aboard first, feeling the deck sink and sway slightly under my weight. Frank leapt after me and held out his hand to Brandi. I pointed her to the bridge. She sat looking out while Frank and I carried on the cooler and a couple of bags with our swim gear and food and prepared to cast off.

Frank had clearly spent time around boats. He coiled onto one hand the line that held the bow to the front of the slip and tossed it to me. Then he jogged to the end of the pier, coiled up the stern line, and jumped the widening arc between boat and pier. He caught Brandi watching him and gave her a big grin. Together we pulled the boat over and released the lines fore and aft from the pilings on the other side.

I settled myself in the pilot's chair and switched on the ignition. My heart leapt in a familiar sense of mastery and anticipation. The engine throbbed and hummed. The boat, reversing, turned in a swirl of foam. And we nosed our way through the great reticulation of piers toward the open water.

A soft smell of gasoline hung in the morning air. The long, slow swells puckered and dimpled, the sea's immutable fluctuation. Upon them the reflections of craft and pilings rode and waveringly broke.

The Gulf Coast is marked by a fringe of islands, a shadowing archipelago. Horn Island, once the haunt of the Mississippi artist, Walter Anderson, is an hour out, with an easy harbor on the bay side and a dazzling white beach on the Gulf. I suggested we go there, anchor and walk across the grassy spit at the east end to swim in the wilder Gulf surf.

We moved out onto the open water, where clustered fishing boats rode like an armada. A blue and white boat, circled by lighting and lifting gulls, trawled off our port bow. A wedge of pelicans flew across the sun.

The sight of land fell away behind us. I turned the wheel lightly in my hand, gazing lazily out over the blue-gray chop of the water as we pressed toward the empty horizon. The gust of our motion carried the pungent bouquet of the sea. The steady throb of sound, the lift and sink of the boat across the waves, possessed my whole body.

Brandi and Frank were a carnival to the eyes by themselves.

Brandi emerged from below with a large orange and yellow towel and carried it somewhat unsteadily up to the forward deck. Billowing out the towel she let it fall onto the white deck and carefully straightened its edges. Then she sat and removed her halter.

I knew that she arranged her sunning from a professional point of view. The patrons of the Reno Palace, she'd explained to me apologetically, liked her torso tanned and her girdle white. "They think the tan-line's sexy."

She drew a large pair of sunglasses from her bag, settled them on her nose, and lay back on the orange and yellow towel amid the glittering white.

Frank emerged from the cabin where he had stowed his clothes and clambered confidently up onto the deck. He wore green swimmer's briefs which set off his golden tan and made his hazel eyes vivid. Some quality in his appearance changed from context to context. Alone with me, he had looked like a rich man's son. As he lay beside Brandi, her artifice gave his exaggerated good looks a cheap cast.

I wore the leisure uniform of my age-mates, baggy khaki shorts and a navy-blue knit shirt. The hair on my bare arms was gray and white, my skin patchy red, as I slouched paunched before the wheel. They were another generation. If they were my children, I'd expect a spontaneous assignment of me to a different human realm, post-sexual, foreign in its significant life-memories, its importance fading as their generation rose toward the center.

But I couldn't bear to be seen in this way by these two. My claim on Becca was a claim to be their peer, as vital as they, a more successful competitor.

My glance shifted back to Brandi. She levered herself up, propping herself with one arm stretched behind her, and leaned back her head to drink. Her fingernails were a red detail on the red, white and blue can of Diet Pepsi. Her pose emphasized her breasts, like the pose of a girl in a men's magazine. Maybe that was one place where she'd learned her sense of gestural decorum. I could not take my eyes from her breasts. They were small, with small, dark nipples that protruded dug-like from her body, strange and glistening with oil as if prepared for a photograph session.

She sank back onto the orange and yellow towel in concentrated passivity toward the sun.

Frank, hearing her move, raised himself on his right elbow, placing his large hand loosely around her wrist in a gesture of possession. The vibrating light of sun and reflection seemed to break up his outline. He leaned over Brandi, speaking and laughing. His eyes were soft with habitual affection. His fingers gently massaged her arm along its delicate inner curve.

A faint line of soft dark hair ran from his navel to the lip of the green suit that rode low along his hips. It was matched by a faint densening of hair at the top of his thighs. Suddenly he seemed too powerful, somehow threatening.

I felt a wash of weakness and self-hatred.

How odd to think suddenly of my father! I was back in an episode I hadn't remembered in years.

It, too, was at the water.

33

I don't know whether my father ever loved me. Perhaps both he and I had simply taken it for granted that he did so, mistakenly assuming that he too was an agent of the love that Mama made a palpable family atmosphere. Perhaps he warmed himself in this love as dependently as I did, and, when Mama died, found himself stranded without resource in the absence and cold that followed. Or perhaps there was something about me as a boy that disappointed him.

At times I still find myself wondering if this was the case, as if it would be a comfort to be able to name my failure and, by taking responsibility for it even now, get beyond it. In any case, after the death of Mama and my brother, my father spent late hours out and when he came home closed himself in his study. And he began to drink.

For me, it deepened a nightmare. I was already drowning in loss. I desperately wanted Papa to tell me that he loved me, that something I had done was all right, that I was not going to die, that he would keep me safe. But the only time he sought me out was when he was drunk.

His behavior when drunk was unpredictable. Sometimes he was full of a dreadful love, more often he was harsh and humiliating. Either way, once those large hands fell on me, the only wisdom was to surrender and wait until his impulse was exhausted. Not that I mean to suggest that he physically abused me. He never hit me and would never have sexually touched me. But I learned to fear the thick perfume of bourbon, sometimes, too, of stale urine, which hung around him, and the smell of tobacco on his hands as he pressed me against his shirt front.

"Do you love me?" he asked. "Do you love me?"

One night, twisting against the suffocation of this embrace, I scraped my cheek against his shirt buttons. I began to cry and he unexpectedly let me go. Looking at me as if in surprise as his glance came into focus, he reached out and with a big, bent finger wiped away from my cheek a smear of blood and tears. He began to weep.

"I know I'm a bad father, Georgie."

Again he drew me, now tenderly, to him.

"When you're grown up you'll understand."

The next day it was as if this episode of drunken tenderness had never happened. But it gave my never completely defeated hope something to hold onto.

In his opposite mood he was more terrifying. I, who wanted nothing more than to please him, found I could displease him with unpredictable ease.

"*Can't* you eat without scraping your knife on your plate?" he asked, during one of the rare and silent dinners he ate at home.

I froze.

"Well," he leaned forward, "Why don't you answer me?"

I tried through a mind filling up with fear to think what answer would be acceptable, knowing in hopeless certainty that whatever I said would not turn aside the stream of blame.

"Well," he continued, "Do you think you make it pleasant for me to come home when you behave like this?"

I couldn't smell the bourbon, but I knew that he had been drinking. "Well? Well? *Well?*" His voice rose with each impatient repetition, and then in an almost sacramental gesture of rage he raised his hands and danced his silverware across the table.

"You have no idea how hard it is for me!" he screamed, his rising body shoving his chair away from the table.

As he slammed the door to his study, I almost wished he had hit me, if it would have made him stay.

Sometimes after these scenes, Addie, who now came in the morning and stayed until I went to bed, would comfort me. But she kept a watchful eye when showing me affection, for she too was afraid of my father.

Grandmere and Papaw made an effort to see me and Papaw must have exerted some mixture of understanding and force on my father, for the next summer we took our holiday at what I am sure was the last place Papa wanted to be, the house on the coast.

One morning while I was sitting at the table with Grandmere, engaged over Addie's ham and eggs, Papa came in and asked if I would like to go with him to his firm's picnic, an annual affair for clients and other people of influence who lived on the coast.

I looked up slowly to see whether this was a trap, one of those offers which would be withdrawn on the grounds of some inappropriateness in my behavior if I showed happiness or cause me to be excoriated for ingratitude if I showed hesitation.

But something in my father's long face looked unguarded and even shy, as if in this house he had remembered or forgotten something.

Before I was required to answer, however, Grandmere placed her old hand with its large rings and large knuckles around my small arm and, looking up at my father, said, "How nice, George. Georgie would love to come."

"Good, George," my father said, with a quiet smile. "We'll leave in an hour."

We drove along the road to Frenchman's Bayou in the old, dusty car that had been retired to the coast house about the time I was born. We rolled down the windows, so we rode in the full draft of the warm midmorning air. On one side lay the beach, a scrubby sheet of gray sand tufted with sea oats; on the other, flowed dunes covered with thickets of beach shrubs, low, twisted, with muted silvery leaves. And, where the dunes fell away, a passing openness revealed the receding flats of water and low-lying islands of the bayou.

I chattered to my father, swirling to notice everything and talking about the nearing picnic as if a tap had been turned on. His face in its relaxation showed a weariness I think he always felt, but whose presence his closed and rigid manner concealed. Yet even in this openness he remained largely silent, as if some tremendous incompetence baffled him every time he was prompted to make a gesture toward me.

Finally, he smiled over at me bouncing and chattering in the passenger seat. The blowing air puffed and flapped his shirt around him.

"I'll tell you what, Georgie," he said, like an unpracticed actor trying to perform heartiness. "How would you like your old man to teach you how to swim? Swim like a champ?"

My father had been a local celebrity for his prowess as a swimmer. My own swimming was an untutored crawl, which I

162

could not remember learning, but which kept me safe in the water around the dock. In Papa's study he had two trophies, the remnants of an indeterminate number of prizes which his talent and versatility had won. I loved these golden urns. I loved the golden swimmer, bent, arms drawn back and ready to dive, which topped each one, and the neatly inscribed lettering in which I could read my father's name, which was also my own. They were part of my importance because they were part of the family's importance. And now he wanted to give some of this prowess to me and help me become a more valued boy.

"Do you mean it?"

He seemed flattered by my appreciation of his offer. Laughing, he threw back his head and raised his hand as in a witness box. "Georgie, I promise I will teach you how to swim like a champ."

"WHOOEE!" I shouted, spinning in the seat and butting my head up against his shoulder as if he were one of Papaw's placid dogs.

We turned onto the narrow road, hardly more than two ruts through the scrub, which led to the private picnic area, fishing camp and overnight campground where the picnic was to take place. The air felt hotter with the sun reflecting from the sandy flat, and even hotter as we slowed down to rattle over a planked bridge above which stretched a sign painted in uneven and weather-bleached letters: ADAM'S EDEN.

Adam was Adam Theroux, an old man with grown sons who helped him in his business. People said that he had listened to more people drunk in Eden than any bartender in town and didn't hesitate to use the secrets he knew if he needed a favor.

At the side of the bridge a boy older than I was, broad-chested and dark-haired, leaned over a piling, pushing a crab net carefully through the water. Beside him on the hot wood stood a bucket through whose wire-covered top twisted a red and blue crab claw. He looked up, caught my face framed in the open window barely a foot away watching him, and raised his left fist as if he were going to punch me. Then the car pulled ahead and I watched him recede, following me with his glance and laughing at me.

Papa pulled up in front of the little wooden store whose screen door this morning seemed permanently thrown open as people came in and out. I followed him up the steps, dodging a man and woman feeling their way down with bags in their arms. This was a place I knew well and I drifted after him through the jammed interior.

Beside the door was a cooler filled with chilled glass bottles of root beer and orange drink, sandwiches and boxes of bait. The shelves along the walls were crammed with fishing supplies and picnic goods. The top of the counter was framed on the left side by the cash register and on the right by glass jars of hard-boiled eggs, pickles and sticks of beef jerky.

My father waited for his turn with one of the busy Therouxs, scanning the cartons of cigarettes stacked above the counter. I repeated to myself in a single string the cigarette slogans that Rose sang with the radio when she cleaned or ironed in the afternoon: *LS-MFT Lucky Strike Means Fine Tobacco Pall Mall I'd Walk A Mile For A Camel Call For Phillip Morris For A Treat Instead of A Treatment Try Kools*. Learning a new slogan gave me the same feeling of something important acquired as learning to name a new make of car. I was loyal to Camels because Papa smoked them.

Restless with the wait, I fixed my eyes on the glass case in front of me. Part of it was reserved for the deceptively candy-like packages that I had learned held nothing to interest me, Ex-lax and aspirin. But beside these were rows of Necco wafers, whose pastel rims glowed through the stiff, milk-papery wrappers; compact boxes of rubbery Jujubes; flat, black squares of Sen-Sen in red metallic packets; sweets whose many pieces could be made to last through the longest movie or the slowest hour. I looked up the length of Papa's body to his face and wondered if I dared ask him for something. But he was tapping his wallet impatiently against the counter and I decided I had better not.

My eye continued beyond him to the slow fan which stirred the air and gently twirled strips of flypaper. Flies, black and iridescent, still or vibrating with an angry, electric buzz, swam the air as the sticky streamers softly lofted and fell.

"Georgie!" Papa's voice startled me. "Want something?"

My desire abandoned the candy and I ended up hurrying down the steps behind my father with a cold paper cup of chocolate ice cream in one hand and a flat, tongue-depressor spoon in the other.

We drove around to the picnic area. Someone had strung up a sagging banner with the name of my father's firm on it between two of the moss-hung live oaks which gave the area patches of warm, damp shade. The place was filled with families, women in bright summer dresses, children racing around or wading at the muddy edge of the bayou. A roped-off swimming section with a sandy beach and a diving-float lay beyond the wooden tables.

Papa pulled up beside an empty site and shut off the engine. I shoved open the door, slid down onto the running board, and jumped to the ground. In those days we didn't roll up the windows on a hot day unless we expected rain and it would have been hard to find a locked car in Mississippi.

Papa led the way to the dressing rooms. These were in a large building divided by a wall to make separate changing areas for the men and the women. The doors were labeled "Adam" and "Eve" and adorned with pictures of a barely covered man and woman in a cartoon hillbilly style. The wall between "Adam" and "Eve" was thin. This later led to the practice of my friends and me standing in "Adam" and listening for the sounds of the bathroom being used in "Eve". These we met, trading glances of excitement and triumph, with boisterous laughter.

But this morning was the first time I had been in the "Adam" dressing room. When my mother was alive, I was still young enough to go into the women's area and my father didn't want to be bothered watching out for a small boy. So this felt, like the promise to teach me to swim, like an initiation into manhood. I glanced at the two rows of lockers and wooden benches along the right wall, where a man and two boys were changing and talking. Ahead were three open showers.

Along the left wall, the wall adjoining "Eve," extended a long trough into which flowed a continuous stream of water. I grabbed Papa's hand. "What's that for?" I asked, in a voice that made the dressers turn. He reddened. "Georgie!" he said sharply, "If you want to ask me something, do it quietly."

Next to the trough in a doorless stall stood a dirty toilet. The cement floor was wet, wet from the shower, wet from the feet of swimmers, and, the smell seemed to say, wet with urine as well. The air was damp and close and buzzing with mosquitoes there seemed no way to brush away.

My father found two open lockers and began to unbutton his shirt. I hated the smell and wetness of the place and I was afraid I might make another mistake. For the first time in my life I felt self-conscious about being seen naked. I bent forward over myself as I slipped off my shorts and pulled my swimsuit over my haunches.

Papa pushed shut the door of his locker. Imitating his gesture, I did the same with mine. Then he threw his towel over his shoulder and walked briskly out into the sunshine. I skipped to keep up with him.

"Papa," I asked, grabbing to catch at his fingers, "are we going to swim now?"

He didn't seem to hear me. As if absorbed by an urgency that walled him in and urged him on, he strode across the dusty parking area, his skin a too emphatic white in the bleaching sunlight, and lifting his left hand to shade his eyes, surveyed the crowded tables.

"I have to see Mr. Jordan for a few minutes," he said, touching the top of my head with his hand. "Then we can swim."

He spotted the man he was looking for and threaded his way through the crowd to join him.

"Charles," he called as he approached.

Jordan was a very fat man, whose eyes were lost in the folds of his face. His complexion was soft but yellowish. I couldn't tell whether he was sick, or the color was cast by the shadow of his hat, or he was partly some race I didn't know. The lips of his small, round mouth looked purple. He leaned against a table and supported himself with hands placed atop one another on a cane.

"Charles, I was hoping I'd see you," my father said, seizing the hand that Jordan barely raised from his cane, every finger large, soft and pendent so that it looked like a yellowish udder, and squeezing it. "I hope that cane doesn't mean anything serious."

"Gout. A little trouble with gout," Jordan said. His voice was as high as a woman's and he wheezed through his round purple lips as he talked. "Hot day, isn't it?" He caught sight of me. "Who's this?"

"Oh," my father said. "This is my son, George. Georgie, this is Mr. Jordan."

Jordan stooped forward slightly, resting more heavily on his cane, so he could reach me with his hand without my getting lost in the great cavern below his belly. The round, puffy, discolored fingers hung before me. I hesitated.

166

"Know how to shake hands?" he wheezed cheerfully, in his high voice.

"Of course he does," my father said sharply. "Mr. Jordan wants to shake your hand, Georgie."

I looked down at the sandy ground, but put my hand out. Jordan's sausagey fingers, hot and sweaty, embraced and held it limply.

Jordan dropped my hand, took a handkerchief from the pocket of his great, loose shirt, and carefully wiped his palm with it. Then he tamped his forehead as delicately as Grandmere did when she was putting on her makeup and stuffed the handkerchief back into his pocket.

"Hot day. *Hot* day," he wheezed, collapsing back against the top of the picnic table whose edge seemed to disappear, without his noticing it, several inches into his flesh. His immense yellow knees had dimpled knobs at the center girdled by heavy folds like collapsing basketballs. He opened the lid of a white cooler and reached inside. "Like something to drink?"

I couldn't tell which of us he was talking to, but my father answered with a quick off-handedness, "Don't mind if I do. It's hot as hell."

Ceremoniously, Mr. Jordan reached into the cooler, lifted out a large bottle of ginger ale and an opener, and pried off the shiny cap. It fell in the white dust; I picked it up and put it in my pocket in case I wanted to play with it later. From the bottle he filled two glasses about two-thirds up. Then he picked up a paper bag, pulled away its top, and from the lip of a bottle inside filled the glasses the rest of the way up. The movements of his great, yellow hands were as precise as a chemist's.

Papa set the glass to his lips and swilled a long drink; I watched his throat move as he swallowed. He emptied the glass and set it on the table.

"Thirsty," he said, as shortly as Mr. Jordan. "Can I have another?"

"The more the merrier," Jordan wheezed, and laughed a long, gasping laugh, as if he had said something especially funny.

Papa took the second glass, but drank it more slowly. It was as if he drew some reassurance simply from holding it.

"And Little George?" Jordan asked, again lifting the lid of the cooler.

"Yes please," I said. He pulled out a green glass bottle of Coca Cola and popped the cap off with the opener.

"Looks like you, George," he wheezed to my father as he handed the bottle to me. "Want to be just like your father, boy?"

"Yessir," I answered.

Again he laughed his long, gasping laugh, but Papa seemed not to notice.

The grownups fell into their own conversation. At first, I followed it, not its content, but its movement, turning my head from Jordan's high wheeze to my father's firm baritone. Then my attention drifted.

The conversation continued, distant, like the murmur of wind in the tops of high trees above me. I wondered how long Papa was going to talk. We were supposed to be swimming.

I fell into a trance, the abstracted patience of children and animals. After a while, I stooped down and stamped circles in the dust with the ginger ale cap I'd rescued from Papa's drink.

Finally I got restless.

"Papa," I said, touching his hand, "I'm going to the store. Will you call me when it's time to swim?"

He continued speaking with Jordan. I was afraid he'd be impatient if I interrupted again. I stood beside him for a moment looking up, and when he took no further notice, I wandered away.

The picnic area was so crowded that it was difficult to move without bumping into someone.

Every table was the center of a family, or more than one family, mothers and fathers, brothers and sisters and friends, grandparents. People were drinking paper cups full of lemonade from coolers or bottled soft drinks. Beneath one table in the shade sat wax paper-covered shapes of cakes and pies. At noon the firm would be serving lunch, but people would be eating all day from what they brought with them.

I watched all this life I didn't belong to. A tiny girl in a diaper broke away from a tangle of older children among whom she was dancing and laughing and ran on windmill legs to her mother, who swung her up and held her close against her breast and lowered cheek. The girl rested there for a moment as if gathering fresh daring and then squirmed to be let down. Her mother set her carefully on the ground and watched as she danced back to the other children. Then she turned and began to rinse some paper cups with water from a pan and set them into a paper sack on the table.

I longed for my mother.

I walked on more slowly now, my head down, scuffing the sandy dust up between my toes. I liked making my mark on the ground as I went. I wandered out from between the cars at the edge of the parking area into an open space under a large live oak still some distance from the store. A sense of someone there made me look up. In front of me stood the boy who had been crabbing on the bridge when we drove in, bigger than I, dark-haired and broad-chested and mocking.

"What's *your* name?"

"Georgie," I said in a low voice.

"Georgie's a name for sissies. Georgie what?"

"Georgie Burden."

I tried to step to the side, but he stepped in front of me.

"I can beat you up."

I didn't know how to handle this situation.

I looked round to see if Papa was watching and might come to help me. My eyes found the place where he and Mr. Jordan had been sitting. I could see Jordan, but Papa seemed to have vanished.

I looked back to the boy who stood in front of me.

"I don't want to fight."

He screwed his face up in mock fear. "Don't *want* to fight," he mimed. Then with the quickness of a thought his expression relaxed. "Give me a quarter."

"I don't have a quarter," I said, desperately asserting the reason of the situation. "I'm just going over to the store to look."

"You can't go to the store unless you give me a quarter." He stepped closer to me: I could smell his sweat. "Get your Ma to give you a quarter!"

I broke into shameful tears, turned, and ran from him.

"If you come back here without a quarter, I'll kill you," he shouted behind me.

My terror grew with the act of running. I reached the table and lurched to a stop, my heart wildly pounding. Papa had moved. He was sitting on the running board of Jordan's car, which was pulled in alongside the picnic table, his elbows on his knees, a drink held lazily in one hand. Catching my breath, I knelt down by the front tire of the car, close enough to feel protected, but distant enough not to call attention to myself, and wiped off my tears.

Papa and Mr. Jordan kept talking across the distance between the table and the car, not taking any account of me. In the drift of their conversation I picked up remarks about Roosevelt. Jordan mentioned Mickey Mouse in his wheezing tenor and they both laughed.

I began to get hungry.

"Another drink?" Jordan asked.

He didn't seem to be keeping up with my father, but he was infinitely hospitable.

"Not yet," Papa said. "I've got to go piss. My back teeth are floating."

He stood up.

"Papa," I said, leaping up. I was afraid he would leave me alone. "Can we go swimming now?"

"No, George," he said. "There are a lot of other children around. Go play with them."

But this was so impossible it made my heart sink.

I knew the signals that marked the currents of adult relationships. I was always watching Papa and Grandmere and Papaw and Addie, the people who chiefly made up my world, carefully reading what they were feeling, so I could place myself as safely as possible in relation to it. If I had learned not to trust the world that took away my mother and was so unreliable in my father, I had also learned to trust my ability to ride the uncertainties of my familiar part of it without being destroyed.

But I'd had no experience with other children. I couldn't fathom how to do this apparently simple thing: go and play with them. And I could not play far by myself. For out there watched the boy waiting for his quarter.

"I'll be back in a few minutes, Charles," my father said, turning to Jordan. "Want me to get lunch?"

"Three dogs," gasped Jordan. While they worked out the details, I prayed Papa wouldn't force me to go look for other children, as he might, if the idea took firm hold on him. But his mind was on his bladder and lunch. He headed off.

"Sorry, boy," wheezed Jordan. He waved his yellow paw with its sweaty handkerchief in the direction of the cooler. "Nothing to give you. Don't have another Coca Cola." He paused. "Like a piece of ice?"

I nodded.

We sat together in companionable silence. He tamped his forehead under his hat-brim. I sucked the sliver of ice. Melting drops from it fell on my chest and legs.

After a long wait my father returned carrying a cardboard box.

"Quite a line," he said to Jordan. He set the box on the table and lifted out three paper plates. Jordan pulled out the bench with a scrape and settled his great bulk on it. Papa picked up a hotdog spilling over with mayonnaise, ketchup, mustard, onions, relish and chile and put it before Jordan. "Two more, Charles," he said. "I'll leave them in here."

Papa handed me my hot dog, with nothing but ketchup, the way I liked it, and took his own. "Here's coleslaw and beans," he added, pulling two larger containers from the box and handing us spoons. "Take what you like."

I waited for the men to serve themselves and spooned myself a large serving of beans.

"Don't eat too much, George," said Papa reprovingly. He turned to Jordan. "How about a drink?"

This common interest, I later understood, was the reason Papa settled himself to the side of the other picnickers and close to Mr. Jordan.

Mr. Jordan went through his ceremony with the ginger ale and the paper bag, handed me a glass of ginger ale and gave Papa and himself their glasses.

"Quite a day," said Papa, looking around appreciatively and lifting his glass to his lips. Then, as if influenced by Jordan's gasping speech, he repeated, "Quite a day."

We settled down in the warm air to the silent labor of eating. Yellow jackets buzzed around the table or lit on the coleslaw and beans. From time to time, shielding his hot dog in one hand, Mr. Jordan pulled out his handkerchief with the other and flapped them away. I worked through my beans and hot dog, carefully catching any escaping ketchup with my tongue. Afterward, I was still hungry.

"Papa," I said, standing up on the bench and leaning against him. "Will you come with me to get another hot dog?'

"You know how to go there, George," he said, "I don't have to go with you. But if you eat any more, you'll get sick. And I'd prefer you to sit down."

"Are we going to go swimming?"

"Not right after eating, Georgie. And if you keep pestering me about it, we won't go at all."

I sat down and remained silent. This was the first voice of drunkenness.

Nothing, I told myself, that I did now would make a difference. If I didn't remind him, he would forget. If I did remind him, he would refuse because I was pressing him.

I slid off the bench and walked toward the bayou. I didn't care if the waiting boy beat me up.

I walked over to a stretch of the water's edge, too grass-choked for comfortable swimming, but open onto the broad flat of the bayou. The sky and farther shore wobbled on the surface in soft, undulant reversal, the brown water skinned with the illusion of transparence as it reflected the transparent sky. I searched for a stone and threw it at this mirrory world. The stone fell with a plunk. The reflection danced away on all sides, shivers of blue and green riding the brown water in fleeing circles. Then it recomposed itself. I threw stone after stone, watching the world shatter and ride together, shatter and ride together.

Finally I tired of this, or the impulse behind it was satisfied. My interest turned to skill. I searched out flat stones, and standing sideways, made them skim like dragonflies across the surface of the water. Two skips...three... But this, too, grew boring.

I lay down at the edge of the water. Among the tangled grass-stems that appeared to bend at the surface and slant in the shallow water flickered shoals of minnows. They were paler than pale silver: they floated transparent between the dark bottom and the air. If I took a piece of grass and dimpled the surface, even in the gentlest way, they fled from the soft disturbance.

Suddenly a shadow fell over us.

172

I turned in terror even before I had time to register the cause of terror. My imagination flooded with the image of the dark-haired, mocking boy.

But it was Papa who stood over me.

He carried a drink in his hand. His face looked numb, as if it were an effort to move his features.

"Do we have to go home?" I asked.

"Would your old man break a promise?" he demanded. "Don't you want to learn to be a champ?"

He gestured down the curving shore to the roped off, sandy swimming beach, crowded with people.

I scrambled to my feet. Happiness broke over my whole body, the more completely because I had given up hope of it.

We drifted along the water's edge, Papa taking each step with shaky precision. An old woman was fishing, a knot of children waded, everything shone. I imagined they were watching me and Papa walking together to go swimming.

Suddenly Papa hit his foot against the root of a live oak that grew across the path and had rounded up as the soil had worn away from it. His glass pitched into the air.

"Grab the Goddamn drink!" he yelped in alarm. I reached for it, but it was already past my hands.

"Papa, I've got it!" I picked it up from the brown grass and handed it to him. There was still a mouthful at the bottom of the glass. My fingers smelled of it.

"Good boy," he sighed. He lifted the drink, swallowed down what was left, and held out the empty glass to me.

"Here, Georgie," he said. His hand was trembling. "Why don't you do your old man a favor and carry the glass."

We reached the crowded sand. I found a place by another tree to set down the glass I was carrying. Papa was already wading into the water.

"How deep can you go, Papa?" I shouted.

I followed him. The water was warm on top, but grew cooler as it got deeper. I bounced in it up to my chest, my arms lifted out to the side to help my balance. My father was further out, deeper.

"Swim to me," he called, turning.

I launched myself forward against the water and paddled smoothly to where he was standing.

I grabbed hold of his forearm and bobbed beside him, wiping the water from my face.

"Is that okay, Papa?" I asked.

"It's paddling, it's not really swimming, Georgie," he said. "It's not a real stroke."

He shook me off.

"I was regional champ at the breast stroke," he said. "Know that?"

He leaned forward toward the water as I bobbed to keep my head above the surface and watch. "Look, this is how you do it."

His words were loud and rapid. He illustrated them by moving his arms in the air above the water as he talked.

"You start with your hands together. Here, in front of your shoulders. Then circle them out to the side, like this. And then you bring them back where you started."

He lifted his head.

"Bring your head up to breathe here, Georgie, when you start to move out your arms." He was speaking loudly enough for the children playing nearby to stop and look over. Suddenly I was overwhelmed by embarrassment. I couldn't follow what he was saying.

"Papa," I pleaded in a low voice, "I don't want to do this now."

"What do you mean, don't want to do this?" he asked in astonishment. "You asked me and you'll do it!"

"Papa."

"It's easy!" He grasped me angrily by the arms and pulled me toward him. "Like *this*." He held my wrists in his hands, drew me level and roughly pushed my arms through the water. "It's just like *this*!"

I tried to move with him, but he was so stretched over me that my far arm made only a broken circuit, and my face kept getting shoved under water: water poured into my mouth and choked me. I began to struggle.

"Let go!" I screamed.

Papa stopped moving my arms. I righted myself in the water and treaded in place. As I wiped my eyes clear of water, I could see other people watching us.

Papa didn't seem to notice them. I thought they were sorry for him because of my sissy behavior.

174

"Let me show you," Papa said. His voice came slower and sounded suddenly dull. He leapt forward onto the water and began to swim away from me. The wake of his kick receded, glinting smaller and smaller on the face of the water. I began to be afraid he was going too far. Then in a wink he was swimming toward me again. His head and his shoulders lifted and fell on the water's surface. But he seemed always to hold me in his gaze.

All at once he was back, but instead of stopping he swam around me.

"Like *this*!" he said, lifting his head and letting the water spill from his mouth. "Like this!" his arms circling and flashing.

As he swam near and circled me I got more and more panicky. I couldn't see exactly what he was doing and knew that when he asked me to repeat it, I'd be humiliated again. My shame gathered as a knot in my belly and rose against the back of my throat.

Unexpectedly, I began to retch.

I vomited. Again. The stinking fragments of my lunch floated about me on the water.

I backed away from it.

"I'm sorry," I whispered, frightened. But it was deliverance, and I also felt enormous relief.

My father stood up. He looked surprised and so exhausted he could barely move.

"I told you that you were eating too much," he said in a faint voice. "It's time to go home now."

We returned to the bathhouse.

Many families were leaving now, the bathhouse was crowded with bodies. The air was warm and moist and strong with the smell of sweat.

I turned my back to my father as I peeled off my swimsuit and fumbled in the locker to find my underpants.

"George," Jordan's high voice rang out in salutation. "And Little George. Go swimming?"

Papa placed his hand on my shoulder and turned me around.

"George got sick," he said wearily. "I told him he was eating too much."

Jordan looked down at me.

"So. Created a sensation," Jordan chuckled in short gasps. His high voice seemed to roll down his mountainous belly until it fell

175

on me like a weight. He reached down and poked me in the chest with the edge of his hand.

I waited, visible and ashamed, for them to speak more about me.

But almost immediately, they resumed their own conversation. I was released to turn away and dress.

34

I sat at the wheel of *George's Dream*, my eye resting on the past. The boat moved in apparent stillness, bisecting always the encircling horizon. Suddenly dolphins leapt near the starboard bow, rising in a loose fall of water.

Omens of good luck!

I turned to point them out to Brandi and Frank.

Frank's hand had slipped down the curve of Brandi's thigh, softly caressing. My glance was captured by the movement and hung there.

As if in response to my gaze, Frank opened his green eyes. His gaze intersected mine. He looked startled and then cast me a smile that was complicit and lewd.

I turned away.

When, after an interval, I glanced toward him again, I found him still gazing at me with the same mocking and complicit smile. Then he turned from me, closed his eyes, and lay back again, setting his face toward the dazzling sun.

After another half hour a portion of the horizon line thickened, disclosed itself to the eye as a stable shape. The shape lengthened out and became itself the horizon.

Frank and Brandi had fallen asleep on the deck. I was struggling not to succumb to the suck of fatigue from the dreamlike night I'd spent driving up and down Mississippi, to and away from Becca. My fight with Becca was like a gravitational center of attention in my mind, drawing me obsessively as I obsessively tried to avoid it. I wouldn't look at it directly.

With a deliberate effort of energy, I brought my attention back to the surface of the day.

Be here, I thought. *Here on the sea, on the light, on the island.* I watched and managed myself as if I were another, an unstable family member with whom I had an intimate relationship of care.

As *George's Dream* moderated speed, Frank raised his head and saw that we were off the island. His face opened like a child's. He shook Brandi's shoulder and leapt up. She examined what faced her at eye-level, reached out for the can of hot Diet Pepsi, and after drinking rubbed her eyes with the palms of her small, dark-red-nailed hands. Then she held out an arm for Frank to help her up.

The boat had been built without an electric winch for the anchor and I hadn't added one when I bought her. I loved the ritual of raising and lowering the anchor by hand.

I leaned forward toward the window.

"Frank," I shouted, gesticulating, "Can you get the anchor?"

"Sure."

He stepped off the orange and yellow towel onto the deck as if it were not hot to his bare feet, a display, I thought, perhaps only a young man would think worth making, and walked to the tip of the bow. Brandi, standing first on one leg, then on the other, slipped her flip-flops over her small feet and followed him. I cut the speed again, churned the boat in just off the beach, and held her steady.

Frank picked up the anchor and dropped it slowly toward the water, feeding the chain hand over hand, the muscles working up his arms and shoulders. Brandi stood beside him looking down, her small breasts now visible, now invisible as she turned, her unripe hips protected by her silvery suit from the professional disfigurement of a tan. She held her hand on Frank's shoulder as if her thin energy had to be renewed by the energy which flowed from him.

It was noon. Vehement light poured from the sky and reflected up from the water and the white deck. Streams of it met in the two young bodies standing in the bow, as if their substance were a mixture of flesh and light.

The anchor splashed through the surface and began to float down. Frank waited for it to grab, stood up, and grinned in satisfaction.

I cut off the engine. Everything was light and silence.

Frank, followed by Brandi, made his way back from the bow into the pilot house.

"Want to get down the dinghy or walk in?" I asked.

"What do we need to carry?" Frank responded.

"I need my bag," Brandi said. Her voice had the familiar push of effort in it. "Something to keep off mosquitoes. And stuff to keep my tan even. And my cigarettes. And drinks."

"We've got a small cooler we can put drinks in," I said. "We'll need shoes to walk across the island."

We had become a knot of three gathered at the side of the boat looking toward the shore. The boat veered around on the anchor chain in the direction of the tide, and gently bobbed on the light swells that rode up and under it.

"It's not much to carry," Frank said. "It would be nice to walk in."

I descended forward into the galley. There were soft drinks and beer in the refrigerator, kept always well-stocked by Julia. I hauled out a small cooler and packed it with half a dozen cans. Then I twisted a blue plastic ice cube tray over them, sending a rain of cubes into the cooler. That should keep us comfortable.

I carried it back to the bridge.

Frank handed Brandi her bag. She had pulled a loose, light, long-sleeved shirt over her suit and carried her flip-flops in one hand so her feet were bare for the water She pressed the straw hat to her head against the light breeze.

"I'm ready," she said with cautious pleasure.

Frank descended the ladder. Gently he lowered himself into the water and then dropped. The water rose around him to his chest, water almost as clear as air over the scalloped bottom. The waves flattened and twisted his green trunks, his legs. Fish, like strips of tin, flashed here and there over the sand.

He stretched up his arms.

"Give me the stuff. I'll take it ashore."

I handed down Brandi's bag. Then I lowered the cooler. Frank waded forward, slowly at first against the weight of the water, then more rapidly as he emerged up the incline to the shore. He set the bag and cooler down on the bright beach and splashed back into the water. Brandi raised her hand to the side of her face and waved as if she were scribbling on the air.

Frank waded out thigh-deep in the almost surfless tide, arced down like a dolphin, and reemerging swam toward us. The wake of his kick glinted on the face of the water.

"You'll love it, baby," he said, rising in a fan of spray and smiling up at Brandi.

"Okay," she said. "I'm coming. But be careful."

179

She set her hat on the deck, turned at the top of the ladder, and watching each step climbed down and crouched above the water.

"Now what?" she called.

Frank reached up, circled one hand around her long waist, placed his other hand under her knees, and with a swoop lifted her from the ladder.

"Whoops," she squealed. "George, get me my hat!"

I handed it over the side and she clapped it on her head.

"Carry me in, Frank!"

I climbed onto the ladder and stood at the top looking down toward the water. Suddenly the distance seemed to widen and I felt as if I were about to fall from a great height. My awareness closed down in a panicky dazzle.

Be here! I told myself. *Here!*

But even the sunlit, solid, presence of Brandi and Frank, laughing as they struggled toward the beach, thinned into a transparency glittering with anxiety. Because of my fear and guilt for what I had done to Becca the night before?

Could I, then, order Frank and Brandi back onto *George's Dream*? How would I explain such behavior?

Why should I trust this sudden shift of feeling, which had proven itself recently such an unreliable prophet?

I let go.

I felt myself drop from the side, plunge down through the water. The sea rushed up through the legs of my shorts, billowed my shirt on the surface. My feet hit the bottom with a thud.

I was in.

35

Wading, I climbed toward the waiting couple. The depths of the water dazzled, as if elastic puddles of light had been caught within them, pulling apart, coming back together. Through the oscillating pools of light a shoal of foot-long fish preceded their fleet shadows, parting to move around me, or nuzzling and bumping my legs. They were as fearless as creatures in paradise.

I reached the damp margin of fawn-colored sand below the white beach and climbed up the shore. This was the bay side of the island, harbored from the off-sea wind and the ocean's surf.

"The island's narrow here," I said. "Down at the ends there's a lot of salt marsh and slash pine and palmetto woods. But here it's dunes across with a few ponds tucked in."

I didn't add that I knew it so well because it was a favorite destination of Julia and the children. "The beach is even more beautiful on the other side."

Brandi stood at the end of a small line of footprints that had carried her past the curves of debris that marked the tidal zone up to the edge of the folding dunes. Her prints in the wet sand were shaped and stiff, those in the dry above soft-edged and fallen in on themselves. The tail of her shirt, which had trailed in the water as Frank carried her in, clung to her, darker and brighter.

She raised her left hand to her sunglasses beneath the slanted shadow of her hat.

"I don't want too long a hike," she said seriously.

Frank broke into a grin.

"You and George walk on ahead," he said. "I'll carry your bag and the drinks."

I took Brandi's arm and turned her toward the dunes.

"Frank," she called looking back over her shoulder. Her voice, slightly anxious, curved over the silent beach. "Toss me my flip-flops from the bag."

Frank poked into the bag in which Brandi had packed her necessary supports and searched around. He rose holding the shoes.

"Look out," he called. The first sailed through the air and hit the sand before my feet. I reached down to hand it to Brandi. As I started to rise, the second struck me on the brow.

I put my hand to my forehead and stood up; Brandi bent and rapidly retrieved her sandal.

"Sorry, George," called Frank apologetically. His face was a blank.

Mask and imputation, the twin lies by which we try to make our lives manageable: the masks we pretend we are, the imputations by which we pretend to ourselves that we really know another. How amid these habitual fictions can we ever know the truth of any human situation?

I decided to turn away and once more taking Brandi's arm supported her over the gentle crest and into the interior of the island.

The dunes rose low. We found passage through a hollow inlaid with tiny shells and fragments of shells. It was like finding our way around and over the contours of a sleeping body of light, the million mirrors of the sand creating a resplendent, precise-edged dream. Shrubs with arrowy leaves and gray branches hugged the dune-slopes at distances that allured and defeated the pattern-seeking eye. Higher stood sparse hummocks of sea oats. Their green-gold, almost transparent heads, pendent as a horse's mane, swayed and darted on tensile stems above collars of stiff, narrow leaves. A red-winged blackbird rose from a knot of oats as we approached over a dune-crest, leaving a bouncing stem to sketch a visible absence. I pointed its flight out to Brandi.

"I'm hot," she said. "I thought it wasn't far."

"Almost there," I said, pointing to a freshwater pond that stretched like a shallow puddle at the foot of the next line of dunes. Cattails fringed it part way round and turtles sunned themselves on the visible bank. A white heron collected all stillness into itself. "That pond's a landmark. I've never seen it totally dry up."

Sand slid from under our feet as we descended the slope and worked its way into our shoes. The heat rose as if reflected from tin; the soft wash of the surf, now audible, was a remission.

"Is there anything to drink?" asked Brandi.

"Not until Frank gets here," I answered.

I turned around. The dunes were bare. A black-headed gull crossed the empty sky, voicing its mocking call. *Ha-ha-ha-ha.*

We rose over a final dune; onto our gaze broke the ocean. In its soft wash a group of six gulls with black heads and gray wings skittered or paddled up food, undisturbed by our sudden appearance. The surf rustled lightly like cellophane.

We descended along the gray sand which edged the dune, through a line of dusty seaweed and pieces of driftwood tangled among flat, beach-clinging vines, and out onto the hard white beach. Some days there were other people here, or boats just beyond the scalloped sandbars. Today the curving shore was empty.

"It's beautiful," Brandi said. "I've never been out here. Let's go down by the water."

We walked down to the tawny margin where the tide advances and recedes. Ocean shells sprinkled the wave-scalloped shore. Here, a sandbar reached out into the shallows, a firm reticulation of sand under a shifting reticulation of light. Brandi stepped into the water.

"It's cold," she said. The creamy surf washed and spread over her feet. "Look!" She reached down and picked up a biscuity sand dollar.

I walked out to my knees and glanced back along the larger curve of shore that this perspective exposed. It was empty.

"What's keeping Frank?" I called to Brandi. If she heard that my voice was troubled, she didn't show it.

"He'll find his way," she said cheerfully. "Frank can handle himself."

We walked back up the beach and sat down. Brandi covered her torso carefully and exposed her arms and legs to the sun.

"My tan line."

I was too uncomfortable to make conversation. I sat silent, watching the layered collapse of surf or turning to glance behind us.

Finally, Frank appeared: dark hair, broad chest, green-suited hips, legs rising successively over the dune-crest, and he trotted down the beach slope toward us. He looked like a college kid ready for pleasure.

"Here at last," he said cheerfully. He set the bag and cooler down on the sand.

"Thanks, honey," Brandi said. She reached first for the cooler and pulled out and snapped open a Diet Pepsi.

Frank edged between us and squatted. I could smell the faintly rank sweat which filmed his torso and clung in tiny drops to the wings of black hair that fanned beneath his arms.

I started to shift away, but Frank's hand curved around my shoulder.

"This was a good idea of yours, George," he said in a cheerful voice, "coming out here. No crowd. We *are* alone, I checked it out."

Frank squeezed my shoulder, as if in a gesture of camaraderie. He kept squeezing until my shoulder buckled to the side and I cried out.

Then the pressure began to relent.

I was allowed to draw back, gasping like someone who's pulled himself to safety from drowning.

It was like the game of the night before, but now unambiguous.

I turned.

Frank was squatting slightly behind us. In order to see him, I had to turn and lift my head. The long exposure of my neck made me feel an all-possessing fear. Looking into Frank's face, I saw something I hadn't seen there before, something elemental: the leaping exultation of contest and victory.

"What's going on?" I gasped.

Frank's smile broadened, but his eyes faded into the impenetrable blankness I'd witnessed before. He drew me to him, bending his face close to my cheek. I felt his warm breath against my skin.

"Will you give me what I want?" he asked in a low voice.

His face drew closer now, so close that his cheek brushed against my cheek and I inhaled his breath like a lover's.

"*Prove* that you love me."

The pressure of his right hand on my shoulder tightened.

"What have I done to you?" I cried. "Why are you doing this?"

My face blubbered with panic and disgust. I twisted against the imprisoning pressure of his effortless strength.

Suddenly he relaxed his grip. He let me pull away the length of his arm. His face grew furrow-cheeked, slack-mouthed, as if he'd aged thirty years. In a moment his young mobile features took on an expression I recognized as my own. He raised his left hand above his shoulder and brought it down hard against my cheek. "Bitch!" he screamed. His voice was perfectly my own to Becca. Then it modulated to his sister's. "Stop it! Stop it! Stop!"

He leapt up and leaned low over me, his body trembling in mimed outrage. His expression and voice were still mine. I put a hand to my face, smearing across my cheek the blood that flowed from the side of my mouth.

"Bitch!" my voice screamed in him. "What do you want?"

It was as if I faced myself from the other side of a mirror and watched in dreamlike reversal my assault on Becca.

I scrabbled up and began to run blindly along the empty beach in shame and dread. The sand slipped from beneath my feet; my shirt and shorts were flapping about my running limbs as I ran bent-over, a desperate old man's run. I wondered if the terror and exertion would kill me.

Looking back, I saw Frank rise and turn. The young man ran with easy, athletic strides toward the crest of the beach, up which I was struggling as if I could cross the island and find safety at the boat.

I turned away and ran down the middle of the sand. It was foolish to continue, Frank easily outran me. But my terror drove me on.

My consciousness seemed to double: my mind stood apart and calmly noted the whole of the drama being played out on the beach, watching my panic and my body running from Frank as if they had no relation to myself.

But before I could think about the strangeness of this, Frank appeared beside and above me and I veered down toward the water. I slipped in the wet sand, scraping my knee, but pulled myself up and plunged ahead. My shirt front was wet from the fall.

Suddenly Frank stood in front of me.

I swerved and headed back toward Brandi, blurring the line of my footprints that stretched now toward me along the empty beach. Brandi sat as in suspended animation, infinitely separating herself from what was occurring between Frank and me.

I could see Frank from the corner of my eye, running along the dune-side to keep me cut off, gaining on me.

Gaining, gained, past me again. Curving in front and turning to face me. He leapt at me, blocking and taunting.

I turned once more and stumbled over my ankle. Falling heavily, my face hit the wet sand.

Immediately Frank threw himself on top of me. His arms reached up and pinioned my outstretched wrists against the beach. With his knees he pinned my thighs. The pressure of his body breathing hard against mine made a hot, sick suffocation of dread choke my lungs.

Then, as his body calmed, he again laid his cheek on my gasping cheek.

The left side of my face was pressed into the wet sand. Opening my right eye, I made out only an odd angle of the shining beach and at a distance Brandi unmoving. An unfolding wave reached up and lifted the back of my hair.

"Please!" I tried to tug free, but the effort to pull away from the sand only put me more fully into Frank's grip.

A following wave reached further up the beach, dashing against the back of my head as it rose, and filling my mouth and nose as it withdrew.

Choking I struggled to raise my head. But the unrelenting pressure of Frank's cheek on mine held my face to the sand.

"I wasn't just making movies in California, George. Becca didn't let you know about that, did she?" His voice had lost its steadiness and genuine rage trembled through.

"Want to be my prison bitch?" he whispered. His hand groped down the front of my body against the sand and pushed into my shorts.

"No. Becca..." I began in despair.

At her name, Frank rammed his knee between my legs. I shook like a fish being beheaded.

"Don't even mention her," Frank hissed vehemently. "Maybe I'll just kill you now."

I fell silent. After a few moments he rolled his heavy weight from my body and dragged me to my feet. I stumbled and retched, barely able to stand from exhaustion, terror and pain.

Frank prodded me forward, kicking the flesh of the back of my thigh to set me in motion.

"I'm ready to go home," he said. "This time you can carry the cooler."

I turned my head and opened my mouth in a last effort to speak.

He gave me a second, more painful kick.

"You aren't in charge any more, George!" he said. "Shut up and move."

36

The passage back across the island, back across the strait, back to the house, as if we were winding up the string we had unrolled through the earlier part of the day, returns in memory with a quality of hallucination. I had scarcely slept for the past two nights. I was punch-drunk from the revolutions of my relationship with Becca, wounds that I had inflicted on myself and on her. I'd kept myself going on keyed-up, on manic energy. Now the terror and exertion of the fight with Frank on the beach plunged me finally into thick, almost unendurable, exhaustion.

I remember the walk across the island from two perspectives that could not have been, but seem in memory, simultaneous.

The first perspective is continuous and immediate. Frank made me carry the cooler. I hadn't the strength to hold it for long, so sometimes I dragged it behind me, stooping to the right, tracing irregular figures in the sand. And then again I embraced it with both arms and lurched forward with a stagger. The sun bore down. I was sick with the heat and the effort. Sweat glued my shirt to my body; it gathered in my lashes and ran down into my eyes.

I kept my glance to the ground, concentrating on the single task of putting one foot in front of the other, of not falling as the sand slipped from under my climbing feet. Frank walked behind me. I could hear his laboring breath and occasionally saw his shadow from the corner of my eye. I wanted to do nothing further to draw his rage against me.

An insect jumped with a dry rattle and skittered away to shelter in the bluish leaves of a shrub. I gave an alarmed cry and stumbled. Frank kicked me with the flat of his foot. I stumbled further, dropped the cooler, and fell. Frank stepped closer. Kneeling, I looked up his long body to his face, a black absence against the fierce halo of the sun.

"Be careful, George," he said. "If you can't carry your weight, I ought to get rid of you."

I scrambled to my feet, clutched the handle of the cooler, and bending again to the right staggered on. One foot, then the other, nothing but *this* effort, *this, this,* all there is.

Brandi walked ahead, the left and right sides of her swimsuit across her buttocks lifting like silver signal flags in regular alternation. She walked with urgency, always keeping me between herself and Frank.

And at the same time memory unrolls that grueling immediacy, I see, as if it were a film shot from a helicopter far above: three tiny figures crawling across a vast emptiness, the sheen of the sun laying like satin on the still sand and unstable sea.

How could I have come to this?

Frank managed to get us onto the boat, keeping me under his eye as he heaved Brandi and after her the cooler up to the deck. This was a moment of transition. I felt a leap of fear that he might be isolating me now in order to kill me and leave my body behind. But this wasn't his purpose; not, at least, yet. He gestured me to the ladder and clambered up quickly after me, turning his head to avoid the drench of water from my clothes.

On deck he held out his hand.

"I think I'd better take your keys, George," he said matter-of-factly.

I fumbled in my pocket and brought out the keys to the boat.

"No," he said, his impatience showing only in the *come-on* gesture he made fluttering his fingers. "*All* your keys."

I dug again in my pocket, pulled out my key chain, and dropped it with indisguisable reluctance into his palm. His hand closed around it. I had given over to him access to my car, to both houses, to my office, and to anyone who might be in them.

What harm had I set in motion?

"And your watch."

I pulled it from my wrist and placed it, too, into his hand. He glanced at it for a moment and then tossed it through the door into the sea.

"I'll be your time-keeper."

"Now we have to make you secure, George," Frank said with a small, malicious smile. He gestured me ahead into the pilot's cabin, then further to the doorway that led down into the galley. Why there?

Some words of Larry Bird floated into my mind. "I have eyes all over my head when I'm on the basketball court." I was growing so afraid of Frank that I had eyes all over my body as I descended the steps into the shadowy galley. But I was so exhausted it was hard to think. Panic kept flooding up in a swelling gush, independent of his immediate acts or my reflection.

I took in the features of the room, used so long that I knew it with the taken-for-granted familiarity with which I knew my houses. The built-in table and the captain's chairs which Julia and I had bought on an afternoon when we were happy. The wall cupboards closed and locked against the wallow and pitch of the boat in a storm. The refrigerator, sink, stove ... I was being drowned in panic, I could hardly fix my attention on anything ... the drawers with the ...

I tried to conceal the recognition that flashed on me. Did I start? I made myself very still. Unless I caught Frank off-guard, he would be on me. But the exploding panic made me reckless.

I lunged and jerked open the drawer which held the knives.

Empty!

Turning my glance in dread behind me, I met on Frank's face in the half-light a smile of comprehension and victory.

"Surprised?" he asked. "I managed to explore the boat rather carefully before I brought the cooler." He walked over and placed a hand on my sweating shoulder.

"I don't have to humiliate you, George," he whispered. "You do such a good job of humiliating yourself."

I stood as still and patient as a dog that has grown used to being beaten, waiting for the blow. But Frank backed away.

"You can still be useful to me, George," he said. "But I *am* in charge now. Doubt that and I *will* kill you." He pointed to the nearest chair.

"Bring that up to the bridge. I want to keep an eye on you."

I grabbed the arm of the chair and dragged it behind me. Then, heavily seizing it, I lifted it awkwardly up the stairs. Frank directed me to the side of the tall pilot's seat and made me wait in front of my chair as he walked over and lifted the top of a bench in which equipment was stored. He pulled out a coil of rope, while he glanced over at me.

"I told you I checked things out."

190

He came back, put his hand on my chest, and shoved me down into the chair. Then he bound my arms to its curved arms, twining the rope around my wrists and elbows, pulled the rope tight around my chest, and tied it.

He stepped back and ran his eyes over his work.

"You look like somebody's trussed you to toss you overboard, George," he said. "You'd go right under. Scream, and you'd choke that much faster. It'd make us both famous, once they found you like that.

"I'd like to be famous. I wouldn't even begrudge you your share of it."

His eyes held mine, every stupid taunt inflating him. They made him feel his power like a mounting sexual charge. It was unreserved self-fucking. My rage fought with my fear. *God help me not do something to encourage him!*

Then he broke the gaze and laughed and again looked me up and down. He took his seat in the pilot's chair, thrust the key into the ignition, and turned it. The engine throbbed into life. He called aft to Brandi, who had spent a long time in the head and then settled in the stern.

She came stiffly up the stairs to the bridge. Her eyes refused to see me tied up, as if by such refusal she could isolate herself from danger or blame. I wondered if she was afraid because she had seen Frank act in this way before, or because this was new?

She held the wheel while he went forward and raised the anchor. Then she retreated again to the back.

Frank settled back at the wheel, looked down at me in the shadowed chair beside him, and swung the bow toward the open bay. The boat throbbed and slapped across the water. From the chair in which I was bound, I could see framed through the doors and side windows disconnected patches of the bay, random stretches of sky blurred with afternoon haze.

Frank was intent on steering. Subdued by the steady movement of the boat, I drifted into a doze, fell forward against the rope binding my chest, and jerked myself awake again. I didn't trust enough to sleep.

But, too, I didn't want to be awake. Because awake, my mind drifted to what it didn't want to touch.

Where was Becca in all this?

191

How well did she know her brother?

I felt it was impossible she would knowingly put me in this danger. Was he a danger to her as well? If that were the case, I'd rather die out here on the water in this mysterious private struggle with Frank than draw her into it.

The rhythmic *shhhhh* of the wash across the bow, the muted lift and sink of the boat, the soft throb of the engine, lulled me. The air smelled of salt from the open doors and a faint mechanical odor of gasoline, oil, and hot metal from the humming engine. I labored to hold myself awake.

Eventually I realized that we must have passed the halfway point. It didn't make sense that Frank, who had so far stopped short of killing me, would now make himself vulnerable by killing me near the mainland. But it no longer seemed to matter. Whatever the case, I could no longer will myself awake: my head fell forward and I slept.

37

I woke at the rough thrust of Frank's hands working the ropes that bound me to the chair. I opened my eyes onto the young man's intent face.

"We're back, George. I'll let you bring the boat in. Then we'll all walk off together. I don't want anyone suspicious."

I rose from the chair. My muscles had stiffened and I needed to urinate.

"Please," I said, blinking against the light, ashamed at the whine of dependence in my thickened voice. "Let me go to the head."

"Sorry, George," said Frank. "You've had your ration of comfort for the moment. It's time to take the wheel."

I rubbed my face, trying to wake up enough for movement.

Frank gathered my shirt front in his hand and shouted like an angry parent.

"I said *take the wheel!*"

So we carried out the charade.

I assumed the pilot's seat. We were approaching the white-roofed piers of the marina. I reduced speed and *George's Dream* threaded the aisles of water toward the berth. To the men on the dock, relaxed in their assumption of the normal, I appeared the master. Frank mimed attentive deference, an eager young man waiting to loop the fore and aft lines to the pilings. In his own mocking reversal of appearance, he seemed to be looking back at me for direction. Only I could see his eyes were full of warning.

A passerby lifted his arm to receive the bow line at the pier. Quickly, flashing him an open grin, Frank tossed it to him and turned and then ran back to the stern. Frank took the stern line and leapt onto the dock.

I'd done this dozens of times with my children. The old man at the fruit truck had taken Frank for my son.

Frank secured the line and quickly leapt back aboard. He made his way back to the bridge and nodded to me to cut off the engine.

Frank extended his hand. "Be sure the keys reach the right pocket."

Obediently I handed them over. He turned toward the stern and called Brandi.

"Now," he said, "we're all going to leave together."

We stepped out onto the dock. Frank put his arm around my shoulder. I could see my car through the thicket of masts and spars that lined the angled dock, waiting across a sunlit corridor of water. A short walk down the pier alongside the restaurant patio. Brandi walked behind us, carrying her bag. Frank glanced back, appeared to say something to her, nodded, and laughed, notating cordiality for any observing eye.

On the red flagstone patio, members enjoying an afternoon drink sat at white tables in blue canvas chairs in groups of three or four. A couple waved to me and I waved back. Frank looked up, caught their eye, grinned, and waved too. It was protective coloration, chameleon-like. By making us so visible in the right way, he was making us invisible.

If as an attorney I were examining myself in court, I would ask with a show of incredulity why I didn't use this moment to shout or run away. This was my last chance before I was isolated with Frank and Brandi in the car or at the house. I was surrounded by people I knew who would have come to my aid. Frank might have hurt me, but it was unlikely that in those circumstances he would have been able to kill me. So why didn't I do something?

I can't make it clear even to myself. My mind was divided. To create a scene would have made my relationship with Frank a public spectacle. That would have exposed my affair with Becca to the world and to Julia in the most degrading way. I worried, too—as if my danger were a contagious condition—that if I challenged Frank, I might open others in some unpredictable way to harm.

Yet against this I had every reason to be certain that Frank intended to hurt me, even kill me, once he had me alone, and my last chance of escaping him was slipping away with every step I took.

When I balance things up in this way, I make it sound as if I were thinking in the same way then. But the truth is I was in such shock at Frank's violence breaking into my taken-for-granted world that my mind couldn't bite down on any aspect of it as real. The ordinary rules of cause and effect as I had always relied on them seemed to have slipped their moorings and left behind a world as incalculable as magic.

Frank's brutality and cleverness in manipulating me and the people waving at us renewed the same helplessness and shame that had paralyzed me as a boy.

All this was swimming around in me, not as formed thoughts but as tags of thought and impulses, pushing me this way and that. I seemed simply to watch it go on with no idea whether I was going to maintain the charade or explode in the next second.

And so in the bright Saturday afternoon I walked past my last hope of escape.

At the car, Brandi took the back seat. In the front Frank and I reversed places. With him at the wheel, we drove back past the shabby daytime face of the strip. He turned left onto the street where Brandi's apartment house sat behind the closed up club. She scooted out of the back on the driver's side, stood for a moment readjusting the elastic of her swim suit with a red nailed fingertip, and leaned forward as Frank turned up his cheek for a surprisingly domestic kiss.

"Bye, hon," she said softly.

"See you, girl," he said touching her hand.

Her eyes still refused to confess my existence. Turning, she headed toward the door.

Frank released the car into motion. His mobile face relaxed into its habitual mask of openness. We cruised along the strip, took the turn-off to Ocean Springs, threaded the roads through town, and turned into the driveway at the black mailbox with its gold lettering: *BURDEN*.

The Lincoln crunched over the shifting oyster shells and gentled to a stop in the carport. I waited for Frank's signal before I stepped out. I didn't want him to become angry and refuse to talk. He gestured me into the house.

"I think I'll put *you* in the guest room," he said, directing me forward to Beth's room which I had assigned to him.

The room, by its familiarity, was almost unbearably comforting. I glanced at the quilt, shabby with loving use, that Julia had long ago sewn for the bed. My need to urinate was now piercing and I opened my mouth to ask Frank to let me go into the bathroom.

"No," he said. "Whatever it is, no. Now you're going to sit and think."

"Please," I said after a moment's hesitation. "What is it you want me to think about?"

Frank didn't answer.

"*What* things?" I repeated. "For Christ's sake, tell me what you want? When Becca comes ..."

Frank spun around, his face beneath his black hair flaming with fury. Drawing back his hand, he rammed it into my solar plexus.

I gasped, doubled up, and fell. I knelt, my hands gripping my middle, my head falling forward until it touched the floor, retching.

Frank grabbed my shirt by the collar and pulled me part-way up from the floor. To my vision, his face seemed to divide, his image to become multiple.

"Don't even try to tell me how much you can give her!" Then he dropped me. "You are not in control here," he said, stressing each word separately. "I am."

I lay gasping as he dragged over to the corner an old wooden chair, originally from a Cajun farmhouse, one of the pieces my mother had found charming and brought into the family. He heaved me up from the floor like a shot deer and threw me, still stunned, into the chair.

"Now," he said, glancing around. "I wonder where you keep rope in this house.

38

I sat facing a blank right-angle of wall, the front legs of the chair shoved to the baseboards. Frank had roped my arms and legs, chest and shoulders tightly to the wooden chair.

Then, without speaking a word, he stripped the bed and removed all the pictures and tossed them in a heap with the rugs he had kicked together, making the room a ruin. Looking it over for a moment, he jerked out the telephone and tossed it onto the pile. Then he dropped the Venetian blinds and left.

Twisting my head I could see in the dim light brighter squares on the wall where pictures had hung. One of the hangers had made a crack in the plaster, covered for years by the picture it held: the crack fanned out on the wall like a spider's web.

I was afraid.

Nothing I had experienced enabled me to understand what was happening inside Frank. Looking back I could find times when he'd reacted angrily, but they had turned so quickly to charm, they hadn't seemed to mean anything. And I'd been so bent on winning him over because he was Becca's brother that my mind wasn't open to signals of real danger. Or else I'd unconsciously minimized them and tried to placate him when they'd registered.

And Frank had seemed as bent on wooing me as I was on wooing him. I wondered sitting here if he had read from the beginning what I wanted from him and had decided to make me feel I was being successful? Had mimed compliance in order to gain control? Had this rage been there from the start? Even looking back, how could I know?

I thought of the muddled and brutal changes, the all-of-a-sudden surprises, of my daily life with my father, whose cues I had so diligently tried to read, but could never master. Now in my fifties I had somehow fallen back into that place. But Frank had made himself even more confusing to read, delighting in a savage game. The only thing I knew was that each outburst of rage was more brutal and crazy than the ones that had preceded it. I dreaded the unpredictable next step.

197

I had to urinate.

Sometimes it went out of my consciousness for a while and then it returned more strongly, clamping my awareness to the painful urgency of my body. I rocked in my chair fighting for control, not wanting Becca to find me in the stink and humiliation of having wet my pants, like an infant or incontinent old man. And then, when the urgency relented, I was returned to the blank wall, the dread, and the obsessive race of my thoughts, my mind like a machine working on its own, beating and beating again at the limits of its knowing.

What was certain?

Frank knew everything about my losing control of myself, no, make myself say the true word: about my *beating* Becca the night before. His frenzied aping on the island flaunted it. *How* did he know?

I knew the probability my mind was refusing to approach.

Becca had to have told him.

Every time I touched it, guilt at what I had done and shame at it being known paralyzed me.

I saw myself above Becca, exposed as if to a circle of all-seeing eyes, my hand open to hit her as she silently wept. I of all people should have understood the humiliation and pain I was inflicting on her in such a way as to stay my hand. But how would Becca have betrayed me to Frank? How could she not know his crazy violence?

Or did our separate forms of violence come to seem to her indistinguishably the same thing?

Or had she betrayed me?

My mind slid to an image of Frank hiding somehow in the house while I tried to coerce Becca to what I desired. It didn't have the feel of likelihood. But, then, the last two days had instructed me in the deceptions of likelihood.

My rootless ratiocination spun on.

Suppose that Frank *were* there. How would he get there? Suppose he had a car hidden somewhere. Or he used Brandi's car, she had to have one. Or some other friend had driven him up to Jackson.

And why did he return? Perhaps he had seen me leave and followed me. Or perhaps he had driven there independently of me and was surprised when I turned up.

So, yes, he could have been at Becca's when I arrived. Where?

Say that when the bell rang, Becca took him into the kitchen. Or he waited in Chris's room, listening through the wall. But if he was present, how would he not have interrupted?

Then maybe he arrived after I left and found Becca awake, weeping.

My ratiocination spun itself out, ramifying, branch after branch, unable to find a purchase on any confirming reality.

I turned to another premise and obsessively sought out its implications, to see if they touched a confirming point that I could unambiguously accept as true.

Suppose there were another person, totally unknown to me, hidden in the house. Why would this person be there? And even if I could imagine an answer to that, could I believe that anyone would be able to listen to Becca's cries and not stop me? Or call the police?

No matter how I thought it through, the surface of the experience remained totally ambiguous. Every possibility my mind spun out might be true and equally might be false. There seemed no footing for certainty, nor even for relative probability.

I became aware I was straining against the ropes, my body reflecting my mind's tense reach for clarity. I fell out of my inner world and found myself gazing at the angled blank of the corner. Perhaps it was better just to let go and wait on the unfolding event to make things clearer.

But I was afraid to let go. My mind spun and spun in the emptiness of exhaustion. I moved to pull myself up in the chair and the ropes cramped and choked me. I almost screamed at the frustration and constraint. My need to urinate was returning and all I could do was helplessly feel it increase. It obliterated my thinking.

My situation was a grim parody of the end of a classical mystery: the master's barely embodied grey cells penetrate all appearances, identify every ambiguity, expose false conclusions, sniff out the true, snare the violent and restore justice.

My thinking was only spinning in emptiness, hyper-alert and exhausted, intricate and ungrounded, fogged by my weakened body, swayed by my fear and desire. I could not find the truth. I had lost control of myself and the situation. All I had always relied on had betrayed me.

What did I really want to know?

Becca's motives.

No, Becca's love.

From deep within my chest, taking me by surprise, shuddered a convulsive sob. My chest heaved again and again. My sobs emerged as grotesque wheezes, strangled by fear of attracting Frank. Under the pressure of this silent weeping, my bladder began to lose control. Drops of urine spread over my shorts, leaving two, small, unequal stains.

I closed my eyes and began to rock back and forth against the ropes, as if the darkness and motion would help me regain control over my betraying feelings and body.

The dizzying, the nauseating pressure of my bladder made me groan. I leaned forward, trying to press against it, but the ropes held me upright. The physical habits of a lifetime struggled and gave way. A stream of urine, thin at first, flowed down my scrotum and under my crotch. Of the body's own accord, it was checked. And then with a spasm of pain, broke forth in a flood that swirled hotly beneath me, puddling on the chair, flowing forward and spilling in streams I watched run down my bare legs.

The crotch and legs of my shorts were wet, and a mist of urine rose in the air, stinking. I tried to lean forward, to drain it away from me, off the chair onto the floor.

When Frank came in, he would see it.

Becca would see it.

I could bear no more awareness, bear no more sense, no more feeling, no more thought.

I sat unmoving, my mind as bare as a baby's.

39

I woke with a start.

The room was almost dark, my body flickering patches of pain. My middle ached from Frank's punch as I tried to turn myself toward a window to estimate the time. My shorts were almost dry, but I stank of urine. I felt the sharp need to urinate again. Some dim light still seemed to flow at the edges of the blinds. It must be about half past seven.

Surely something had woken me, but I heard nothing now.

My ears strained into the silence.

Yes, I heard voices, but too far to make out whose they were. They approached and then receded as if the speakers had turned away.

My heart began to pound. I wanted it to be help, but knew it might be death. The voices began to approach again and this time didn't turn away.

The male voice was raised. It was Frank's.

The female voice was harder to hear.

And then in a moment I knew it was Becca's and heard the familiar step of her walk.

The handle turned and the door opened inward, admitting an angle of light. I twisted my head toward it. There was a pause, and Becca stepped in, immediately followed by Frank.

They were still for a moment. Frank's large hand held Becca's upper arm, in support or restraint. Seeing them beside one another, isolated in the light, I was struck once more how alike they looked and how beautiful. The black hair, the green eyes, their finely-proportioned features, the ease and life of their bodies which was in them a kind of lordliness, paired them for my imagination, as if the light in which they stood was a nimbus of gods, standing across an impassible divide from me in the darkness.

I knew this was the first time Becca had been in the coast house. But her presence felt to me like a restoration. Her searching glance found the pile of bedding and rugs and pictures in the middle of the floor and then made out the chair in the dark corner and my turned eyes.

As soon as our glance met, I felt connection and trust.

It was as if my experience with Frank had torn me away, not only from my relationship with Becca, but from any context in which I could strike root or depend on my tacit understanding of my horizon. I no longer had a world.

Now, no matter what should happen within it, Becca restored the world. Even if she should walk in and shoot me, I would know there had been between us connection and love and that would always remain *also* present.

My gratitude for this enormous fact calmed me.

Becca reached up and placed her hand softly on Frank's chest.

"Please," she said in a low voice, looking up into his face. "Let me do this as I asked."

Frank glanced over at me and his face spoke his rage.

"Please," she repeated. "I promise I won't be long."

He turned abruptly and walked out into the hall.

Becca found the wall switch, flicked it on, and closed the door. The ceiling fixture spread a thin, dull light across the room. She walked slowly over to me, on her face a look of sadness and resignation.

"I can't untie you," she said softly, as if stating a condition we were both forced to observe. She pulled over a foot stool which Frank had kicked in my direction when he was tearing apart the room and sat down beside me. Resting her hand on my thigh, she looked up into my eyes. I knew she had to smell the urine.

"Becca," I began, but my face crumpled and I started silently to weep. She stayed beside me and didn't turn away, waiting for the weeping to pass. "Becca, I'm sorry. I'm so ashamed about last night."

I started to weep again and tried to move my hand beneath the rope to reach for hers. She removed her hand from my thigh and closed it over the tips of my fingers.

"I know you're sorry, George," she said quietly. "I know you're sorry."

She sighed and fell silent, as if any further word she might say would have to be hauled up against great resistance and she couldn't yet steel herself to that labor.

202

"Tell me," I finally asked, "What's going to happen?"

When she spoke, it was as if she were trying to answer a different, more urgent question, one that perplexed her. She kept her gaze fixed on mine, her voice tender. But even so close, she seemed withdrawn behind an opacity that made her elusive.

"George, I was so grateful to you, from that first day we met at Dr. Stoddard's. You seemed so sad and I was so lonely and when we talked in the donut shop, I suddenly found myself laughing. There was lightness in what we made together outside the rest of our lives. You seemed as happy as I was with what we had. I told you, I never wanted more."

"Becca."

The fall of the dull light in the bare room on her pale cheeks and dark hair was somehow so moving that I could hardly register anything else. But I flinched from the finality in her voice.

"You imagined it all, George. *Why* didn't you listen?"

Her voice took on an edge of baffled frustration, as if she were a fairy tale princess cursed to return and return to a knot she would never be able to untie.

"You're not listening now. You're just thinking about the next thing you'll say to try to change my mind.

"You invaded my house in the middle of the night. *You beat me up*! There isn't anything more to say."

My mind returned to its earlier question.

"Becca, Frank knew all about last night. How did he know, if you didn't tell him?"

She shook her head.

"How do you think, George? Who else do you think your violence has threatened? You're so self-absorbed you can't even grasp the fear of a five year old boy! When Frank called this morning, Chris got the phone. Chris told him you came in the night and hit me in the bedroom. He was afraid you were going to kill us. When you left, I couldn't calm him down, he was terrified you'd come back."

Her voice rose, full of anguish. Hearing herself, she glanced at the door and lowered it. "Frank made me tell him everything. Chris was still so upset, how could Frank do anything else?"

"Why didn't you tell Chris I was sorry I shouted and promise I'd never do it again? I know Frank is your brother, but he hasn't been around in five years. For God's sake, I know he's been in prison. He's really a stranger passing through our lives."

"George, *you're* the stranger passing through my family's life!"

"That's not true! You *must* feel it."

"George, listen to me. It doesn't matter. I want you to hear what I'm telling you. There *is* no more us! This is your madness."

Becca leaned her head forward, set her elbows on her knees, and rested the palms of her hands against her eyes. It was a gesture of fatigue. But she was also withdrawing into that inward place of privacy of which I was so jealous.

"What is it?" I finally interrupted her silence, coaxing. "Are you worried about Frank? If he lets me go, I promise I won't press charges. You can tell him that. I know there's something wrong with him, but I won't make it my business. I can even give him some money, if that will help. It could come from you, if he wouldn't want to take it from me. Becca, you could afford to help him now."

At every word she seemed to close herself more tightly within herself. My voice faded off. I didn't know what more to say.

I was afraid that Frank might come back, maybe more violent.

"Is that it?" I asked, continuing my thinking aloud. "Are you afraid that Frank may hurt you? Or hurt Chris?"

Becca didn't turn or remove her hands from her eyes. But she seemed to have taken a decision: She began to speak over an obvious unwillingness in an utterly weary, flat voice.

"Frank won't hurt Chris."

Her voice alarmed me.

"Becca, what's wrong?"

"Frank *won't* hurt Chris, George. Chris is his son."

She let out a long sigh and again fell silent.

"I don't understand. Frank's not your brother?"

She turned toward me, her eyes open, but as empty of feeling as her voice.

"He *is* my brother."

"My God," I said, "My God."

"You wanted to know, George."

"Becca, it makes no difference to me. Honestly. You don't have to say any more than you want."

She let her gaze slide toward the floor. Her impassive voice stumbled on, as if she were reading a story deeply engraved within, but never spoken before aloud. I couldn't tell whether she was speaking now to inflict it in rage on me or on herself as merciless penance.

"Frank and I always belonged together. The other kids in the family were too much older to want to play with us. We were the surprise. Mom didn't want to raise another bunch of kids. She said she'd gotten wore out with the others; that was her joke. But I knew she never loved us as much, loved us the way I love Chris. Daddy was still moving around a lot, so we couldn't keep friends. So Frank and I were always with each other. It became another family joke, we were the Siamese twins, we couldn't be separated.

"When we were eleven, Frank met a kid who had spied on his sister and her boyfriend. He showed Frank all the things he'd learned. That afternoon Frank took me up to the attic, where my mother had made a little room for visitors. He locked it from the inside."

Becca paused, and her brow gathered as if she were carefully scanning her remembered experience, in order to get it right. I didn't know how I could endure to hear what she was enduring to say.

"There was light through the shutters. Frank kissed me. And then we undressed and he took my hand and led me to the bed. He showed me the things the boy had shown or told him about what could be done with bodies and hands and mouths. Then we lay side by side, facing each other, our arms beneath each other's bodies, nothing hidden, then or ever."

She raised her eyes to me and repeated with a pale emphasis, as if demanding that I appreciate this, "Nothing hidden. *Ever.*"

Then her voice returned to its uninflected telling.

"Touching him, opening myself to being touched by him, was the sweetest thing in the world. Looking into his face, sweaty and dirty from playing, his big green eyes and tangled black hair, was like gazing into a mirror, and I was a mirror for him. But now in our lives there were things we couldn't tell anyone else, things we had to fake, I *became* fake, so no one would say I ought to be ashamed or try and separate us. I prayed that Mom and Daddy

205

would die and the older kids be sent somewhere else. I asked God that Frank and I be left behind to live in the house forever."

Again a pale emphasis troubled her even flow. She paused, drawn for a moment into what she had remembered, and then let it go.

"I can't remember much about the very end of elementary school," she resumed. "We decided we'd have to act like the other kids, so no one would suspect us. We played apart from each other more. In middle school we began to hang out with groups of friends, pretending to confide with laughter what boys or girls we thought were neat and who we wanted to like us. I never stopped watching myself, for fear I'd let a word slip or someone would find us together in love. In high school we had steadies like everyone else, though I never stayed with one boy too long, I didn't want anyone to get to know too much about me. It didn't even bother me when I started sleeping with other boys, because it never felt real."

I was very still. I knew something about pretending, not inviting friends home, not telling about my father falling down stinking on the floor of every room in the house, or the terrible, unending games when no matter how careful I was I'd say or do something that would make him humiliate me.

But I didn't understand *this*. Maybe she knew it, because she addressed me directly, my name admitting my presence.

"George, sometimes I felt like I was from another planet, living on earth, pretending to be a human being. I needed to keep what we were a secret so people wouldn't hurt us. I'd look around at other kids and teachers and people in stores or in church and wonder if they were faking too, if the real part of their lives was something only they knew and *all* I saw was pretending. It made me feel sick to think about it. How could I know?"

I gave her my grave attention, but remained silent. She seemed to be satisfied by this. Or did she notice? As if she were working a piece of sewing, she bent her attention to her story.

"And then the year after my senior year I missed my period and after a while I knew I was pregnant. I was between boy friends, so I knew the baby was Frank's. We went up into the attic, lay in each others arms, and talked. I told him I would never get an abortion, because the baby was *ours*.

But I was scared to go ahead and have the baby. I thought if Daddy found out I was pregnant, he'd never speak to me again, because of the shame it would bring him in the church. Frank said I should sleep with a boy who was hanging around me at that time, Mike, and then tell him it was his baby. He said Mike was the kind of boy who would marry me, if he thought the baby was his.

"That's how Mike and I got married. Later, I told Mike the baby was early. I think a couple of people may have smelled a rat in the woodwork, but they didn't look closer. It added up and I'd kept the families respectable. By this time Frank was away. He made everyone believe he'd fallen in love and gone to California chasing a woman."

Becca was speaking more fluently now. Her sadness inflected her voice, but it was muted, as if the woman she felt sadness for were someone else.

"I asked Frank not to come home. I wanted to make Mike a good wife. I couldn't stand to think what would happen to Chris, if the truth came out. I'd felt lonely before, there was so much I couldn't talk about. But then I'd always had Frank. Now I felt like he'd died. I was so lonely I wanted to die too.

"I thought this was the way it would always be now. I couldn't stop crying. Mike saw how depressed I was and tried to help me, but what help could he be?

"I couldn't tell him what was wrong.

"Mike almost cried himself when he told me he couldn't make us work out. He'd fallen in love with another girl. But I was relieved. All I wanted was for him to keep loving Chris. And he has, though that bitch he married has tried to make to make trouble between them."

Becca stopped. Although *she* was speaking with little emotion, I was washed with her ache and shame which her numbness was holding at bay. I felt I'd do anything to keep her from feeling it. And I wondered if this was the end of what she had to say? The end falling for her *before* our beginning?

She reached again for my hand, for the tips of my fingers, but didn't look at me.

"Now you know," she said in an exhausted voice. "That's why I could never have let you think of us marrying."

"No," I said quietly. "Maybe now I know why you need me more than ever."

Becca remained silent. After a few minutes, she rose wearily, smoothing out her daffodil skirt with a brush of her hands.

"I'm leaving, George."

"When will I see you?"

"You won't. I quit my job yesterday and notified my landlord. Chris and I are leaving the country with Frank."

I began to shake, as if in the hot summer evening I'd caught a chill. I couldn't make my mouth work.

Becca stood looking down at me.

"Frank knew you were going to ask to marry me," she said, "way out there in California. I didn't believe him." Her voice caught, broke. "I didn't *want* to believe him. I liked being with you, George. I hurt Mike and I didn't want to hurt you. Frank didn't even say he was coming; he knew where we were going to meet and just turned up. He wanted to see you. He told me I have to go back with him."

"Becca, just let me talk with him!"

"That wouldn't be good, George. But don't worry, he's not going to hurt you. He'll leave you here tied up. Monday, he'll call Brandi and tell her to come out and cut your ropes, in case you haven't got yourself loose."

"Listen to me! Frank has no claim on you. You don't have to be afraid of him. *You* cut my ropes. I can get help."

She looked at me with an expression of deep surprise and then her lids closed over her great eyes.

"But I just told you," she said. "I *want* to go with Frank. I'm in love with him. I'd never let anything keep us apart again. "

40

Becca turned away and walked out of the room, pulling the door shut behind her. I heard no more voices, only some subdued sounds of movement. Then the heavy front door slammed. A car faintly started and faded away.

I was alone.

With a surge of rage, I threw myself against the ropes and struggled to shove and pull the chair toward the bathroom, looking for something to cut myself free.

At first I found I could walk the chair in little steps by pivoting on the left leg in the rear, thus swinging the right leg forward in the front, and then with a kind of shuddery push-and-drag bring the left leg in front even with the right.

It took all my concentration and strength. At times the effort was so great that I felt nausea rise in my throat and behind my eyes. Then, pivoting onto a hooked rug which Frank in his anger had kicked out of place I tilted back too far and fell.

I lay on my side. Pain shook my body and faded. Now it was harder. I tried to brace the side of my foot into the knots of the rug, and push myself and the chair to which I was bound a little bit forward.

The ropes moved with greater resistance across the rug than the wood of the floor and chafed at my arms and legs.

I paused to catch my breath and then continued.

Finally I reached the bathroom. Moving along the tile, by comparison with rug and floor, felt almost as smooth as skating. But still I could only progress by inches.

This room was darker. It received less of the light from the ceiling bulb in the bedroom and had no windows. There were drawers and cabinets along the front of the sink. I always used the bathroom off the master bedroom, so I didn't know just what was here. It seemed to me that I would be more likely to find something sharp, scissors or a razor, in the upper drawers. If I could perform a miracle and get the chair upright, I might be able to pull out a drawer and reach even a tied hand over the side. Or better, pull the drawers out, so they would fall to the floor and spill their contents onto the tile. Then I could tilt myself over, painful though it would be, and feel among them.

I had to keep trying. I couldn't bear the thought of staying immobile and helpless, flooded without defense by the feelings I knew were waiting.

The bathroom had no tub, only a shower stall fronted by a frosted glass door. So the lowest fixture with a rim was the toilet. I inched across the tile toward it. If I could get my head up to the rim, perhaps I could use it as a lever to pull myself in the chair upright. In the half-darkness I could make out the shape of the bowl from beneath. I set my feet against the metal strip that held the shower door at the floor and edged my neck as close to the toilet as I could get it. Thus braced, I raised my head and slid the side of my head and cheek up the side of the bowl.

The play of the rope was sufficient for the top half of my head to crest the bowl's edge. I pushed against the metal strip with my feet and against the cold porcelain edge with my head and the chair lifted like a ramp between floor and toilet. But I couldn't get leverage to raise myself further. The porcelain edge of the toilet bowl cut fiercely into my temple and the strain of lifting myself was too much to bear.

I collapsed back to the floor, my head hitting the toilet and the tile with a heavy jar. The clatter of my fall rang out through the empty rooms.

I lay there for what seemed forever. Finally a different possibility occurred to me. If I could manage to break the door of the shower stall while protecting my face from the falling glass, I might be able to get a piece of glass in my hands and somehow manage to cut the rope with it. I contemplated the danger and the slim probability it would work. But since it was the only further step I could think of, I decided to give it a try.

Trembling with fatigue, I wriggled in the chair to find a purchase between my feet and the floor in order to shift my position.

I discovered something then I hadn't planned. In the fall from the rim of the toilet the bottom arm of the chair had pulled free from the back.

210

The chair was wooden and old. Its joints were weak. I rocked over on my back and worked the loosened arm down the rope until it fell out. My own arm was still in the rope, but it was no longer splinted to the chair and could move more freely. Now I set more methodically about loosening the joints and releasing my limbs. It was slow, but after half an hour I had made myself free.

I was so stiff I could hardly pull myself up and walk. Leaning against the wall, I slid down the hall to the family room and then along the draped sea-facing wall to the French doors. Pulling back the curtains enough to reach the handle, I threw open a door. I stepped through it like a magician stepping out onto stage.

It felt like magic, though the magic was not mine, but the wonder of finding that the world was still there. The air was damp and warm and filled with life. The mosquitoes whined at my bare skin and the rackety nonstop throb of the frogs flowed everywhere. The gray spaciousness of the lawn under moonlight extended down to the calligraphy of waterside trees and then met the polished reach of the gulf. I sank down against the glass of the door and prayed for this world to pour through me, to ground and cleanse me, to make me sane. I began to feel myself uncramp and then I slid into sleep.

A few drops of rain woke me up. I brushed at my face with my hand and struggled into consciousness. It was still night, but there was the faintest thinning of darkness. I pulled myself up, stepped back into the house, and locked the French door behind me. Moving cautiously, I made my way down the hallway to the master bedroom and groped across it into the bathroom.

After a moment's hesitation, I flipped up the light switch. A row of large, clear bulbs over the mirror and sink flashed on with the suddenness of a scream. I strode over to the toilet and urinated. My earlier mood of release was disintegrating and I was building up an adrenalin-bathed urgency.

What should I do first?

Call the police!

But as soon as I thought it, I knew I couldn't do it. What would I tell them? And through them the media? And through the media Julia and my colleagues and our friends? About the lover's triangle between the socially prominent attorney, George Burden, his young mistress, and her psychopathic brother, with whom she had shared a nearly lifelong incestuous relationship? That's the way they'd flatten it out. And I feared what Becca had meant when she said she'd never let herself, Frank, and Chris live apart again. I walked over to the sink and turned on the tap. As I placed my hands under the water, my eyes met those of the face in the mirror. What did I read?

The reflected face was sunburned and filthy, grimed and scraped from dragging myself across the floor, welted with the bites of mosquitoes. I was unshaven, my eyes hollow with exhaustion, my hair matted. My shirt and shorts were filthy and torn, my shorts stained with the stale urine, of which I stank. I looked like my father at his most drunken. And in the reflected eyes were the passions that haunted his, loss, craving, hurt; humiliation and stubborn rebellion; despair and willed dullness of mind.

The eyes in the mirror said: *I know you for who you are, your lies won't work with me.*

I couldn't bear their gaze. Like a mechanical toy, wound up and released into its jerky, programmed walk, I hurried back to the guest bedroom and began to order it. Trembling but meticulous I remade the bed, hung the curtains in place, restored the pictures and rugs, plugged in the telephone. I wanted to remove all signs of Frank's presence, not for Julia or whoever else might come into the house, but for myself. I needed to obliterate it, make it not have been. I grabbed up the rope and the pieces of the chair and carried them out the front door, threw the chair on what was left of the woodpile from last winter and covered it over with logs, then carried the rope around to the shed from which it had come.

Now the sky was thinning into true dawn. Everything rested at peace in the dim, misty stillness, as if rising into existence from the roots of created being. But I was apart, enclosed in the compulsion to go back inside and finish the labor I'd started. In the kitchen I grabbed a towel and washed down the counters, took the dishes from the sink and placed them carefully on the shelves. Then I reached under the sink and pulled out the beery garbage. I took the bags outside to the trash cans. Then I looked over the room. Nothing here that wasn't mine, wasn't me!

In the dining room I washed down the refectory table, in the family room the top of the coffee table and the phone. If anyone

212

had tried to stop me, I would have shoved them away. I *had* to do this! I walked back down the hall to Frank's room -- *no*, to the guest bedroom -- and on into the bathroom. This, too, I washed down, even the toilet, viscerally not wanting to leave uncleansed anything Frank had touched or used.

I stood in the doorway surveying the bathroom, then turned and surveyed the bedroom. Everything was the way it should be. Or almost everything. The clock from the night stand had fallen under the bed. I fished it out. It had stopped at three, the time of Frank's rampage. He must have pulled it from the socket and dropped it. I didn't know where my watch was.

Picking up the telephone, I dialed the local time number. The mechanical voice droned over the line.

"The time is Sunday, July fourth, seven-twenty a.m."

July fourth.

This was the morning of my birthday. It had fled from my mind. I remembered Julia making me promise not to let anything interfere with our being here to observe it. Julia enjoyed birthdays, days of festive attention to the people she matter-of-factly cared for all year.

What had I accomplished in this year of living?

I felt the weight of my self-congratulatory disloyalties to Julia, the year of intentional betrayals. I felt the suffering I'd ended up bringing on Becca. What hypocrisy there was in the reputation for integrity I wore like a well- tailored suit! And harder to grasp was this: although I lived the evidence daily that this reputation was empty, I continued to believe that it was true. I'd been able to know and not know at the same time what I'd been doing.

To me this reputation, shaped from the opinions of others, was more intimate than a garment, it was as intrinsic a part of my self as my body. Even at this moment of confronting its falseness, I couldn't face the prospect of losing it. I didn't think I could bear the humiliation of people knowing what I had done and what I had suffered.

Thank God, I thought, *Julia's not here to insist on our going to church!*

This paradoxical prayer spoke out my deepest betrayal. I knew I was thinking like a child, that no place was nearer or farther from God. But there, before Christ in the host, unable in my heart either

213

to receive or deny him, I wouldn't be able to hide from myself how appallingly known I was by him. *Even before a word is on my tongue, lo, O LORD, thou knowest it altogether.* I'd loved to pray Psalm 139 when I could believe in my own integrity! Now I felt what it was to have something I couldn't confess, because I couldn't let *myself* fully know it.

And how could I pray for forgiveness? I couldn't tell God from my divided heart that I repented all I had done. Sometimes I did, sometimes I didn't, and whichever feeling was possessing me at the moment always carried the opposite as its destabilizing shadow. Whichever way I turned, I faced an intolerable surrender: of grief or desire; hatred or love; the wish to let go or the wish to plunge out and find Becca. I didn't want to come before God's eye.

I didn't want to bear the weight of God's forgiveness.

Time pressed on in a lucid chaos of distraction. My thought shuttled back and forth, back and forth in its impasse of passion. Memories laden with urgencies of feeling, with desire, fear, and shame, leapt into exaggerated presence as if randomly lit up by flashbulbs. Everything seemed foreign; I seemed foreign to myself, observing as if in another the float of anxiety weightless as a hallucination. I wondered if an injury irretrievable had happened to me. I wondered if I'd passed over into madness.

I thought, *If I sit here, my body will begin to convulse.*

It was like a bad drunk. I *was* drunk, with panic I could no longer shove away. Without being able to push my thought through to purpose, I stood and fled into a larger space, to the family room, to the curtained French doors, onto the morning lawn spreading away to the water.

Always through a difficult night, I waited for this: the emergence of day out of darkness, the reestablishment of the solid world. Every step of this transformation was familiar, and every time it unfolded, I ached with a surfeit of wonder. The air was fresh and warm, the lightest morning breeze lofted a hint of salty dampness up from the water. Now again the early morning sunlight was tangled in the treetops, brilliant as rippling water where the leaves moved. Soon sunlight would run down the trunks, pool on the grass, overflow the shadows; would brighten and brighten. Before me was the path I'd taken on thousands of days down to the pier and the water.

This morning the day didn't mute my agitation. I walked down toward the water. The grass was damp to my feet. The great pines and magnolias rolled past my eyes on both sides. I was walking, but it seemed as if I were being borne on an escalator through a theme park re-creation of the setting of my life. It was all empty surface, there was nothing behind it, the edges of everything softened to dreamlike insubstantiality in a flickering halo of light. My alarm was unbearable. The light was swallowing everything up, the lawn, the trees, the sea, it was going to swallow me up.

Suddenly all my energy gathered into a single intention. I ran down to the beach beside the pier. The periwinkles swayed on the black rush, the hermit crabs lay hidden in the whelk or snail shells scattered along the sand. My times were getting mixed up. I couldn't remember clearly where in my life I was. I thought of my mother, felt myself rocking, rocking in her lap, seeing my brown shoes. I tugged off my clothes and stood naked beside the water. This at least was one act over which I had power. I walked forward and the arms of the water embraced me.

The water was warm near the shore, but as I waded out, it grew colder. The sun was a hot eye, whose vision drilled through me. In the long, shallow sweep of the bay I had trouble getting beyond my depth. I swam toward the channel. The distance seemed to stretch endlessly.

Finally, the bottom withdrew beneath me. I lay down upon the water as on a bed. Then, with my arms I pushed myself under. Down and down until my lungs could bear it no longer and I sucked in water.

Convulsively my lungs rejected the water, my body doubled. I flailed to keep myself under, but found myself rising. My head broke the surface, I gulped in the hated air.

As soon as my body grew calm, I once more forced myself under. I tried to hold out longer this time, until the automatism of my lungs more greedily sucked in the water.

I'm going to make it happen!

Choking and confused, I tried to force a second flow of water into my lungs. But the sea seemed to reject me. It thrust me up and up, back into air.

Water streamed from me. My eyes seemed to take in for the first time the reality of the day. The day, I thought crazily, is larger than I am. It curved over and around me and extended beyond the horizons of my vision. My loss and rage and shame had loomed larger than the world; it had willed the world to exist only as my backdrop and witness.

Now suddenly the sun was again the sun, the sea again the sea, and I was just a middle-aged man—this middle-aged man in this passing moment, whose mistakes and suffering were part of the common human lot.

It came over me that to God my being out here in the channel laboring to drown myself was seriously funny.

I struck out toward the shore, swimming easily, feeling the flow of the water around my body and the pleasant warmth of the sun. My mind drifted to the questions I faced now that I was going to live. A fresh tendril of anxiety wrapped itself around these questions in my mind. I became anxious at the anxiety. What could I do, I thought urgently, to hold onto this access of peace?

And then I found myself laughing, doubling up in the water, splashing to keep my head up. What I *had* to know I really already knew. I needed to heal my torn relationship with Julia. I needed to do my ordinary job. Perhaps there was proper unfinished business about Becca and Frank, something I couldn't assess or respond to alone. It was an illusion to think I could meaningfully plan, and therefore control, these things by any further effort now. I had to wait on what I could not know in this moment.

That was the big joke. Getting urgent about this peace, I would only destroy it. I had to be willing to wait on God's time, God's surprises.

Rolling over on my back, I let go and floated.

###